Justice
Denied

A Novel

Carroll Multz

Justice Denied

Revised Edition

Published by
ShahrazaD Publishing
859 Quail Run Dr.
Grand Junction, CO 81505

ISBN: 978-164764111-5
ISBN: 978-1-61739-017-3

1 Fiction/Legal 2 Fiction/Suspense

Contact the author at:
carrollmultz@charter.net

Also By Carroll Multz

Adult Novels

Deadly Deception · *License to Convict*
The Devil's Scribe · *The Chameleon*
Shades of Innocence · *The Winning Ticket*

With Judith Blevins

Rogue Justice · *The Plagiarist* · *A Desperate Plea*
Spiderweb · *The Mejico Connection* · *Lust for Revenge*
Eyewitness · *Kamanda* · *Bloodline* · *Pickpocket*
Ghost Writer

Childhood Legends Series®
A series of novels for middle-grade readers
With Judith Blevins

Operation Cat Tale · *One Frightful Day* · *Blue*
The Ghost of Bradbury Mansion · *White Out*
A Flash of Red · *Back in Time* · *Treasure Seekers*
Summer Vacation – Part 1: Castaways - Part 2: Blast Off

TABLE OF CONTENTS

Dedication

*This book is dedicated to
my late wife, Rhonda,
my helpmate, soulmate
and inspiration.*

A Note From The Author

Writing a novel is like living a fairy tale. Despite life's many trials and tribulations, all the windmills ordinarily are turned right side up by chapters' end and everyone goes on to live happily ever after. With a stroke of the pen, the characters' destinies are forged and are limited only by the author's imagination.

If it had not been for my life experiences, I would have been unable to paint the picture of the lives of the characters I have created herein. My life experiences have been enriched by those with whom I have come in close contact and those whom I have observed from afar. To all of them I am grateful for the walk together.

In a novel about the law, how it functions, and our whole system of justice, I would be remiss in not recognizing those who encouraged me to embark upon my legal journey and coaxed me along the way. At the fore were my parents, who taught me values, and observance and respect for the law, and who never gave up on me.

To my father, the first attorney I knew and admired, and my mother, whose love and inspiration will be with me always, I owe everything. To

Associate Justices John C. Harrison and Hugh Adair of the Montana Supreme Court, for whom I law clerked—their belief in my writing skills have brought me to this point, and without their patience, this book and the others might never have been written.

The trial scenes depicted in *Justice Denied* were the product of fifty plus years in court and were due in no small measure to the mentoring and encouragement of my father, Edwin Multz, and to Richard Beacom, Larry Long, Robert Russel, Donna Salmon, and Len Chesler. My thanks to them for helping me along the way and for making me look good.

This novel would not be what it is had it not been for family, friends and associates. I am most grateful to my late wife, Rhonda, Sherri Davis and my daughter, Lisa Knudsen, for their assistance and great skill in preparation of the initial manuscript. And to Judy Blevins and Margie Vollmer Rabdau my thanks for their assistance in preparation of this second edition. But for them and the prodding of my youngest daughter, Natalie Lowery, this novel would have gone unwritten.

I'm immensely grateful to longtime family friend and former editor of *The Colorado Lawyer*, Arlene Abady, now deceased. Arlene, who was familiar with my writing, having edited over twenty of my articles for that publication, painstakingly edited my first attempt at fictionalization. She cannot be thanked enough for her efforts which are reflected herein.

Three of my fellow professors at Colorado Mesa University, Drs. Don Carpenter and Jerry Moorman of the Department of Business and Dr. Dan Flenniken of the Department of Mass Communications, provided invaluable insights and perspectives in reviewing the initial manuscript for which I am most grateful.

Finally, to the designer of the cover and interior of the revised edition, Frank Addington, my profound thanks.

Additional Remarks: Although the first edition of *Justice Denied* was heralded for its technical approach, it has been rewritten to appeal to a wider base. The same is true of *Deadly Deception* and *License to Convict*. No longer pedagogical in nature, the three are still designed to inform, inspire, and entertain—in that order. For those who are intrigued by courtroom drama, I have left the court scenes virtually untouched. Sit back and enjoy!

Cursed is the man who
withholds justice...

Deuteronomy 27:19

PART ONE:

PREPARING FOR THE FINAL CHAPTER

CHAPTER 1
BY A TWIST
OF FATE

Wild and crazy thoughts were racing through his head even before he began the journey to Steamboat Springs, Colorado.

Even though he had trained himself to think of the positive rather than dwelling on the negative, his mind was taking him in that other direction. Forgive and forget, he had been teaching his bible school students, and now he found himself doing just the opposite.

Even though Max was only twelve years old at the time, the ordeal had left some deep emotional scars, some that had required professional help. He thought of a time before the ordeal when life was the ideal. Reflecting on those turbulent times, he could count the ways his life and the lives of his family had been changed—and not for the better. Their lives had been turned upside down and even destroyed by a twist of fate.

He believed with all his soul that God had a destiny in store for him. However, to revisit past disappointments was an emotional detour he didn't need, and especially at this time in his life, couldn't afford to take.

As his plane descended through the intermittent fluffy cloud cover, he couldn't help but think of the lazy summer afternoons growing up in Steamboat Springs. Lying on his back gazing upwards, his childhood musings were inspired by the heavenly transformations of the floating powder puffs. He envisioned giant polar bears, poodles, and snowmen momentarily materialize and then disappear forever.

As a child, his much deeper concentrations found him daydreaming about superhuman feats, the beginning of the universe, its Creator, and the most perplexing, infinity. So deep and serious was his pondering that his consternation would be marked by crying episodes, requiring the consolation of his mother and father.

He had many dreams and visions about events that had not yet happened but did ultimately come to fruition. His dreams were spiritual and philosophical, and he heard music he would later play, and when he became older, would copyright. He was frightened about things that happened that only days before he had seen in a vision.

A therapist he saw as a child told his parents he was clairvoyant. It was only after he told his parents of a dream he had about a cousin in a distant state being involved in a swimming accident that they believed. That, however, was only after they were notified by relatives a week or so later that the boy had drowned.

Max didn't want to get his hopes up too high about the nature of the late-night call from his father's former attorney, Lawrence Whittaker. He had been at this stage before only to be turned away disappointed. Hopefully things would be different this time, but he had no false expectations.

• • •

It was a drab, dismal day when the 747 landed at Denver International Airport. The runway was no smoother than the airways from the time the plane began its descent until it landed. It was obvious that the winter freeze had taken its toll.

Max was never much of a fan of bumper cars, roller coasters, or his daughter's favorite carnival ride, "The Whip." At the thought of returning to Steamboat, his stomach was churning. Now, he was doing everything he could to keep from using the convenience bag provided by the unusually striking flight attendant, who had obviously witnessed his sudden and ghastly change of complexion. With the two elderly passengers seated on each side of him enduring the turbulence rather well, Max felt like a wimp.

• • •

One never knows what to expect in the wintertime in Denver. He could be trimming trees in running shorts and a tank top the day before Christmas and shoveling snow the next. He also remembered the terrible winter storm they had in May the year he moved from there. This February winter day was no different from that which he was hoping to escape when he left O'Hare International Airport earlier that morning. The deicing procedures in Chicago accounted for an almost two-hour delay.

Max was not a very patient man and every time he flew was dumfounded by the inefficiency of the airline industry. With the screening process, he thought the industry had taken ten giant steps backwards. He marveled at the elderly and single moms laden with carry-ons holding babies and dragging small children behind as they traversed the airport maze.

This would be the first time Max had flown into DIA. The terminal building was built to resemble snow-capped mountains and its rising ivory-white canvas inverted cones stretched heavenward making travelers think they had landed in the Alps. DIA was located some distance from the downtown area. Max liked the old Stapleton International

Airport which was closer to the center of town and easier to negotiate.

So much for his whining. His only concern now was to reach the gate that would take him to his destination, Steamboat Springs, Colorado.

JUSTICE DENIED — CARROLL MULTZ

CHAPTER 2
A TIME
TO THINK

The weather delay in Chicago and late arrival in Denver caused Max to miss his connecting flight. The concourse designation and gate number provided by the gate attendant proved to be faulty. Apparently, a change was made after the announcement. Had he checked the monitor he might have made his connection on time. Now he was looking at a six-hour wait for the next available flight. This gave him much too much thinking time.

Having checked in at the posted gate and receiving his seating assignment, he felt more confident now about the anticipated departure.

Partly as a diversion, partly for information and mainly to kill time, Max kicked back in the uncomfortable chair in the waiting area and stretched his legs out in front of him. He picked up the Wednesday, February 4 edition of *The Denver Post*. Face up was a photograph of one of the most recognized athletes of the time, Michael Phelps. The winner of an unprecedented eight gold medals in the swimming events at the 2008 Summer Olympic Games in Beijing, Phelps was not pictured with his patented victory sign or with medals draped around his neck or endorsing a product.

Instead, the American idol and sport icon whose photograph had been plastered on the front of the Wheaties cereal box, promoting the "Breakfast of Champions," was pictured smoking a bong purportedly containing marijuana. Max was shocked. *What? It can't be! Probably trick photography or a spoof.* Yet, this wasn't the National Enquirer. The role model that Wheaties eaters everywhere attempted to emulate wouldn't do such a thing and certainly wouldn't be stupid enough to allow the incident to be memorialized, let alone disseminated to the public at large.

Max had always been intrigued, if that is the proper word, by those who risk so much for so little. For the moment he was putting the speculation of emotions he would be experiencing upon his arrival in Steamboat on the back burner. His mind wandered to Paul Horning, who was a quarterback and a Heisman Trophy Winner at Notre Dame and was suspended for allegedly betting on NFL games while playing for the Superbowl Champions, the Green Bay Packers. He also thought of "Charlie Hustle," Pete Rose, a major league baseball player who had not been inducted into the Baseball Hall of Fame because of his alleged gambling exploits. Or how about the NBA referee whose questionable calls were called into play when he was connected to a gambling scandal? If each had done a cost-benefit analysis, none would have opted for the low road.

Max remembered that over the years several Olympic gold medal winners were required to surrender their medals because of the use of steroids or performance-enhancing drugs. Jim Thorpe had to forfeit his Olympic medals because he had received payments for playing semi-pro baseball. *Great athletes all*, Max thought. *If only they had weighed the probable consequences of their actions.* Max wondered whether their ill-advised decisions were based on inadvertence, ignorance, or just plain blatant disregard for the rules of the game.

Max thought there were some actions not quite as innocuous. One couldn't be as understanding or sympathetic when the action taken was egregious, deliberate, and premeditated. A case in point was the O.J. Simpson case. O.J.'s alleged deliberate and premeditated acts reportedly cost the lives of two people and caused an emotional upheaval to the loved ones who survived. Worse yet, if the allegations were true, O.J. deprived his own daughters of growing up with a mother.

For every cause, there's an effect—even when

the cause is unintended. And in no way did Max intend to minimize the effects of self-destruction on the destroyer. *I guess in some respects the inevitable consequence to the destroyer is deserved,* he thought. *Turnabout is fair play! Eh? At least the destroyer is in charge of his or her own destiny. Too bad the victims aren't afforded the same privilege.* Max shook his head as he stared into space.

Max believed his venting might be viewed as self-realization or self-fulfillment. It was important to him at this juncture even if it served no moral, political, or societal purpose whatsoever. It did bring to the fore the massive and pervasive effect the ordeal had on him and continued to have on all those he cared about.

CHAPTER 3
THE MAIN CHARACTER

If it hadn't been for Max's father having been unjustly accused, there would have been no ordeal or at least not the ordeal. The second of five boys, James Curtis Cooper was born on July 15, 1938, just outside Steamboat Springs, Colorado, in Routt County, to G. Forrest Cooper and his wife, Bessie.

The Cooper Ranch, as it became known, was acquired by U.S. Patent on November 27, 1915. The land was homesteaded by Max's great grandfather, Joseph Michael Cooper, born in 1876 and thirty-nine years of age at the time of the grant. Max's grandfather, G. Forrest Copper, was born in 1908 and would then have been seven years of age. The original grant deed was given to Max by his grandfather and hung proudly on Max's law office wall.

Max's father, whose nickname was Jamie, was the largest of the five boys and save for his father, was the strongest and hardest worker in the family. Since he was the smartest, according to his mother, he was the only one to attend and graduate from college. He obtained his Bachelor of Science Degree in Business Administration in 1959, graduating with honors from Colorado State University in Fort Collins. He lettered in football and basketball all four years.

Max's father would return to Steamboat in the summers during his college years, dividing his time between the Cooper Ranch and the Steamboat Bank & Trust Co. (SB&T Co.) The night processing job at the bank was financially rewarding and not only accommodated his ranching duties but provided him with skills and training he was only too eager to learn. During the summer vacation between his junior and senior years and the Christmas vacation his last college year, he was given responsibilities usually reserved for the full-timers. Upon graduation from CSU he was offered and accepted a position with the SB&T Co. as a loan officer and within a short period of time also held the title of chief operations officer and later first vice-president.

While attending high school in Steamboat Springs, as Max's father would tell it, he met an attractive and talented cheerleader and track star who had just transferred to his school by the name of Jennifer Mae Carpenter, the daughter of a prominent physician who later became the Steamboat mayor. They were inseparable and Jennie, as she was fondly called, and Max's father married during Christmas vacation his senior year at CSU. The new Mrs. Cooper, who had been working in her father's clinic since high school, resigned and resided with her new husband in a small apartment near the CSU campus until spring graduation. Fifteen months later, specifically February 21, 1960, Max, christened Maxwell Deven Cooper, was born. His sister, Collette, Max's only sibling, was born on March 23, 1963.

· · ·

Alden E. Stillwell, the son of the president of SB&T Co., attended school with Max's father and mother. In fact, he had a mad crush on Max's mother to such an extent that Dr. Carpenter had hired a local attorney for the purpose of obtaining an injunction to prohibit what Dr. Carpenter's attorney described as stalking and harassing. Alden had been vying for Max's mother's affection since grade school days. The bespectacled nerd, as Alden was referred to by his classmates, was the classic pest and an annoyance to the Carpenter household. The Carpenters believed if Alden was Jamie's competition, there was no contest.

Reflecting on the past, Max always wondered if the genesis of the ordeal was sparked by the perceived grade school rejection. If that were true, then the ordeal was ignited by the high school pairing and ultimately fueled by his mother's marriage to his father. After all, his father, grandfather, and great-grandfather were all servants of the soil and toiled to raise the crops that fed the cattle that kept the banking Stillwell family fattened.

During the Great Depression, farmers and ranchers who couldn't keep up their loan payments to SB&T Co. shuddered when they heard the Stillwell name. Alden's father, Brandon, and grandfather, *the* Wellington D. Stillwell, had been presidents of the bank and were directly responsible not only for the community's success but also for its very survival, at least according to them. Unless you bowed and kissed their ring, you could end up on the bank's blacklist. Many a proud farmer or rancher with hat in hand and bended knee was humbled by the ritual required to obtain even a small loan from SB&T Co.

The only decent Stillwell, according to local folklore, was Brandon, who had taken a liking to Max's father. Brandon was noticeably disappointed in Alden even though Alden was the heir apparent to the Stillwell dynasty. Although Alden said nothing and in fact congratulated Jamie upon his appointment as first vice-president of SB&T Co., a move relegating Alden to a position inferior to that of Max's father, Alden showed no outward jealousy. It's not difficult to imagine that the sting of depriving Alden of what he considered the ultimate put-down by his own father must have been more than he could bear. Max rationalized that could have been the crowning blow that sparked the ordeal.

CHAPTER 4
INTO THE WILD
BLUE YONDER

The six-hour wait at DIA proved to be less painful than Max expected. He amused himself with a plethora of reading material. The Denver Post was not as substantively charged as he had remembered, and he was disappointed at how much copy consisted of circulars of various descriptions—none of which interested him. He apparently was not the only one of the same mind as piles of discarded inserts were strewn about the airport seating areas.

Although he wasn't hungry, Max indulged in a hamburger with the works, fries, and a soda which he purchased at one of the many hurry-and-wait stands at DIA. It was almost as expensive as lunch at his favorite deli in Chicago. Though billed as the mother of all hamburgers it still tasted like cardboard. His stomach was churning as much from anticipation as the hamburger and fries he had just devoured. *They don't serve much food on flights these days and the muffin, fruit cup and orange juice don't go very far.*

The waiting area filled with travelers who spilled out into the aisle. The gate crashers boldly crowded forward and stood in the first-in-line slots ahead of those who had been courteously waiting to form the appropriate lines when called. In any case with seating assignments, the offenders didn't really gain an advantage; they still had to wait their turns.

• • •

The flight attendants on this flight were picked from a different pool than those on the Chicago to Denver fight. Observing the one assigned to Max's section, it was obvious to him she had been a prison guard in her previous life. Pretty enough, she was gruff, and as the gentleman next to Max was heard to comment, "It's too bad she didn't finish the Dale Carnegie course." She did her job. The ski bunnies and playboys bound for the ski slopes, stylish in their bright after-ski (or was it pre-ski?) wear were kept in check.

Max had always had a problem with too little leg room, and other than that was comfortably seated in a window seat that was not over the wing. He saw a lot of white ground cover on the mountains west of Denver and once they passed through those large white cotton balls in the sky and reached their cruising altitude, he saw the rich blue skies over Colorado. Not quite the big sky country of Montana, but almost.

　　　　　JUSTICE DENIED — CARROLL MULTZ

Once the captain announced his permission, Max adjusted his seat, closed his eyes and drifted into the wild blue yonder. As if a time machine had turned back time, Max watched himself as a small boy. He was with his sister and parents on an outing, hiking the steep trails near Fish Creek Falls just outside Steamboat.

The panoramic scene from one of the trails was just as breathtaking as ever. It was as if he had never left that place. There was a serenity he experienced there that was not equaled anywhere else he had ever been. He had always felt safe and free and the freshness of the air was still and friendly. As he was watching the clouds drift by, he ventured too close to a cliff's edge. He heard his father yell, "Max, watch out!" Just then, he tripped and as he was tumbling over the edge, his father grabbed him by the hand.

This surprised Max because his father had been some distance away and it was implausible to him that his father could have been at his side instantaneously with his fall. His father was pleading with him to hold on tight and extended his other hand to pull him to safety. Impulsively, Max jerked from his father's grasp causing him to cascade uncontrollably into the black abyss below. It was as if Max was not actually falling but floating in space and felt he had the power to float back into his father's waiting hands. It was as if two energies were tugging at him from opposite directions. One voice was begging him to go back; the other was telling him no. Max's consternation was vivid, and his indecisiveness rankled him. It was as if he were paralyzed in time.

Amid Max's quandary, he felt a tugging at his arm. Max immediately jerked awake and he noticed that his startled look caused the flight attendant to smirk. With a tray in one hand and a mini pack of pretzels in the other she asked what he wanted to drink. Irked by the interruption of his dream as much as the interrupter, he flippantly said, "Something strong and a lot of it."

Sipping on a cup of hot black coffee with his irritation over the interruption fading, interpretation of the strange dream became all-consuming. Did it have a meaning? If so, what was it? Was Max's father speaking from the grave? Max had been bombarded by meaningless dreams on a nightly basis lately. Maybe it was just one of those. Maybe his subconscious was just playing games and the dream was not a blueprint designed to chart his course or lead him in any particular direction. Yet it was so real and the invitation for him to break its code so irresistible.

Max knew the ordeal was not his father's fault and certainly nothing over which his father had control. As Max matured, he realized his father had been set up to take the fall. Then why did Max withdraw from his father as his father reached for him in his dream? Why did he reject his father and in doing so when he chose to fall, reject life itself? Didn't the dream demonstrate that even though he didn't think his father was right there beside him and at the ready, he was and probably had been all along?

Maybe Max's father experienced unwarranted guilt over the ordeal even though he didn't deserve the consequences it brought upon him and his loved ones. Maybe the dream was meant to show that his father was reaching out for Max's hand begging Max to forgive him. Perhaps taking his father's hand symbolized Max's acceptance of his father's unnecessary apology. His father was begging for reconciliation and Max, by withdrawing his hand, conveyed his unequivocal rejection. That must have been disappointing to his father. Max thought: *If only when he reached out I had given him my hand! Yet, when I looked into his face and our eyes met for what seemed like an eternity, I did not see or sense contentment or peace. He conveyed instead a longing, an anxiety and an anticipation that I could have fulfilled; yet for whatever reason, did not do so.*

When Max had slipped away in the darkness, he did not fall. His rejection was not irretrievable. Max had the power within him to retract his rejection and return to his father's waiting hands and arms. Since he had not hit bottom and the issue was still in doubt, it was probably not too late. He wondered: *How do I convey my love, acceptance and unconditional forgiveness? How do I obtain forgiveness in return? If I've been a disappointment to my father and my family in general, how do I reverse that? My dream tells me it's not too late!*

All this had been overwhelming, starting with the ordeal in 1972 and all that followed including the recent late-night telephone call Max received from his father's former attorney, Lawrence Whittaker, prompting his having booked this flight and now this disturbing dream. Max had always operated under the assumption that there was a reason for everything. His wife of 34 years, Pam, had always said, "God didn't create us to torture or punish us but to bless us and we must put faith in him and trust that he will do just that."

PART TWO:

RELIVING THE ORDEAL

CHAPTER 5
THE ARREST

The stillness of that July morning in 1972 was broken by the sound of sirens screaming from two police cruisers pulling up to the front of the Steamboat Bank & Trust Co. Their abrupt stop was signaled by the screech of brakes. Two officers from each cruiser bolted to the door of SB&T Co., which was opened by an all too eager Alden Stillwell, the thirty-four-year-old son of its president, Brandon Stillwell.

With guns drawn and one set of handcuffs jingling and flashing they were ushered into the office of one of its vice-presidents, James Curtis Cooper, also known as Jamie Cooper. Assistant to the president, Jamie had worked for the bank since graduating from college in 1963. He had risen from the ranks and was Brandon Stillwell's right-hand man, much to the chagrin of Alden Stillwell, Brandon's son. Jamie and Alden were the same age, had gone to school together, and worked at SB&T Co. the same length of time.

It was almost with glee, as one of the officers would later testify, that Alden hurriedly led the officers to Jamie's office. He slammed open the door and pointing at Jamie, shouted, "There, that's the thief who stole thirty thousand dollars from the bank."

A stunned Jamie jumped up from behind his desk, "Wha...what's going on?" he asked.

"Don't pretend like you don't know," Alden shouted and immediately threw $1,000 of fifty-dollar bills strapped together bearing the Federal Reserve Bank of Denver stamp on the desk separating Alden and Jamie. In doing so, the strap tore, and the bills scattered on the desk and floor.

Before Jamie could respond he was thrown to the floor. His hands were cuffed behind him and he was jerked up into a standing position. Despite his cooperation, Jamie sported a torn shirt, split pants, a large bruise on his forehead and a bloody nose from being slammed to the floor.

After the rough treatment, Jamie, stunned at the sudden turn of events, sat without saying a word. Although he was confused, he didn't protest or offer any resistance as he was advised that he was under arrest for felony theft, specifically embezzlement, of $30,000 of bank funds. Jamie was manhandled as he was forced into the back seat of a cruiser that had no door handles on the inside and a steel mesh curtain separating him from the officers in the front seat. The police officers left almost as quickly as they had arrived, only this time with a prisoner in tow.

During the ride to the police station one of the officers turned to face Jamie and read from a card, "You have the right to remain silent. Anything you say can and will be used against you in court of law. You have a right to an attorney. If you cannot afford an attorney, one will be appointed for you."

When the officer asked if he understood his rights, Jamie nodded, still too dumbfounded to speak.

. . .

Once at the station Jamie was locked in a small room with a table surrounded by three chairs. After the cuffs were removed, he was roughly shoved onto one of the chairs. Although the gushing had subsided his nose still dripped blood and from the way it felt, Jamie surmised it had been broken. He was in so much pain that it hurt to turn his head. The overhead lights were so bright he couldn't have looked up even if his nose hadn't been broken. As he sat cradling his head with his hands Jamie could hear shuffling behind a large mirror on the wall directly in front of him. He correctly surmised that a gallery was assembling behind the two-way mirror which no doubt included the Stillwell father-son team. "Blood is certainly thicker than water," he mumbled to himself. *How soon they forget*, he thought, lamenting the callous treatment he was receiving despite his seven years of dedicated service to SB&T Co.

• • •

Jamie didn't know what he was arrested for specifically. He hadn't seen the strapped stack of fifties until they were thrown on his desk. The $30,000 that Alden accused him of taking was a complete mystery. When he asked for clarification, he was told by the officers that he was being uncooperative and that would work unfavorably in the setting of bond, disposition of his case, and in sentencing. He was terrified and confused. To make matters worse, his broken nose made it difficult to breath.

After several relays of officers attempted unsuccessfully to elicit a confession and Jamie's repeated request for an attorney, he was finally allowed to make one call. He had worked with Lawrence Whittaker and Whittaker's partner, Gordon Brownell, on some trust matters. He knew Mr. Whittaker had done some criminal defense work, so he called Larry.

When Larry was allowed to visit Jamie at the jail the next day and after discussing the arrest, Larry agreed to represent him. When Jamie inquired about his fee Larry told him he needed $1,000 up front.

Later that day Larry met with Jennie, Jamie's wife, at the family residence. The Cooper children, Maxwell, twelve, and Collette, ten, were helping their mother prepare dinner. It was evident that all had been crying and were upset. While Larry was outlining the various criminal procedures, Jamie's father, G. Forrest Cooper arrived. He had ten one hundred-dollar bills rolled in a bundle and handed them to Larry. Larry assured him that would be sufficient for him to get started on Jamie's case.

Jamie had been arrested early on July 11, and as it turned out, wouldn't be making his first court appearance until the fourteenth. That meant Jamie would be spending three nights in jail before he would be taken before a judge. Routt County Judge William Dearborn, as part of the court rotation process, had been assigned Jamie's case. Because of a medical emergency in the Dearborn household, the judge had continued Jamie's first appearance from the afternoon of July 12 until the morning of July 14.

CHAPTER 6
MAKING BOND

Jamie awoke to an eerie gloom on that Wednesday July day. His first night in the slammer was fitful at best. He couldn't remember the last time he had not awakened next to Jennie. He knew the call of morning was Jennie resting her head on his chest, long blond hair spilling across him and that scent that was uniquely hers. This morning was different in more ways than he could describe.

Although the jail doctor had re-set and taped Jamie's broken nose it still throbbed, a sensation he had first experienced on the school ground in the sixth grade and later the football field and basketball court. He was not surprised when he awoke and looked in the small metal mirror affixed to the cell wall and saw what appeared to be a raccoon staring back. The two black eyes came with the territory. They were the inescapable result of the nose trauma he sustained at the hands of the over-zealous arresting officers the previous day.

He had already been fitted in jailhouse garb. The jumpsuit was the color of the hunter orange parka he wore during deer season, only more faded. It was tight and he felt like one hundred pounds of potatoes being squeezed into a ten-pound bag. At six-foot-five, he couldn't expect the jail to keep in stock jump suits his size. Besides, he was not going to church or a wedding; he was only going to court.

Jamie was not happy with the continuance. However, Larry convinced him the delay might work in his favor. Larry reasoned the wrath of the Stillwells might diminish, public opinion might soften, law enforcement aggression might subside, and the prosecuting attorney might reconsider filing charges considering the scanty evidence.At least the rationale, faulty or otherwise, made the stay at the county hotel more bearable. Jamie's major concern was how Jennie and the kids were coping.

• • •

Jamie awoke early that Friday morning. Although he couldn't see the sun rising in the eastern sky, he could feel the prayers of his family and friends and a new optimism permeated his being. *This is the day made by the Lord. The day I will be allowed to return to be with Jennie and my family.*

Larry brought a fresh set of clothes for Jamie to wear to court. However, the jailer refused the tender citing jailhouse rules. Jamie felt self-conscious when he entered the courtroom wearing the orange jump suit and lace-less tennis shoes. *Not fitting attire for a bank officer and president-elect of the Steamboat Springs Chamber of Commerce.* He hung his head in embarrassment.

It was 9:45 a.m. when Larry arrived at the Routt County Courthouse. The locals were already assembling and scurrying down the hallway to get the best seats in the courtroom.

Jamie was ushered into the courtroom by the deputy jailer whose green uniform resembled a Christmas tree. It was adorned with decorations consisting of a badge, patches, two-way radio, keys and other official paraphernalia that ballooned his otherwise frail frame.

Apparently. the onlookers were accustomed to seeing Jamie in a business suit, white shirt and tie. Today when Jamie entered the courtroom, the spectators gasped.

After the initial shock everyone sat in stone silence waiting for Judge Dearborn. Larry appeared to be relaxed and was positioned at the defense table next to Jamie. He had open in front of him case books and the Colorado statutes. Larry had no more than taken off his glasses and set them on the table when the bailiff banged his gavel and announced court was in session.

Amidst all the fanfare Judge William Dearborn pranced in wearing a black robe much too large for his miniature frame. The judge had black horn-rimmed glasses and a mustache that barely covered his upper lip. In a squeaky voice, he said, "All right, you may all be seated. Before the court is the matter of James Curtis Cooper, also known as Jamie Cooper." Leaning forward and peering over his glasses, he asked Jamie, "Are you Jamie Cooper?"

Larry nudged Jamie in the ribs thus prompting him to rise. Standing erect, Jamie responded, "Yes."

"Very well," said Judge Dearborn. Then directing his attention to the prosecutor, he queried, "Bob, is the District Attorney's office prepared to formally charge Mr. Cooper at this time?"

"We are, Your Honor," Corbett responded without looking up from his notes.

How is it I'm required to stand and bow to the judge while the other side doesn't even have to look at the judge when speaking to him? Jamie thought.

Larry then stood and asked the judge if Jamie's handcuffs could be removed for the remainder of the proceedings. The judge nodded and instructed the deputy sheriff who was seated behind Jamie to do so. Thankful to be free of the tight cuffs, Jamie vigorously massaged his wrists to restore circulation.

Corbett would soon become one of the key

players in the drama that was about to unfold. Robert or Bob, as he was sometimes called, was currently completing his second term. In November he would be running for his third consecutive term. With that goal in mind and to cement his reelection, Corbett was on a quest to win, win, win.

Corbett was in his forties, sturdily built and had sported a crew-cut since his days at Penn State where he played linebacker. He had no facial hair and dressed conservatively, usually in tweeds and never without a tie. His word was his bond and even his detractors said he was honest. His competitive spirit sometimes, however, got in the way of his better judgment. Once he made up his mind to do something it was difficult to persuade him otherwise.

At the hearing, Jamie could see Larry was bracing himself to make the much- anticipated objection to the district attorney's request to file the complaint. His moment came right after Corbett handed the charge form to the bailiff, who in turn handed it to the judge while Corbett simultaneously deposited a copy in front of Larry. Larry barely looking at the tendered complaint said, "Your Honor, we object to the filing of this document."

"What?" Judge Dearborn asked incredulously.

"I know it's elemental and that Your Honor no

doubt has already considered it, but Mr. Cooper was arrested on Tuesday without an arrest warrant and today is already Friday. This is the first day that an attempt has been made to file criminal charges. Colorado law frowns on arrests made without a warrant and allows that to be done only under very unusual situations such as exigent or emergency circumstances." It appeared to Jamie that Larry was just getting warmed up and Jamie sat fascinated, listening as Larry continued.

"Rule Five requires that when an arrest is made either with or without a warrant the arrested person shall be taken without unnecessary delay before the nearest available county or district court. The rule doesn't say may. It specifically says shall which means 'must!' Again, Your Honor, Mr. Cooper was arrested early Tuesday morning and today is already Friday and the time, according to the courtroom clock, is ten eighteen a.m."

The judge appeared to be unabashed by Larry's recitation of the law and in a condescending fashion, interrupted saying, "The Court is aware of the date and time, Mr. Whittaker!"

There he goes again, Jamie thought. *He calls my attorney by his last name and the prosecutor not by his last name or even his first name but by his nickname. If that doesn't look like a double standard, then I don't know what does!*

Larry was now shifting into high gear. "Rule Five then goes on to mandate that after a defendant has been taken without unnecessary delay before the nearest available county or district court a felony complaint, information, or indictment shall be filed, if it has not already been filed, without unnecessary delay in the proper court and a copy thereof given to the defendant. Judge, the rule doesn't say two, three, or four days later and the choice is not up to the district attorney."

"The prosecution," Larry continued, "has not advanced any reason whatsoever, let alone any cogent reason to justify Mr. Cooper's arrest without a warrant or the delay in his being taken before a judge or the delay in the filing of a felony complaint." Larry glanced toward the prosecution's table apparently to punctuate his point. "Also, my client was precluded from calling either his family or an attorney for almost ten hours after his arrest. Again, a violation of Colorado law and his constitutional rights."

The judge interrupted Larry again and said sternly, "Your client's constitutional rights are not for this court at this time, but for another court at another time."

"That was another of Judge Dearborn's canned

rulings and a clever way to sidestep making a decision," Larry would later tell Jamie. "He must have learned it at Judge's school."

Judge Dearborn, noticing Larry's long pause, said, "I'm sorry, I didn't mean to interrupt you. Please proceed and please hurry this along as we have other matters to address."

Fired up once again, Larry continued, "Your Honor, justice cries out for denial of the prosecutor's tendered filing of a criminal charge in this case. Because of the delay in the three respects mentioned, inadvertence would hardly be an acceptable legal excuse. Even the attempt to file a charge impugns the integrity of the court. To allow the filing would fly in the face of the letter and spirit of the law."

Now it was Corbett's turn. Turning to the DA, Judge Dearborn said, "Bob, do you desire to respond?" Before the DA could even respond, the judge turned to Larry and said apologetically, "Part of the delay here was due in no small measure to my unilateral continuance for medical reasons. Somehow, I don't see how that should be imputed to the prosecution, do you Mr. Whittaker?"

"Judge, even if we lop off one day, our argument still appertains," Larry quipped. "Even if you weren't available, Judge Tibbits was. I know, because I had a matter before him on Thursday. And I know you were available both Tuesday and Wednesday because I was on your docket. Regardless of whether it was your fault, the fault of the DA or the police, or all of you, an unnecessary delay resulted in Mr. Cooper's being denied his constitutional rights. Rejection of the filing is the only proper remedy."

Without Corbett having to say anything, the judge categorically denied the defense motion. The judge ruled, "Even though the prosecution hasn't shown exigent circumstances to circumvent the arrest warrant requirements, the court can and does take judicial notice of the substantial amount of money involved and how law enforcement might have been justifiably concerned about Mr. Cooper's fleeing the jurisdiction to avoid prosecution."

He paused and added, "Especially since the bulk of the money has not been located and is presumably in Mr. Cooper's possession or control."

• • •

Larry rubbed his eyes thinking, *That remark is in direct derogation of the presumption of innocence guaranteed Jamie by both the federal and state constitutions. If this is an example of the judge's mindset, we may as well just throw in the towel. Jamie deserves better than this!* With a puzzled look, Larry whispered in Jamie's ear, "How does he know all that? We don't even know that. Who in the hell is bending his ear?"

Apparently noticing the side bar and Larry's inability to conceal his chagrin, the judge, bent on justifying his decision, added, "Mr. Whittaker, now just what would the fine folks of our community think if I were to dismiss this case on a mere technicality?"

"They would have applauded your having the courage to do the right thing," Larry wanted to say. *What a sorry excuse for a judge*, Larry thought. "Dearborn's maladroit ruling typified his cowardly nature," Larry would later tell Jamie.

Judge Dearborn then began reading the complaint to himself, but loud enough for those seated at the two counsel tables to discern, Umm, Hum and Aha. Finally addressing Jamie, he said, "Young man, please stand while I read the charge against you." Obliging, Jamie slowly rose to face the judge. "The complaint alleges that, 'On or about the tenth day of July 1972, you knowingly, feloniously and without authorization obtained control over a thing of value, specifically thirty thousand dollars in cash, without authorization from its true owner, Steamboat Bank & Trust Co., with intent to permanently deprive the aforesaid bank of the use or benefit of the aforesaid property in violation of the theft statue, a felony carrying a possible penalty of one to ten years in the Colorado State Penitentiary and/or a fine of from two thousand to thirty thousand dollars.'"

Judge Dearborn then asked Jamie if he understood the nature of the charge brought against him and the possible penalty in the event of a conviction. Jamie nodded. The judge scolded him, telling him the court reporter could only record that which was audible—not nods. Embarrassed, Jamie said, "Yes, Your Honor, I understand both the charge and the possible penalty."

Larry then requested that bond be set since theft was a bondable offense. The judge asked Corbett what amount he was requesting, and Corbett responded, "Fifty thousand dollars."

Larry stood and said that such amount would be acceptable if the judge would grant a personal recognizance bond. He also indicated that Jamie's father was present in the courtroom and had agreed to co-sign with Jamie if a co-signer was required.

"What say you?" the judge asked Corbett.

Corbett said, "I oppose a PR bond on the grounds that I don't think it's appropriate, considering the circumstances."

Judge Dearborn said he was "inclined to agree."

Of course he does, Larry thought. *Another set-back for the defense: Prosecution 2; Defense 0.* Larry then asked for a reduction of bond, citing Jamie's age, marital status, length of time in the community and lack of any criminal record. Corbett graciously said he would leave the matter up to the sound discretion of the court. The judge reduced the bail to $25,000 announcing "cash, property, or surety." With that, the judge removed his glasses, raised his brow and looked at the Stillwell family sitting in the front row immediately behind the prosecution table. He then hastened to add, "Unless...unless, of course, the thirty thousand dollars mysteriously reappears, then the court might...just might... consider a further reduction."

It was apparent Larry was having difficulty disguising his rage when he said to the judge, "Your Honor is presupposing Jamie took the money. An accusation doesn't equate guilt."

The judge surprisingly said nothing and standing, smiled wryly at Larry. "The attorneys will please schedule the preliminary hearing with my clerk before leaving here today." With that he briskly announced, "This court is adjourned."

Larry was grateful that the judge hadn't taken exception to his remarks but wondered if he would pay for them in the future. The judge was known for his short fuse and was particularly impatient with attorneys. By instilling fear, he had made attorneys afraid to challenge or embarrass him because of his lack of legal knowledge or common sense. A good ploy practiced by many a judge.

• • •

Jamie's father owned Cooper Ranch outright. Since it was unencumbered, a property bond in the amount of $25,000 could be and was posted. Upon Jamie's return to the Routt County Jail, he was processed and released.

Although they had a lot to discuss, Larry knew Jamie was desperate to be with his family and distance himself from the ordeal. Larry couldn't blame him and after he, Corbett and Jamie met with the clerk and the preliminary hearing had been set for July 31, Jamie made a beeline home to the waiting arms of his wife.

• • •

When Jamie went to Larry's office the following morning the handshake turned into a bear hug. They were jubilant at having succeeded at the bond hearing. Jamie was free for the moment at least. Had they known that the worst of the ordeal was yet to come, there wouldn't have been such a celebration.

On his way out the door, Larry handed Jamie

a small beautifully wrapped box and said, "By the way, happy birthday number thirty-four!"

Taken by surprise, Jamie queried, "How did you know?"

"That's my secret. I know more about you than you think," Larry quickly responded.

"But you haven't asked whether or not I stole the money," Jamie said with a frown.

"Don't have to, but if you want to tell me, now is your chance," Larry responded.

"You know I didn't," Jamie said emphatically.

Just then Larry's investigator, Bobby Dean, nicknamed Bodean (pronounced Bow-Dean), poked his head into Larry's office as Jamie was leaving. Larry had hired Bodean to work on the case right after his first visit with the Coopers.

"Come on in here, Bodean," said Larry. "I want you to meet our new client, Jamie Cooper."

Jamie extended his hand as Bodean entered and Bodean took it in his meaty paw and gave Jamie a warm handshake. "Pleasure to meet you, Mr. Cooper," he said.

"Likewise, Bodean," Jamie responded. "But please call me Jamie. That way I won't feel like an outcast."

"Roger that!" Bodean chortled. "Welcome to our legal family."

CHAPTER 7
ESTABLISHING THE ATTORNEY-CLIENT RELATIONSHIP

When Jamie arrived at the law offices of Whittaker & Brownell, promptly at eight that paradisaical Monday morning, he was greeted by Verna Weager, Larry's highly competent legal secretary for the past ten years. Verna was neatly attired and looked every bit the schoolmarm. Jamie instantly liked her, and they chatted as she led him to Larry's office. Standing and quickly rounding the desk, Larry shook Jamie's hand with zeal.

Larry ushered Jamie into the conference room with his left arm draped around Jamie's shoulders in a fatherly gesture.

Positioned on the credenza was an electric coffee pot emitting that coffee aroma that had stimulated Jamie's senses even before he walked into the room. There was a creamer with fresh cream and a small bowl filled with sugar cubes. Verna soon reentered carrying a large tray with an assortment of various pastries.

As Jamie and Larry comforted themselves at the large conference table facing each other, Jamie was the first to speak. "I can't begin to thank you enough for taking on this rebel's cause. You have provided the hope I needed to believe that there may be light at the end of the tunnel after all."

"Don't thank me yet," Larry said. "You don't know anything about me or my firm. We may prove to be dismal failures. However, the challenges your case presents are not beyond our capabilities. You need to know that even though we may do everything according to Hoyle and the stars may be aligned in our favor, that doesn't ensure that justice will be done. I can promise you, however, that we will do everything within our power to uncover the truth and if that truth is your innocence, to fight for your acquittal and exoneration with great intensity."

"That's quite a promise!" said Jamie, as the two smiled at each other.

Though only twelve years older, to Jamie, Larry seemed much older and much wiser than that dozen-year spread. Jamie was most impressed by Larry's caring and sensitivity. *Larry's positive attitude is contagious!* Jamie thought. *I'm no longer adrift in a sea of discontent!*

• • •

Verna stuck her head into the conference room and announced that Bob Corbett was on the phone and was anxious to speak to Larry. Larry said, "Okay, I'll take it but please hold the rest of my calls."

"Hello, Bob, what's so important that you needed to interrupt my morning nap?" With that, laughter. "Uh huh," Larry repeated several times, nodding. "How does two-thirty this afternoon sound? Umm, okay, see you then."

After he hung up, he told Jamie that Corbett had some investigative reports to give him and that Corbett thought the two should touch base and see if some of the evidence to be presented at the preliminary hearing could be stipulated to. Corbett also suggested the defense might consider just waiving the preliminary hearing all together and allow the case to be transferred to district court. Larry said he agreed to meet Corbett at two-thirty to pick up whatever information the district attorney had, as well as explore the possibility of streamlining the preliminary hearing, or depending on what the district attorney offered in exchange, waiving the preliminary hearing altogether.

"Whatever you think," Jamie responded.

• • •

Jamie had known Larry since 1959 when Jamie returned from CSU. Larry was a frequent bank customer, and both were active in the chamber. However, they really didn't socialize or run in the same circles. Larry defended some high-profile defendants and did mostly criminal work and was known mainly for his successful defenses.

. . .

After court was adjourned on Friday, July 14, Larry kept Verna busy typing various motions including a request for preliminary hearing. Before day's end, the documents had been filed and Larry was already thinking about the preliminary hearing and its importance.

As he would explain later to Jamie, the preliminary hearing was the screening phase designed to weed out the cases that would be unlikely to succeed at trial.

Larry went on to say, "From the prosecutor's perspective, why take a case that is a dud to trial when there are so many worthwhile cases standing in line. Normally, a DA will not file a case he does not expect to win. For that reason, most cases survive the preliminary hearing stage."

From the defendant's perspective, the preliminary hearing was an opportunity to showcase the inherent weaknesses of the prosecution's case as well as get a sneak preview of the prosecution's evidence. "Because the preliminary hearing is so matter of fact and the outcome so predictable, the prosecution's witnesses are not usually well rehearsed. This gives the defense the opportunity to seal their testimony in concrete so that statements they make are difficult later to revise or recant. Impeachment by prior inconsistent statements is one of the defense's most effective weapons," said Larry.

"The defense does not have to call any witnesses but sometimes does depending upon the type of evidence sought to be elicited," Larry advised. "Seldom, if ever, does the defendant testify at a preliminary hearing." Would Larry chance it in this case? He had entertained the idea but immediately erased the thought for fear of its potentially dangerous consequences. How about calling Alden Stillwell to the stand as a defense witness? It might backfire, yet that was a possibility.

Patience was not one of Larry's long suits and though anxious, he knew he must await receipt and review of the offense and investigative reports, prosecution witness statements, inspection of the physical evidence and as importantly, Bodean's investigative results.

Larry had tried to dissipate the doom and gloom surrounding Jamie's case and bolster Jamie's morale. Hopefully Jamie was gaining some confidence and absorbing some of the optimism Larry was seeking to emit.

●●●

Jamie had not read the newspaper accounts that had appeared in Thursday's newspaper. His wife had been shielding him from the negative press since his arrest. He told Larry that his wife had withheld the negative communications sent through the mail as well, again so as not to depress him any further than he was already. Jennie had also been screening most of the telephone calls since not all were friendly.

Larry asked Jamie if there was any other fallout and if he could detect the mood of the community with which he was associated. Jamie said he and the family attended the 11:00 a.m. service at their church the Sunday before and found everyone cordial and sympathetic. The minister had said a prayer asking for God's hand and grace in Jamie's court case and nearly everyone told him they would be praying for him.

Jamie, Jennie, Max and Collette had lived for years at the Cooper Ranch in a house originally belonging to Jamie's grandfather. When Max had started grade school, however, they moved to Steamboat Springs. They purchased an old stately house which they remodeled that was close to the bank, schools, hospital and shopping.

●●●

Larry knew Jamie had history in Routt County and that the family had been pillars in the community. Larry was counting on a sympathetic jury and hoped the prospective jurors had long memories. Larry was shocked to learn of the animosity Jamie would later relate and hoped it wouldn't divide the community into the *for* and *against* Jamie camps and generate a letter-to-the-editor war in the local newspaper. Trial by newspaper would not be particularly helpful for Jamie.

"In a small community like ours," he told Jamie, "everyone knows everyone else and you don't always know who's related and who isn't. Everyone seems to know everyone else's deep dark secrets."

He slid Thursday's newspaper across the conference table to Jamie. "Here, read this," he said, pointing to the front page. "This is just the beginning and you might just as well get used to it."

Jamie took a deep breath and read the following:

BANKER BUSTED

The community was still buzzing and shocked at press time over the arrest of prominent bank employee and lifetime native, Jamie Cooper. Cooper was arrested on Tuesday morning shortly after he reported for work at Steamboat Bank & Trust Co. where he held the title of first vice-president.

According to a reliable source, it took four armed police officers to subdue the six-foot-five-inch, 245-pound former high school and college football and basketball star. Bank employees watched as Cooper, showing the effects of the struggle, was ushered into the parking lot and loaded into a waiting squad car.

Cooper, according to deputy jailer, Dick Towner, was booked into the Routt County Jail about 3:30 p.m., Tuesday, July 11, without incident. He was fingerprinted, photographed, and issued a set of jail coveralls.

Apparently, although it has not been confirmed, from the time of his arrest shortly after 8:00 a.m. until 3:30 p.m., he was being interrogated by the arresting officers at the police station.

Although criminal charges have not yet been filed against Cooper, it is expected that will take place later today. No bond has been set by the court and according to court sources that will take place at the bond hearing scheduled for 10:00 a.m. on Friday, July 14. The case has been assigned to County Judge William Dearborn.

Jamie read the article stoically at first. It wasn't long, however, before Larry could see anger building. Jamie's face flushed as he said in indignation, "How do they have the audacity to suggest that I resisted arrest and had to be restrained?" It was more of a statement than a question. "When the police first arrived and told me I was under arrest, I thought it was some kind of joke or stunt. I was having a birthday in a couple of days and sensed some kind of surprise, but not this. I smiled and stood when the police entered. I never at any time said or did anything to provoke them."

Pausing for a moment, Jamie continued, "The pummeling I took was totally unjustified. It came out of the blue, and believe it or not, one of the arresting officers was like kin. Clint Coleman had helped me mend fence at the Cooper Ranch the weekend before."

In obvious resignation Jamie said, "Larry, I can't believe this is happening to me."

• • •

Larry didn't know what to say. Fumbling for words and wanting to calm Jamie, he blustered, "I guess we don't know who our true friends are, do we? But it's not a bad article and the reporter was only reporting what she was told. It's obvious the 'reliable source' was the police department.

She'll be hounding you for a statement if she hasn't already. And of course, you'll decline comment."

"I guess the reporter was just doing her job and the nasty happenings in the community are newsworthy," Jamie said. "As you said a few minutes ago, I might just as well get used to it. Things aren't going to get any better, are they?"

"No, probably not," Larry replied. "Take a look at the editorial page. That won't make your day either."

As Jamie turned to the editorial page, he told Larry the editor, Eric Sweeney, was a former classmate of his and still considered one of his closest friends. Jamie's jaw dropped as he read:

CAN'T JUDGE A BOOK BY ITS COVER

No matter how well you think you know someone, you probably don't know them well enough. Appearances are deceiving and if you think someone is too good to be true, they probably are.

It pains me to write an editorial about someone I have admired and respected over the years. That someone is James Curtis Cooper, or known to those of us who have been fond of him, "Jamie" Cooper.

I grew up with Jamie. We attended grade school and high school together. He was the valedictorian of our high school class and captain of both our football and basketball teams. He had the lead in most of our plays starting with The Little Dutch Boy in the second grade. He dated and married the most popular girl in our class.

Jamie's sister was my date for our senior prom. Many a summer I spent at the Cooper Ranch working alongside Jamie and his father, G. Forrest Cooper, the son of Joseph Michael Cooper, who homesteaded the land that was the start of the 1000-acre Cooper Ranch and was a long- time county commissioner and mayor of our fair city.

Tuesday was a day my heart stood still. When one of our reporters swung open the door to my office without knocking and informed me of Jamie's arrest for embezzlement of funds from our town bank, I experienced that same sick feeling in the pit of my stomach that I experienced upon learning of the death of John F. Kennedy.

Jamie certainly has the presumption of innocence and we would be ill-advised to rush to judgment without knowing all the facts, but things don't look good for him. For his sake, I hope all of this has a plausible explanation. Only time will tell!

Larry could tell the editorial had a frigorific effect and that Jamie was fighting the stream of frustration. The tears that he had been storing since his boyhood days began to flow and then all the sadness, frustration, disappointment, regret and guilt gushed forth. Larry turned his head away in order not to embarrass Jamie.

When both retained some semblance of composure and looked into the other's eyes, a bond formed between them stronger than between brothers. This was a bond that never would be broken and one that would carry them through the perilous course of the ordeal and beyond.

"You need to have a bucket ready for me the next time this happens," said Jamie, managing a smile. Both chuckled.

Jamie pulled a small box from his pocket. It was the box that contained the birthday gift Larry had given him the previous Saturday. He removed the solid silver medal and chain, "I can't possibly accept this."

"Is it against your religion, or you just don't like it?"

"Oh, no," Jamie replied. "It looks like a family heirloom that has sentimental value."

"The medal," said Larry, taking it from Jamie, "has indeed been in the family for generations, actually for over a century, according to my father. As you no doubt noticed, the crucifix on this side and the Blessed Virgin Mary on the other," he said, pointing to each side of the half dollar size silver medal, "are quite worn. It was worn by my grandfather during World War I and later by my father in World War II. I wore it until several years ago when the circular attachment wore through. While it was being repaired and the chain replaced with a more durable solid silver one, my wife presented me with a solid gold medal and chain that I dare not wear.

"There is a lot of history connected with this medal," Larry continued, as he held it up and allowed it to sway at the end of the chain. "It was given to my grandfather by his father and to my father by his father. It was worn during many a battle, including legal battles. We all wore it at different times, not only because of the religious implications, but and I hate to admit, as a talisman of sorts. It was meant to and did in fact, bring us good fortune."

Handing the medal and chain back to Jamie he

said, "I have no son to pass this on to and I want you to have it. By wearing this you will show your faith in the Lord, and while you wear it, it will be a symbol that Jesus and his Blessed Mother are always with you and that no harm will come to you. They will always be at your side."

Jamie hesitated and then put the medal and chain around his neck. There it would remain throughout the whole ordeal and beyond.

CHAPTER 8
A POST MORTEM OF JAMIE'S FIRST COURT APPEARANCE

After all the tears were shed and all the forms signed the real work began. Almost on cue Larry and Jamie rolled up their sleeves, sharpened their pencils and licked their fingers. The bell for round one had rung.

Larry began by handing Jamie a copy of the criminal complaint. They read and studied it together as well as a copy of the Colorado statute Larry had duplicated for Jamie. Larry explained that not only was the wrongful act required to be proven but the culpable mental state as well. "Here," Larry explained, "the prosecution has to prove that if and when you did it, you had the intent, the specific intent, to permanently deprive the bank of the money."

Jamie nodded. "What about the police denying me the right to make a telephone call and questioning me for seven hours despite my request for an attorney? Is that really 'for another court at another time' as Judge Dearborn stated?"

"Yes," said Larry, "but our time will come.

By the way, Jamie, did you see J. Henry Ross, the bank's attorney, present at the bond hearing?"

JH, as he was sometimes called, was Brandon Stillwell's yes man. Both knew him as the weasel and a man who would do anything for a buck. He was built like a bull with a thick short neck, heavy features, cold steely eyes topped by black bushy brows and thick black unruly hair. People speculated that he did a full body shave every morning before leaving for work. The weasel had stayed behind and was speaking with Corbett when Jamie was led out of the courtroom.

"Yes, I did see him," Jamie responded. "What do you think that was all about?"

"Well, the present action is a criminal action for which the state seeks its pound of flesh mainly to punish you for what it perceives is a wrong committed against society. Its purpose is not to collect the thirty thousand dollars; that must be done through a private civil action pursued by the bank. That's obviously why the weasel was there."

"You're kidding! You mean I can anticipate a civil action that I will have to defend on top of everything else?" Jamie shook his head in apparent disbelief. "It's too bad you don't have children, Larry, because I have a feeling I'll be paying enough before all this is over to send two sets of twins to college."

"The answer is yes to your question. And as to your comment, your contribution to the Whittaker fund for the needy is much appreciated." Both laughed.

"Do you have any other questions… or comments?" Larry asked.

Jamie again shook his head. "I'm afraid to ask anything more for fear of what the answer might be."

Larry began to gather the scattered paperwork into a file folder. He looked at Jamie with sympathetic eyes. "I think we've covered most of the negative possibilities and we'll deal with them as they arise." Larry noticed Jamie looked downcast. In light of all that transpired, why wouldn't he? And he couldn't be blamed for feeling forlorn.

In order to change the mood, Larry said, "You no doubt noticed the Stillwells sitting all prim and proper in the front row on the prosecution's side of the courtroom—all in Sunday attire—Alden with his wife, Debbie, and Brandon with Alden's mother, Laura. Some of the other members of the Stillwell family were seated in the second row directly behind them. I only caught a glimpse, but Debbie didn't seem very happy to be there."

"I didn't look at any of them," said Jamie.

"I didn't want to give them that satisfaction. Also, I was having blurred vision and trouble breathing. You were wise in advising Jennie and the kids to stay away. I didn't see my father until the bond phase when he emerged from the crowd, bless his soul."

"Court proceedings are like weddings," Larry commented. "The community invariably takes sides. You can tell whose side they're on by where they sit. Those favoring the prosecution usually sit on the side where the prosecutor sits; those favoring the defense sit on the side where the defendant and his counsel sit."

"As you've often times commented, you don't always know who your friends are," said Jamie, "or whose side they're on. I guess now all I have to do is look to see where they're seated."

Larry went over the questions Jamie was asked by the police and his responses. The long and the short of what was a fairly long interrogation, considering Jamie asked for an attorney, was Jamie's denial of all allegations. Larry suggested that they wait until after he received copies of the police reports and the transcribed interrogation before proceeding further. Jamie agreed and stated that, as far as he knew, the interrogation was not recorded.

Larry frowned. "Very unusual!" he said. "I guess they can fabricate whatever story they want now without having to worry about measuring it against a tape recording." Instantly Larry wished he hadn't said that when he saw the look of despair cross Jamie's face.

•••

It was approaching noon and Larry was scheduled to have lunch with his law partner, Gordon Brownell, who was driving in from Denver. Gordie, as he was known, had been on vacation with his wife and two teenage sons the past two weeks. Larry was eager to discuss the Cooper case with this former federal prosecutor.

Jamie had planned to drive his family out to the Cooper Ranch to meet with his father to arrange a loan and working schedule so that he could support his family and pay Larry's legal fees.

Larry hoped Gordie wouldn't be late as Larry had scheduled an important meeting with Corbett at 2:30 p.m. at the district attorney's office. Larry had also scheduled an appointment with Jamie for the following morning to review with Jamie whatever discovery and information he obtained from Corbett, Corbett's mind-set, disposition overtures and anything else helpful to Jamie's case. At the same time, Larry, Bodean and Jamie would be briefed on the results of Bodean's investigative efforts. Depending on Gordie's schedule, Larry was hoping to introduce Gordie to the case and to Jamie.

•••

Gordie arrived with his wife, Marilynn, and their two teenage sons, Taran and Trenton, at 11:45 a.m. Gordie was charged and raring to get back into the groove.

After lunch at River Bend and catch-up talk, Larry introduced Gordie to the ordeal. Gordie had a lot of questions Larry couldn't yet answer.

On the way back to the office, Gordie said he wanted a piece of the action. He had turned a few windmills right side up in his day and though he had not practiced law as long as Larry had insight and court sense beyond his years. Gordie was a welcome addition to the defense team, subject to Jamie's approval.

•••

When Larry went to meet with Corbett, he took Gordie with him. Gordie and Corbett were good friends and went to the same church. Their sons were about the same age and had learned to ski together. That wasn't the reason Larry took Gordie with him. He wanted Gordie to hear directly from the horse's mouth what the prosecution's case against Jamie Cooper consisted of—its strengths and weaknesses. Larry didn't want his biases to slant his version of the case.

Corbett was cordial and greeted Larry and Gordie with handshakes and smiles. Corbett had prepared a packet of discovery. The first sheets Larry saw when he opened the folder, were a mug shot of Jamie, front and side, and a copy of the fingerprint card. Next was the National Crime Information Center (NCIC) and Colorado Crime Information Center (CCIC) summary sheets. Neither indicated Jamie had any contact with the law, not even traffic violations. *Good news so far*, Larry thought, passing the documents to Gordie.

There was more to the offense report and witnesses' statements than Larry had anticipated. Impressed, Larry said, "Your boys have been doing their homework on this one."

"Looks like they must want this one pretty bad," Gordie chimed in as Larry passed the offense report and witnesses' statements on to him.

At that moment, Dennis Harlow, Corbett's investigator, walked in with a packet of photographs fresh from the developer taken at the bank.

"Let's see what you have, Dennis," said Corbett, reaching for the packet. As he examined each photograph, he passed it on to Larry, who in turn passed it on to Gordie.

In addition to the photographs of Jamie's desk and office there were photographs of the vault, the vault door, the timing mechanism and a money drawer half full of fifty-dollar bills strapped in $1,000 bundles. There was also a close-up of the Federal Reserve stamps and a torn strap next to twenty fifty-dollar bills strewn on the top of a desk Larry presumed had been Jamie's. Yellow crime-scene tape was seen in the background encircling Jamie's old desk with the lower right-hand desk drawer pictured ajar and its contents clearly visible. No other desk drawers were ajar or pictured open. There were other bank photographs, the significance of which Larry had no clue.

"Dennis, is one of these sets for the defense?" Corbett asked.

When Dennis nodded, Corbett handed the empty film envelope that had contained the photographs to Larry and stated that the set they were examining was theirs.

"I would suggest you two review the discovery at your leisure. After you've done so we can regroup and discuss where we go from here." Corbett paused and then said, "There's no easy resolution of this case. It doesn't appear there is any middle ground. In the eyes of a certain segment of the public we're damned if we plea bargain the case. In the eyes of another segment we're damned if we don't. By letting a jury decide, the jury can take the heat."

Another coward's way out, Larry thought, as he rubbed the back of his neck, apparently considering his next remark. "Why didn't you call a county grand jury on this one? That could have been accomplished in a half day and saved all of us the time and expense of perhaps months and maybe years of hearings, trials, appeals and re-trials."

"I considered that," Corbett replied, resting his chin on his left fist. "I opted to go this route for a number of reasons. As you know, the grand jury is a secret proceeding which takes the place of the preliminary hearing, the latter being a public hearing. I feel the public has a right to know and I believe in transparency. It might have been politically expedient for me to have taken it before a grand jury. But then that would have deprived you of the sneak preview the preliminary hearing provides. Who knows, maybe you'll be able to convince the judge there's no probable cause. That way you and Gordie can be the heroes and I'll be the goat."

Gordie wasn't about to let that one slip past. "Sure! With a preliminary hearing, if the case is dismissed, you can always blame the judge, right?"

He punctuated his remark with a wink.

Corbett's face turned crimson. Whether from rage or embarrassment Larry and Gordie couldn't tell.

"I guess Gordie's right. The determination in either event will be the judge's—not mine," Corbett agreed. "I don't have an axe to grind either way. I'm not out to get Jamie. Nor am I in the hip pocket of the bank. My job is to see that justice is done— not to convict or acquit. What better way to do that than let Jamie's peers in the community make that decision should Judge Dearborn find probable cause? For now, I'll raise the flag with the evidence at the preliminary hearing and see if the judge salutes it."

Corbett was implacable. Larry knew that without ammunition any argument he might advance for dismissal would fall on deaf ears. He must wait for the proper time and that time was not now. *After all, Corbett's reelection bid was on the horizon and he couldn't afford to alienate his following,* Larry thought. *The hell with justice!*

All agreed that plea discussions were premature and that after review of discovery, negotiations could ensue. Also, there was still time to consider how to streamline the preliminary hearing.

Walking Larry and Gordie to the door, Corbett

took a parting shot. "Your client's returning the bank money would go a long way in allowing us to make a sentence concession. Admission, contrition and a firm purpose of amendment would certainly sway the court in your client's behalf. Otherwise, denial, lack of regret or remorse and failing to make restitution will be considered aggravating factors."

"It sounds as though you've already made up your mind as to our client's guilt," Gordie said in disgust.

"And that you have an open and shut case," Larry added.

Unblinking, Corbett responded, "You never know what a jury will do. You lose the cases you think are the strongest and win the ones you think are the weakest."

"If that adage holds up, then according to your assessment, the defense will easily win this one," said Larry.

• • •

Larry and Gordie had plenty of reading material for the night. Their favorite novels would have to wait. They knew that the prosecution's blueprint of the ordeal awaited them and all they had to do was decode it. They hoped the adverse evidence would not get in the way of an acquittal.

CHAPTER 9
PREVIEW OF COMING ATTRACTIONS

It was one of those rare overcast July Steamboat days. Larry and Gordie had both reviewed the discovery the previous night. They were sitting in Gordie's office discussing Jamie's case and nursing cups of the day's brew when Verna arrived with fresh, hot banana bread.

"Who died?" she asked, with her usual sarcasm.

"Who's asking?" Gordie retorted, slathering a generous amount of butter on a slice of banana bread.

"The two of you look as though the Cooper discovery wasn't to your liking. Isn't it a bit premature to be jumping to conclusions?" Verna asked as she departed.

"She's right you know," Gordie said to Larry as Verna closed the door. "We've been here before. There are two sides to every story. As one of my law professors used to say, 'All is not always as it appears.'"

Larry knew they were both right. Jamie would no doubt have a plausible explanation for all those calls to a Las Vegas casino the past two months.

Just because Jamie and Jennie had been there in June didn't mean they were serious gamblers or that Steamboat Bank & Trust Co. was bank rolling their trip or gambling losses, if any. As his father and grandfather used to say, "Rhetoric is not reason and emotion is not evidence!" Larry was now feeling guilty about doubting Jamie's innocence.

No doubt sensing what Larry was thinking, Gordie opined, "It's obvious that Corbett thinks he has found a motive and that the calls and trips to Vegas equate to gambling and gambling equates to losses and losses lead to bank loans, whether approved by the bank or not. I can hear Corbett's final argument now. In his eloquent style he will say, 'Ladies and gentlemen of the jury, the downfall of this once honest and respectable banker was his compulsive gambling and need to borrow money from the nearest available source, the Steamboat Bank & Trust Co. Unfortunately, the bank didn't know about the loan until after they found their money missing!'"

"Bravo," Verna exclaimed, as she reentered Gordie's office to refill their coffee cups.

Gordie held his cup up for a refill, "Does this mean you forgive me?"

"Hell, no!" Verna said, and retreated back to her office.

Larry learned long ago not to get between Gordie and Verna. After Verna left, he said to Gordie, "You're exactly right! And Corbett will have the telephone toll records they obtained from Ma Bell to prove it along with the testimony of the credit manager from Tampico Casino in Las Vegas, who they will no doubt subpoena along with the casino's records."

"Although the records account for only twelve hundred of the thirty thousand missing funds plus the one thousand claimed recovered by Alden, Corbett will claim the other twenty-seven thousand eight hundred was the cash belonging to the bank that was left on the gaming tables in Las Vegas," Gordie offered. "No wonder Corbett thinks he has a slam-dunk case."

"Let's not fall into that defeatist trap Corbett has set for us," Larry said, not just trying to convince Gordie but himself as well.

Just then there was a buzz on the intercom. Verna announced Bodean had just arrived. "Send him back," Gordie yelled into the speaker.

Bodean entered carrying a brown leather briefcase in one hand and a cup of steaming coffee in the other. His black leather vest, jeans and western boots, long reddish-blonde wind-blown hair and matching mustache belied his meticulous and truculent reputation as an investigator.

"Hey, Bobby Joe," said Gordie. "Would you like to borrow my comb? You look like you got caught in the cross winds."

"At least I can change my looks," jibbed Bodean. "By the way, Gordie, did you ever talk to that plastic surgeon I recommended the last time we saw each other?"

"Whew," said Larry, "I'm not getting into the middle of this one either."

About that time the intercom buzzed again; this time announcing the arrival of Jamie—the focus of the summit conference as Larry had billed it.

"Usher him into the conference room," Gordie replied. "We'll all go in there."

• • •

Jamie looked tired and not his chipper self. It was obvious he had the same fitful night as Larry and Gordie. *And he hasn't even reviewed the discovery yet!* Larry thought.

"I gave the check to Verna as per the fee agreement," he said to Larry.

"Thank you," Larry replied.

Verna had previously placed four complete copies of the discovery on the conference table. Larry and Gordie already had their copies tabbed for speedy retrieval. Jamie and Bodean were given copies that were in the stack. They each took a pen and soon their copies were beginning to look like Larry's and Gordie's.

When Jamie started to react to the contents, Larry said, "Please, everybody just read through the whole thing and we'll dissect each and every bit, paragraph by paragraph, sentence by sentence." Although he showed some reaction, Jamie was restrained and followed Larry's instructions. Jamie's face turned white and red and everything in between. *And for good cause*, Larry thought. *I would be upset too, if I were him.*

The journey through the discovery was long and arduous. The plan was to save the photographs for last. Page by page, paragraph by paragraph, line by line, and sometimes word by word, the four plowed through the discovery.

It was only when Verna brought in lunch that the four realized it was lunchtime. Taking time to custom build their sandwiches and select their drinks, everyone began to relax as they ate. They made small talk between bites and sips at first; then the counter-offensive began, not heated or vituperative, but emphatic.

Jamie would have made a good attorney, the others thought, not realizing until after Jamie had left that their observations were shared. Jamie zeroed in on the most damaging evidence and surprisingly dispassionate, discussed the erroneous inferences that were drawn from the facts. Appearances indeed were deceiving Larry and Gordie would soon realize.

Jamie started out by saying the Las Vegas calls and June trip were all true. However, he was not much of a gambler, and he and Jennie usually went to Las Vegas for rest and relaxation and to see the shows. He said he was surprised that the authorities had obtained such private information in such a short time. To add levity, he said he thought what happened in Vegas stayed in Vegas.

In June, Jamie related he and Jennie met his Uncle Matt, his father's youngest brother, Matthew Thomas Cooper, at Caesar's Palace, where they usually stayed. "Uncle Matt's middle daughter, my cousin Patty, had been incurring gambling debts at a rapid rate at various casinos there. She was a high school math teacher living in Vegas and had convinced herself that she had developed a fool proof system of playing blackjack and could beat the odds. The system hadn't worked, and Uncle Matt was picking up the pieces."

Jamie sat for a minute pushing his potato salad around with his fork before saying, "To make a long story short, Uncle Matt couldn't keep up with Patty's trail of losses or cover her IOU's, so he called my father. Dad sent Jennie and me out to Vegas with twelve hundred dollars to pick up a chit at Tampico Casino. He paid for our airline tickets and other expenses. Virtually everything was done in cash, as Tampico would only accept cash.

"The dozen or so calls we made to Tampico were to first ascertain how much was owed and then help Patty make arrangements for payment and to re-negotiate when she was delinquent or incurring new losses. I guess Uncle Matt was losing credibility on the strip and making too many empty promises. He was becoming tapped out as well. Anyway, Tampico was threatening legal action as well as criminal prosecution. The calls were to stave them off long enough for Patty and her father to cover the losses and redeem the chits.

"The problem was that Patty was continuing to sink deeper and deeper in debt. She said the reason was because she had been doubling up on her bets expecting her luck would change and with the winnings would pay off all her debts and ultimately, she'd be able to reimburse her father.

"So, the calls that preceded the June trip were to negotiate payment and settlement and to forestall civil and criminal action. The twelve hundred dollars delivered to Tampico was accepted as payment in full. Thinking that the crisis was over, Jennie and I returned to Steamboat, only to find that Patty was up to her old tricks. Hence the reasons for the calls after the June trip."

"Were the roundtrip airline tickets to Vegas paid in cash or by credit card?" asked Gordie.

Before Jamie could respond, Bodean chimed in, "By credit card, and I have copies of the credit card receipt provided by Jamie's father." With that Bodean produced a photocopy of a credit card receipt showing that G. Forrest Cooper had indeed purchased a pair of airline tickets on June 9, 1972.

Confidence was beginning to swell as Jamie analyzed the so-called evidence in a methodical and almost lawyer-like fashion. "The main vault," he explained, "had a time clock that was set when the tellers completed their balancing and placed the cash in the vault. The head teller, Rita Baker, counted *all* the cash in the vault in the presence of Alden in accordance with bank policy which required dual control.

"On the night preceding my arrest, Rita and Alden closed the vault and set the timer for seven the following morning. I know because I had an office close to the vault. While talking on the phone, I watched Rita check off the various rituals she was performing and observed Alden initial the closing check list and hand it back to Rita.

"No one could open the vault door until seven the next morning. And only the officers, such as Alden and me, had the combination. Even though I was the last one, other than the cleaning people, to leave the bank Monday night and had the combination, it would have been impossible for me or anyone to gain access.

"When I arrived at the bank the next morning it was almost eight and Alden, and I can't remember who else, was already there. I know Rita was there and one of the bookkeepers because I saw the light on in the bookkeeping department and I heard voices. Alden was already there with his office door closed. His office was next to mine and he also had full view of the vault through the glass windows on the front of his office.

"Normally, I'm there at seven thirty, but that morning I had a breakfast chamber meeting at the Tomahawk Cafe at the Cross-Bow that started at six thirty. By the time I walked from there to the bank it was almost eight."

"You walked?" Bodean questioned.

"Yes, I enjoyed the fresh morning air and usually walk when I can," Jamie replied. "I had parked at the bank and just walked the half block to the restaurant and walked back. It of course was not far. I guess nothing is in Steamboat. I had barely settled into my office when the police arrived."

"Was there any money in any of your desk drawers that you know of?" Bodean asked.

"No, none that I know of," Jamie replied. "The first that I'd seen of the fifty-dollar bills was after the police arrived and after Alden had flung them on my desk."

Jamie was bombarded by questions on all fronts. When asked how long he stayed at the bank the night before the arrest, he said, "Until approximately six fifteen." Then he answered no to each of the following questions: Did he ever send money to Tampico? Did anyone other than Brandon, Alden and himself have a combination to the main vault? Did he ever call Las Vegas from the bank? Did he know why Alden turned on him? Did he know where the twenty-nine thousand dollars went? Did he ever take money from the bank without authorization? On and on they inquired and to all such questions he continued to answer no.

When they showed him the photographs, he identified his office, desk and drawer. He said the bottom desk drawer was not open at any time he was there, so he didn't know why a picture was taken of it open. The files pictured in the drawer were stored there and appeared the way they always did. The photographs of the inside of the vault and the inside and outside of the vault door were reasonable representations. The photograph of the cash drawer in the main vault half full of strapped currency looked contrived and would ordinarily have filled the front half of the drawer and not the back half. The other photographs merely showed the layout of the bank and he noted nothing unusual about them.

Jamie refilled his water glass and held the carafe up silently as if to ask if anyone else wanted a refill. No takers.

Jamie said he would like to review the witnesses' statements more thoroughly and asked if he could take them home. Larry replied that he could take the whole packet of discovery; that was his to keep. When asked about the accuracy of his so-called interview, Jamie said it wasn't an *interview*, it was an *interrogation*. He said the four police officers played good cop/bad cop and did everything they could to get him to incriminate himself. He answered everything truthfully. They made much out of the fact that he was the last bank employee to leave the bank the night before his arrest and hounded him about where the money came from that was allegedly found in his desk drawer. They continued to pressure him and told him things would go easier for him if he just confessed and told them where he hid the money. When persuasion didn't work, he said they made veiled threats concerning him, his family and his property.

Jamie's attention was drawn to page 17 of the discovery, entitled "Interview of Defendant" and asked to re-read it.

Interview of Defendant

Name: James Curtis Cooper alias Jamie Cooper
Date: July 11, 1972
Place: Routt County Jail
Charge: Theft F-4

Defendant had been advised of his Miranda Warnings upon his arrest at the Steamboat Bank & Trust Co., County of Routt, State of Colorado, by Officer Gary Boyle, in the presence of Officer's Michael Heath, Lloyd Kinsey and Clinton Coleman.

During the booking process, defendant appeared uncooperative and kept asking why he had been arrested and what he was accused of having done. No statement was reported.

At approximately 0900 hours, he was questioned by Officers Boyle, Heath, Kinsey and Clinton.

Each attempted to interview him separately, and he was uncooperative each time refusing to answer any questions.

When he requested to talk to an attorney, the interviews ceased, and he was placed in a jail cell.

"What the report indicates and what you told us are diametrically opposed," Larry commented. "Unless they claim you made statements later, it won't make much difference. But you're certain you made no statements or admissions of any kind, correct?"

"Yes!" Jamie responded emphatically. "But might my version, which is the truth, have a bearing not only in this case but in a civil action we might bring for false arrest, false imprisonment, malicious prosecution and violation of my rights?"

"Possibly," replied Larry, surprised at how astute Jamie was for someone who had no legal training. *Sounds like Jamie has been doing some homework. I'm impressed!* thought Larry.

"Let's take a break before Bodean takes his turn in the barrel," Larry then suggested.

After they stretched, freshened up their glasses and had their sidebar discussions, Bodean took center stage. Bodean said he was not allowed by Alden to take any photographs in the bank and was told that upon advice of the bank's attorney, no bank employees would be allowed to make any statements.

Bodean, who had been a broncobuster and former rodeo bull rider and used to taking the bull by the horns, persisted, "I was banking, excuse the pun, on being able to interview the officers and employees who had been at the bank on either the tenth or eleventh of July. Their testimony would be critical in ascertaining who might have had access to the money and whether the money even ever existed. When I ran into Brandon at Lions Club yesterday, he appeared willing to talk and said he had left for Salt Lake City on the Saturday before all the fireworks started and didn't return until the following Wednesday. He said he knew nothing about what took place in his absence other than what Alden later had related. With Jamie no longer employed at the bank, he said Alden was now the bank's first vice president."

Bodean thumbed through his notes. "I've talked to the cleaning people and they said when they came to clean on Monday, July 10 at six p.m., Jamie was busy working in his office, the main vault door was closed, and everything appeared secure. They said Jamie left shortly after their arrival. When asked, they stated they noticed nothing out of the ordinary.

They indicated they checked all the outside doors before they left, and all were locked. When I asked them if while cleaning, they might have noticed any loose stacks of currency anywhere, they said no."

Larry asked the names of the cleaning people and Bodean replied "Ron and Betty Skyler." Bodean said their names, addresses and telephone numbers were in his report.

Next Bodean stated he interviewed Ursula Russell, the owner of the title company across from the bank. "Ursula's office faces the front door of the bank and she has an unobstructed view of the bank. She remembered the day of Jamie's arrest and said she had arrived at work about six thirty a.m. and noticed, about that time, Jamie, who she knows through her chamber membership, drive into the parking lot in his Ford Galaxie and after parking his car, walk directly down the street. She confirmed he never entered the bank.

"She said that the chamber monthly meeting was usually held on the second Tuesday of each month starting at six thirty a.m. She said she was updating an abstract with a deadline she was rushing to meet and hence the reason she didn't attend the meeting that morning. She saw Alden drive into the bank parking lot in his Cadillac sedan around six forty-five. She thought that was unusual because he didn't usually arrive at the bank until around seven thirty.

"When asked about Monday night, she said she had left work about six thirty. and the only vehicle in the bank parking lot at that time was Skyler Cleaning Service's panel truck. She said there were no other vehicles in the bank parking lot.

"In light of Jamie's narrative, it's more imperative than ever that I interview Rita Baker to determine who set the timer on the vault door," said Bodean.

"The only way we can force a statement from her," said Gordie, "is if the bank brings a civil action against Jamie. Then we can take her deposition despite the bank's objection."

Larry then stated, "We could always subpoena her as our witness at the preliminary hearing if one is held. The only thing she could do is plead the Fifth to avoid testifying. And if that happens, bingo, we have an alternate suspect."

"We still have plenty of time before the preliminary hearing," said Gordie. "I think we need to regroup and schedule another strategy session."

"Unfortunately," said Larry, "I will be tied up in court the next several days and won't be available until Friday. Would Friday work?" That was convenient for all and the next summit conference was scheduled for July 21 at 8:00 a.m.

Bodean said he would type up his report and have it ready on Friday. "Happy hunting," Gordie yelled as Bodean headed for his car. Jamie was right behind him, obviously looking forward to spending the rest of the afternoon with Jennie, Max and Collette.

CHAPTER 10
THE CLOAK OF ANONYMITY

When Jennie returned from the post office with the mail and newspaper Thursday, July twentieth, Jamie, Max and Collette were playing badminton in the yard along with one of Collette's neighborhood friends. Their dog, Maya, a four-year old Bishon Frise, was stealing the shuttlecock every time it became errant.

Maya had arrived at the Cooper home in a shoe box when she was less than two weeks old. She had been one of a litter of four that Jennie's parents were getting rid of in anticipation of their move to Florida upon Dr. Millard Carpenter's retirement. Max and Collette welcomed the new addition and would have taken the whole litter if their parents had allowed.

The challenge of the badminton game was trying to retrieve the shuttlecock as Maya exhibited the speed of a greyhound and the dexterity and leaping ability of a flying squirrel. If you were lucky enough to get the shuttlecock back, she would be poised, waiting for the next opportunity to steal it and resume her game of keep-away.

•••

Jamie's fun in the sun was short lived when he opened the daily newspaper. He had never liked anonymous comments in the *You Said It* column. He thought such comments were nothing more than unsubstantiated gossip. Besides, he regarded the nameless and faceless hate mongers as cowards. In his opinion, if they were unwilling to reveal their identities by signed letters to the editor, their comments should not be printed. *It was a dangerous practice for Steamboat's weekly to print them,* he thought.

He was shocked to see a whole page of comments in this issue. *Normally they're lucky to have one or two*, Jamie thought. They were all about him and with dread he read one after another. The tone of the comments ran the full gamut, everything ranging from love and kisses to lock him up and throw away the key! The bulk of the comments were vitriolic and venomous. In a fit of rage, he tore the newspaper into a thousand pieces. *The very thing Larry feared would happen happened,* Jamie thought. *I'm being tried and convicted in the newspaper. And they haven't even heard my side.*

•••

Larry, having just read the newspaper and its anonymous postings, felt a sickness much like when one of his best friends had died. He telephoned Gordie at home and Gordie said he had much the same reaction.

"In a community of less than ten thousand," said Gordie, "there's a pretty good chance that everyone knows of the scandal and has formed an opinion that probably can't be erased."

"We have no choice," Larry said, "but to file a motion for change of venue and change the place of trial. There's no way we can pick an impartial jury in Routt County."

Both Larry and Gordie had originally thought that the community would be biased in favor of this deeply entrenched and highly respected family. But the Cooper name, it appeared, had been tarnished beyond salvaging by this incident and the defense would have to go to plan B.

Both Larry and Gordie thought one of them should call Jamie as a sign of support. Larry was surprised when Jamie answered. "Cooper residence."

"Hi, Jamie, this is Larry."

"Hi, Larry." After a pause, Jamie continued, "I suppose you've read the You Said It column in this morning's paper."

"Yes, and it made me sick to my stomach."

"Me too, only worse," said Jamie.

"I spoke to Gordie and we're of the opinion we need to file a motion for change of venue. What do you think?"

"Don't think we have a choice," Jamie said. "If the comments are any indication, there's no way I can get a fair trial in Routt County. Hiding behind the cloak of anonymity, as you all have aptly described it, has shielded the authors of those comments and I'm afraid that some of the authors may end up on our jury."

"That's a strong possibility and not something we can ignore. However, we need to consider where the trial might be moved. The last time I made such a motion and it was granted, the judge was willing to move it only to one of the adjoining counties in our district. That means the choice is either Moffat or Grand."

"That doesn't sound like much of an option," Jamie said. "Word of mouth doesn't stop at the county line. I'm sure everyone has heard by now about all the sordid details and is willing to supply the rope, as one writer has already volunteered."

"What got me was the comment that said the theft was 'generational,' whatever that means," said Larry.

"Definitely a shot below the belt, particularly with all that our family has done for western

Colorado since they settled here over half a century ago," said Jamie. "To curse me is one thing, but to curse my ancestry is going much too far. I guess they're blaming the tree for the bad fruit."

"Well, we'll be seeing you tomorrow anyway. Sorry this happened. Anymore crank calls?" Larry asked.

"Not been paying attention to those anymore. Figure it comes with the territory. I just hang up quickly and let them talk to themselves. I was, however, involved in an incident when I went into Castle's Hardware Store yesterday to purchase some sprinkler supplies. When I came out someone had spat gooey chewing tobacco on the driver's window of my father's pickup."

"Hope you had the window up," Larry said. Neither laughed. "Appears the resentment is evolving into more than a war of words."

CHAPTER 11
PREPARING FOR THE COUNTEROFFENSIVE

When Jamie arrived at the law offices of Whittaker & Brownell that fresh Steamboat July morning, Verna greeted him with "Thank God it's Friday" and "come on, they're waiting for you." She then led him down the short hall to the all too familiar conference room.

Larry and Gordie were already there and had been since 7:00 a.m. Jamie noticed there were two other notebooks sitting on the glass-covered conference table. One was placed in the spot where he usually sat, and a tag bore his name.

"We made reservations for you," Larry said with a smile while pointing to Jamie's place.

"We've got to quit meeting like this," Jamie said returning the smile.

Gordie, head buried in a notebook, said, "We're going on the offensive or should I say we're going to be offensive."

At that moment, Bodean made his presence known by the loud clatter of boots on the tile hallway leading to the conference room. Banging open his briefcase on the glass table as he boldly entered, he said in a contrived western drawl, "Howdy!"

"Did you hear something?" Larry asked looking at Jamie.

"Didn't hear a thing," Jamie replied, deliberately avoiding looking at Bodean.

Gordie looked up and sizing up Bodean's appearance, teased, "While you were at the secondhand store selecting that outfit, you should have bought a comb. If you don't have the money, I can loan you a couple bucks."

Bodean just grinned from ear to ear and drawled, "You're just jealous."

Even with all the worries generated by the ordeal, the bantering between Gordie and Bodean generated a laughter Verna characterized as "boisterous" as she brought in a fresh warm batch of cinnamon rolls.

"I see you resurrected those old clay mugs I had been hiding. What's the matter? Doesn't the coffee taste as good in the china cups?" she said, directing her remarks primarily at Larry.

"These are the tough man's badge of courage— no more sissy stuff. We're tired of having sand kicked in our face," Larry said, gritting his teeth and snarling.

"I think he means it," said Gordie. That set the tone for the remainder of the day.

The first item on the agenda was the matter of the comments in the You Said It column. What to do about them. Gordie said he thought they had tainted the jury pool and that even if a prospective juror had not already prejudged Jamie he or she might succumb to peer pressure and vote for conviction for fear of alienating his or her neighbors, or some paranoid fear of reprisal. What if they filed a motion for change of venue and it didn't succeed? Wouldn't that engender public resentment? Suggesting an accused couldn't receive a fair trial in Routt County would obviously be perceived as an insult. But that was not as urgent a matter now as finding a way to stifle all the hate speech.

Larry was convinced that a letter should go out immediately to the newspaper, attention Eric Sweeney, its editor, objecting to the libelous nature of the posted comments and demanding that the newspaper immediately cease and desist from printing any further such comments. The threat would be a lawsuit and/or the obtaining of a court order or injunction prohibiting all such postings. All that the adverse pretrial publicity was accomplishing was an excuse for the court to grant a change of venue. They all agreed it was probably already too late to counteract the negative public opinion generated thereby.

What about the libel aspect? Although truth is a defense, much of what was contained in the letters was false. It was not only what was said but was not said. The implications, innuendos, and double entendres were libelous as well. Although it was not technically hate speech under the law because it was not directed at ethnicity, for example, it was hate speech nonetheless. The newspaper was propagating this questionable activity by providing the vehicle of dissemination and allowing libelous anonymous comments. They doubted any of the comments would have been submitted had they required signatures.

They felt the newspaper would not risk a libel suit and certainly would opt ethically to take the high road. The same number of newspapers would be sold regardless of whether future derogatory comments were printed, and Eric had the reputation of doing the right thing.

Since a libel action could be brought at any time within one year after the publication of the false defamatory statement, all agreed further consideration should be tabled. However, the letter to Eric Sweeney should proceed as proposed. After they adjourned for the day, Larry said he would draft and have hand delivered such a letter.

Jamie said he didn't want to take matters out

of order but was worried about the bank filing the contemplated civil action. He asked if Larry or Gordie would explain. Larry took the lead and said that the bank had only one choice if it decided to proceed and that was to file a conversion action. That meant that they would seek to recover monetary damages for the lost funds, attorney's fees, and court costs. Ordinarily, the interest would run on the $29,000 from the date of judgment and it would be unlikely that the court would award attorney fees.

Having been in the banking business until ten days ago, Jamie was aware that because the bank was federally insured, there might also be a federal action. Gordie said even though the state and federal governments both had jurisdiction, the feds, in all likelihood, would relegate to the state and let them do their thing. He said it was good that Jamie was aware of the possibility, but not to worry since it was highly improbable that the feds would step in.

Everyone seemed willing to allow Jamie to direct the course of the meeting, at least for now. They knew Jamie's emotions were fragile and that he needed time to heal some of the wounds opened by the despicable newspaper postings. They were willing to give him space and address all his concerns before delving into the tedious preliminary hearing preparation.

When asked what other concerns Jamie had, he replied, "What's the possibility of bringing a civil action against the police department, the jail, and maybe even the district attorney's office? I was falsely arrested. During the arrest they searched me and did a strip search at the jail, all without a search warrant. At the time of my arrest, they also searched my desk and briefcase without my consent. While one searched my office, another, again without my consent, confiscated my car keys and entered my locked vehicle that was parked in the bank parking lot. In fact, the second officer was searching the trunk of my car as the other two officers whisked me away."

Referring to a notepad, Jamie continued, "Jennie informed me that on the afternoon of my arrest, she spotted a marked police cruiser parked in our driveway. When she went outside to investigate, two uniformed officers exited the side door of the garage and walked across the yard and through the gate to their cruiser. She said the double bay doors facing the street had been closed and locked and that the officers would have had to enter through the door they exited."

Still referring to his notes, Jamie continued,

"Obviously, the officers detained me against my will at the bank, police station, and again at the jail. When I was not in my cell, I was handcuffed and accompanied by at least one officer.

"The officers mistreated me at the time of my arrest and assaulted me at the bank and again at the police station. When I was put in the police cruiser in the bank parking lot, one of the officers shoved the end of his baton into my rib cage and tried to slam the cruiser door on my leg. My leg still hurts! They denied me medical attention for my broken nose for over twelve hours. At the booking, they twisted and sprained the index finger on my right hand while fingerprinting me. They used excessive force even if the arrest itself was legal.

"They apparently were having comic relief during my interrogation at the police station, as I could hear laughter behind the two-way mirror throughout the whole ordeal. I don't know who was back there, but I suspect there were several. When I was led out, I saw the chief of police, Jarred Hammerville, and one of the arresting officers, Clinton Coleman, exit the room immediately behind the mirrored interrogation room. Both were laughing and the chief was patting Clinton on the shoulder in a congratulatory gesture.

"They harassed me during the arrest, while

being transported to the police station, at the police station during booking and while I was being placed in my cell. Actually, the jailers were civil and were the ones who ultimately called the jailhouse doctor."

Setting aside his notepad, Jamie stated, "I've noticed the police following me in their cruisers since my release and my father has indicated that the police have been snooping around on his land without permission. Periodically, I see a strange vehicle parked not far from my home with someone sitting in it. The other day, Max, while riding his bicycle in the neighborhood, said he came upon a strange vehicle with a man looking through binoculars in the direction of our home."

When Jamie paused momentarily rubbing his forehead, Bodean, who had been writing feverishly, said, "As a retired police officer and having taught at the police academy, I can tell you they did all the things they were taught not to do. As Jamie talked, I listed ten crimes they committed: false arrest; false imprisonment; malicious prosecution; assault and battery; official misconduct; abuse of official position; harassment; stalking; invasion of privacy, and criminal trespass."

"Wow," said Gordie, "I'm impressed. Here I thought you were just another pretty face."

"Jamie, the three of us have been in law enforcement in one capacity or another," said Larry, "and have great respect for those who lay their lives on the line to protect society. For the most part, I've found police officers to be a conscientious, dedicated, and an honorable lot. What concerns me, is why the police officers, one of whom you described as being like kin, did all these terrible things to you."

"I was wondering the same thing," said Gordie. "I can understand Alden's motives, but I can't understand what motives Clinton Coleman and the others, particularly the chief, would have. Have you done something you haven't told us about?"

Before Jamie could respond, Bodean interrupted, "I've always considered myself one of them and socialized on occasion with most of the Steamboat officers. As an alumnus, I'm usually invited to the Police Officer's Association annual meetings and banquets. Now, after my involvement in your case, I'm a personam non gratis. They go out of their way to avoid speaking to me if they can. Back when I broke up with a high school girlfriend, her friends treated me the same way. I was bothered by it then and I'm bothered by it now."

"My father called me last night after he had read the weekly scandal sheet to provide a little encouragement and to let me know that both he and mom were praying for me," Jamie said. "Dad told me he had been trying to figure the whole thing out for days and particularly after reading the scathing comments in the newspaper. He said he was in a quandary and after discussing it with mom, was finally able to connect the dots."

Leaning forward, Larry, Gordie and Bodean listened in anxious anticipation as Jamie continued. "Some years ago, when my Uncle Lewis was still alive, he and my father found signs of poaching and butchered cattle on the far rocky reaches of the Cooper Ranch. Apparently, this had been going on for several years. So, when they found fresh slaughter hanging from a tree ready to be retrieved, they lay in wait. Sure enough, after it got dark a four-wheel-drive pickup drove down a seldom used dirt road not much wider than a cow trail and stopped less than twenty yards away. Holding a rifle, a large, rugged man emerged with a young boy he guessed to be twelve. In addition to the rifle, they were carrying butchering tools and canvas bags. Both were wearing miner helmets with mounted lights. After the large man set down his rifle against a tree, he began finishing his carving project while the boy laid out packaging material for the prey.

"Uncle Lewis and my father, emerging from

their hiding place with rifles drawn, approached the poachers. When they caught the poachers in the beams of a large portable spotlight, the poacher's crimes were exposed. The man reached for what turned out to be a loaded 30-30. Just as he was about to take aim, my father shot it out of his hand, permanently injuring him. The young boy apparently frightened just froze in his tracks, quivering and unable to move.

"After the man was treated by a medical doctor who lived near the Cooper Ranch, he was transported by a deputy sheriff to the Routt County Jail. He was charged with cattle rustling and a hunting violation. He pled guilty to both charges and served time at the Colorado State Penitentiary."

Jamie stopped and grimaced when he took a sip of his now cold coffee. The suspense of course was raising havoc with the three listeners. Like kids, they bombarded Jamie with a myriad of questions, all at the same time. What happened next? Who were they? What happened to the boy? What's this got to do with your case? When did this happen? Was the boy related to the man? How old was the boy?

"I now know what it feels like to be cross-examined," Jamie said. "I'll try to answer your questions as I remember them. This happened in

1944. The boy was the son of the man. The man was thirty-eight years old at the time having been born in 1906. The son was twelve years old at the time having been born in 1932; now he would be forty years old. Both still live in Steamboat. The father has a withered right hand." Jamie stood up and handed the weathered news clippings he had been holding to Larry. "Dad dropped these off this morning before my appointment with you."

"Oh my God," the three said in unison. "The father is Summer Hammerville, and the son is Jarred Hammerville, our Chief of Police."

"Any other questions, gentlemen?" Jamie asked. Stunned, silent and shocked, they just sat there staring at each other. Jamie then said, "I rest my case!"

None of them could think of anything clever to say. Finally, Larry said, "This is a good time for a lunch break."

Verna had deli sandwiches, Larry's favorite hot pastrami on pumpernickel with German potato salad, coleslaw, and kosher pickles. "Just like going to Ken's Grill on Copley Square in Boston," Bodean said, corralling his allotment.

"I love kosher food too," Gordie chimed in.

Selecting their favorite soft drinks, they all settled in for some cozy chitchat.

Taking a bite out of his pickle first, Larry said he had a confession to make. "Call me a doubting Thomas," he said to Jamie. "I feel like I've been on a roller coaster since becoming involved in your case. I did what I tell my jurors not to do: don't jump to conclusions; listen to all the evidence first before making a decision; and keep an open mind. I learned a very valuable lesson today. Even though I've been leaning your way from the start, I must confess I let some stinkin' thinkin' creep into my mind the past twenty-four hours. You've countered every accusation with a plausible explanation. I guess it's easy when you're telling the truth. And in my heart, I know you are."

Gordie and Bodean followed suit. Confession, contrition and a firm purpose of amendment are needed for forgiveness, and they were asking for forgiveness. Jamie said he didn't blame them for how they felt and only hoped he could help them help him.

"How do you keep such a positive attitude, especially after having read the comments in the newspaper, most of which contained pejorative remarks?" asked Gordie. "I think Larry and I, and maybe Bodean as well, were more traumatized than you. And they weren't even about us."

"Thank you for the compliment. I'm practicing

an art I learned from a book I read some years ago about a prisoner of war who had been confined by the enemy to a birdcage of a cell for a number of years. When he was liberated, he was asked by his liberators how he was able to survive. He said in his mind he played golf every day, he lounged at various resorts around the world, and drank mint juleps every afternoon. He called it disassociation. That's what I'm doing. I have to cope because of all the people out there who depend on my strength—especially now."

Larry, still intent on making up for his lack of trust, said to Jamie, "You thanked me for taking on your case. Actually, it is I who should be thanking you. I will certainly be more circumspect."

"Win, lose, or draw," Jamie responded, "I'll never be able to adequately thank all of you for your taking on this rebel's cause and more importantly, for the friendship I sense is developing between all of us." He rose and walked around the table, shaking each man's hand as if he were campaigning for a political office. Upon returning to his chair, he and the others finished the lunch that had pretty much gone untouched up until that moment. Even then they ate very sparingly.

When Verna cleaned up the lunch mess and collected the leftovers, she said, "What's up with the picky eaters? Didn't you like the food? You all ate like birds. I'll put the leftovers in the fridge, and you can help yourselves when your appetite returns."

* * *

Everything seemed to take on a new hue now. With renewed vigor they began to dissect the case against James Curtis Cooper alias Jamie Cooper. They started with the police officers' witness interviews. The first interview was of Alden Stillwell.

Alden told Officer Coleman that he was an officer at the Steamboat Bank & Trust Co. He, his father and Jamie were the only three who had the combination to the main vault where the bulk of the bank's money was kept. The bank had a system of dual control whereby the head teller, Rita Baker, and one of the three officers, usually himself, would count the money at day's end and set the timer on the vault door for 7:00 the following morning. One would close the door and spin the combination in the presence of the other. This procedure was followed on July 10. Normally his father would open the vault. During the week of July 10 through July 14, however, his father was out of town and so Alden opened the vault on each of those days.

Alden, according to the discovery, told Officer Coleman that he opened the vault door on Tuesday,

July 11. He then went to his office to begin work for the day and when he went into Jamie's office to retrieve a file, he discovered $1,000 in one of Jamie's desk drawers and confiscated it. He immediately went to the vault and when he examined one of the cash compartments in the vault discovered that $30,000 in straps of $1,000, some containing fifty-dollar bills and others containing one-hundred-dollar bills, were missing. Each strap had a stamp on it bearing the Federal Reserve Bank of Denver. He then searched the other drawers in Jamie's desk but didn't find the other $29,000. He stated that he was the first to arrive that morning and that Jamie's Ford Galaxie was in the parking lot when he arrived. He didn't see Jamie. Jamie didn't arrive at work until almost 8:00. When Alden left the bank, the previous evening at approximately 5:45, Jamie was still there.

According to Officer Coleman's report, he next interviewed the bank's head teller, Rita Baker. She stated that she and Alden counted the money in the bank's vault at day's end on Monday, July 10. She and Alden set the timer on the door of the vault for 7:00 the following morning and together they closed the vault door locking it behind them. She double-checked to make sure the vault door was closed and locked.

She arrived at work the usual time the following morning July 11, which would have been around 7:45. Alden greeted her with the $1,000 he said he obtained from Jamie's desk drawer and told her that he checked the vault and discovered $30,000 missing from the main cash compartment. He told her he then searched Jamie's office for the other $29,000 but was unable to locate any sign of the missing money.

In Rita's presence, Alden called the police, and while waiting for the police to arrive, the two searched the rest of the bank in an effort to locate the other $29,000. While they were in the midst of conducting the search, Jamie arrived. Within minutes thereafter, the police arrived on the scene and arrested him.

She, Alden and the rest of the bank's employees again searched for the money after the police left but again to no avail. Alden then ordered her to have all the bank locks changed, to box up and bring to him all of Jamie's personal effects. After the police searched Jamie's car, Alden ordered her to have it towed away.

"Officer Coleman has been a very busy man," Larry said sarcastically.

"Sounds more like an over-zealous cop to me!" Bodean said emphatically. "He's shooting for rank and more pay and it's obvious he's trying to curry the chief's favor."

"The chief wants a Cooper's head on a platter," said Jamie in disgust. "With what's happened at the bank, his wish has been granted and a Cooper's head, namely mine, is just falling into his lap."

"You wonder how many sleepless nights he fantasized about the devastating and painful ways he would exact his family's perceived pound of flesh for what happened to his daddy," Gordie speculated.

• • •

The investigative report indicated that Coleman had contacted the custodian of records at the telephone company, seeking the toll records for the calls made from Jamie's home telephone for the months of June and July 1972. Copies of those records were included in the discovery. Checked off were seven calls in June and five in July made to a Las Vegas number. The numbers, according to Coleman's report, were traced to Tampico Casino, a well-known gambling establishment on the Las Vegas strip.

Another page in Coleman's investigative report centered on the verification of a trip Jamie and Jennie made between the telephone calls in June. He had also obtained records from United Airlines confirming the issuance of roundtrip airline tickets in Jamie and Jennie's names to Las Vegas with a departure date of June 23.

"Hmm," Jamie said in a huff, "I have the damn tickets sitting on my desk at home as we speak. If they had asked, I would gladly have given them those along with the Caesar's Palace hotel receipts, the limousine receipts and anything else they wanted. Remember, our airline tickets were purchased by my father and were put on his credit card. He would, of course, have those records."

Coleman's report noted that he had contacted Katherine Tilley, a bookkeeper at Caesar's Palace, who verified that a Mr. and Mrs. James Cooper had checked in on June 23 and checked out on June 26. Because it was a recent transaction, Ms. Tilley said she would be able to retrieve and forward a copy of the registration to the Steamboat Springs P.D.

"I can't believe they would just give that information out over the telephone," Gordie commented. "Since no copy of the registration form is in the discovery, I assume the police department doesn't have it yet."

"By the way, Jamie," asked Larry, "How did Coleman know to check at Caesar's?"

"Everyone at the bank knows where I stayed. Whenever I went out of town, I made sure they knew how to reach me," Jamie replied.

Perhaps the most damaging piece of discovery was a photocopy of a receipt from Tampico Casino for the payment of $1,200 issued to Jamie on June 23, 1972, "in full payment and redemption of chit #72-PD4485." Noted on the bottom of the photocopy was the following handwritten scribble, "Officer Coleman, I assume this is what you wanted. If we can be of further assistance, please feel free to re-contact us." The notation bore the signature, Horace Green, Head Bookkeeper, Collections.

"The PD designation on the chit number, I assume," Gordie said, "means past due."

"This is the guts of Corbett's case!" said Larry as he shook his head.

Although the case was still young, there were already over fifty pages of discovery. When Bodean was spending more time on particular points than he thought necessary, Larry prodded him along. This would have been the longest of the sessions, and when 5:00 and then 5:30 passed, it was decided to call it a day. They had accomplished all they had hoped for and more.

As they exited the conference room, Gordie turned and asked, "What do you think of Jamie taking a polygraph?"

Jamie said he had no problem with that.

Larry said he felt confident Jamie would pass.

Bodean said he thought a lie detector test was a good idea.

"Who would administer the test and when?" asked Jamie.

It was agreed that Bodean would scout out a polygrapher who didn't have a prosecution mind-set, someone preferably outside the area.

Exchanges of endearment, some kibitzing and then the goodbyes. If this day was but a drop in the bucket of the emotions they would experience on the long journey through the ordeal, they didn't want to know about it—at least not just yet.

JUSTICE DENIED — CARROLL MULTZ

CHAPTER 12
THE CLOCK TICKS

When the summit conference was over on Friday, Jamie and Bodean walked to their cars. Small talk at first, then Bodean reflecting his ex-cop curiosity said, "Jamie, there's something that's been bothering me all afternoon."

"What's that?" Jamie asked.

"Regardless of whether it was you or someone else, how could the money have been removed from the vault from the time the bank vault time lock was set until it expired at 7:00 the next morning? In other words, even if you or that someone else had the right combination, the door couldn't have been opened. They would have had to wait until the time ran down, right?"

Jamie, tossing his notebook, folder and legal pad into the front seat of his car replied, "The bank's vault time lock was an antique and from time to time we upgraded it. The lock has two movements to provide redundancy in case one fails. The theory behind two is that if there was only one movement and it failed; it would almost take dynamite to gain access. Going in and out of the vault for thirteen years, I do remember that when I first started working at the bank and the door didn't open, even when Brandon had dialed the right combination, he went to his office and called the manufacturer. He was gone for quite a long period of time while the tellers waited. He finally returned and referring to numbers on a small slip of paper dialed a bypass combination which apparently overrode the time lock. I'm not aware that ever happened again."

"That's what I wanted to know," Bodean said, nodding. "Apparently, up until that time, no one at SB&T Co. knew the secret combination—not even Brandon. What about you and Alden? You had the regular combination, but did either of you have the secret combination?"

"I didn't," Jamie responded. "I don't know about Alden. Someone must have had the bypass combo and the most likely person was Alden because Alden had access to his dad's office."

Speculating, Bodean said, "He could have been looking for something in his dad's office while his dad was in Salt Lake and stumbled upon the secret combination."

"Either that," Jamie said, "or Alden had the window of opportunity from 7:30 a.m. when the vault opened until 7:45 a.m., when the first bank employee arrived, to remove and stash the loot."

"It doesn't appear in the discovery or anywhere

that anyone ever searched Alden's desk, office or Cadillac. In fact, it appears that he was assisting and directing everyone else in the search. Maybe the operative description is deflecting their attention away from him."

Shaking his head, Bodean concluded, "It's like the fox guarding the henhouse."

"It's pretty clear that Alden pointed everyone in my direction," said Jamie. "For whatever reason, I can only speculate. Maybe revenge, jealousy or to deflect suspicion. Who knows? The officers had tunnel vision. I was accused, charged and convicted all in one quick swoop. All that awaits is the hanging. And flavor the mix with a chief of police and henchmen who want to vindicate the dignity and restore the reputation of the chief's father who was convicted of a felony and went to prison all because of a Cooper."

Bodean was beginning to feel a respect and admiration for a man who was being wrongfully accused, denied by those he thought were his friends and sold out for thirty thousand pieces of silver—much like someone he has known in his heart and who lived, suffered and died almost two thousand years ago. The disparity Bodean attributed to inflation.

The case would hinge on who the jury would

conclude to be the most likely candidate to have stolen the money—the son who would steal from his own father and really from himself since he presumably was the sole heir or an employee who had a gambling addiction and couldn't cover his losses. Bodean knew he had his work cut out for him.

Bodean told Jamie he had a former roommate at Michigan State whose family had been in the banking business and he would call him to discuss the bank vault time lock (BVTL) aspect of the case. He said he had been thinking of calling him for some time now and this would be a good excuse. Because of the impact of the BVTL aspect of the case, Jamie and Bodean agreed to meet at Larry and Gordie's office on Monday at 1:00 p.m.

• • •

On Monday, July 24, Jamie called Bodean and said he, Jennie, Max and Collette were all at the Cooper Ranch and had been there since Saturday morning helping his father mend fence. He asked if they could postpone their appointment until 4:00 p.m. Bodean said that would be better for him as well.

As the clock on the town hall struck 4:00, Jamie and Bodean drove into the parking lot at Whittaker & Brownell, Jamie in his drab 1971 Ford Galaxie and Bodean in his bright red 1972 Ford Mustang. Jamie's mode of dress was similar to Bodean's. He was still wearing his fence-mending garb, not having had time to change.

"I see you got the memo," Bodean said playfully as both hurried across the tile floor, *clickity-click, clickity-clack.*

Verna, diverting her attention away from the typewriter while lowering her gold wire-rim glasses, was greeted by two unkempt and ruffled ranch hands. No doubt surprised by their casual attire, her mouth gaped, and she just stared.

"We just came back from a wedding," Bodean teased. "We figured you missed us."

"Can't get rid of a bad penny," Jamie chided. "That's an old banking joke."

"You two are just too funny—funny acting and funny looking," she said with contrived indignation. "Isn't the leash law in effect today?"

"Aw, come on. We know you missed us," Bodean taunted. "Do you mind if we use the conference room? We need to plot strategy. The walls have ears in all the coffee shops and soda fountains, and we dare not go into the bars. You know how gossip starts."

"Larry and Gordie are still in court and have been all day. The door is open, just move the books aside. Help yourselves to the cold drinks. But, please do me a favor!" Verna added.

"What's that?" Bodean asked, brushing dust from his shoulders.

Verna scrunched up her nose. "Just don't let anyone suspect I know you two. If anyone asks, just say you couldn't find your way to the box cars and stopped to ask for directions."

"Nice, Verna, and we used to like you, too," Bodean murmured as he and Jamie clicked their way to the all too familiar conference room.

• • •

"Did you make contact with your former roommate?" Jamie asked.

"I did," Bodean replied. "It was good to talk to Dustin Davies again and he provided a lot of valuable information. He's been working in the family bank at a branch in Kalamazoo, Michigan. Apparently, the bank just replaced a dinosaur made sometime in the 1800s with a time lock containing what he called a three-movement, double redundancy time movement, made in Switzerland.

"Dustin said each BVTL was different depending on year of manufacture, type, model and manufacturer. He said the early locks contained a mechanism that when a special combination was dialed, the time lock would be disengaged.

He also referred to the special combination as a bypass or secret combination known only by the manufacturer. The manufacturer would only reveal the secret combination to upper-level bank personnel in the event of BVTL failure and the urgent need to open the vault.

"Dustin said the BVTL evolution was marked by two or three movements, providing redundancy in the event one timer malfunctioned. Otherwise, the door could only be opened by what he called extreme and sometimes destructive methods.

"He confirmed what you had already told me about the regular combination needing to be dialed even after the timer ran down. In other words, the vault door does not automatically open at the appointed time.

"He said he would send me copies of whatever he had and would come up with the name of an expert in the field if we intended to call one. He also indicated that such experts were expensive and that they usually wanted their money up front. I told him we would let him know if we went that route."

About that time, the "Perry Masons of Steamboat" arrived. Peering into the open door of the conference room, they engaged in dialogue about disciplining whoever left the back door to the office unlocked allowing vagrants access.

Once Larry and Gordie had deposited their carry-ins in their respective offices, they returned with their *People v. Cooper* folders. Both were appreciative of the crash-course on BVTLs and having learned a new acronym. They all briefly debated the pros and cons of bringing up the BVTL issue at the preliminary hearing or saving it for trial. All agreed that if they did, it would be them providing the sneak preview at the preliminary hearing, and thus, by placing the prosecution on notice, would be allowing the prosecution to arm itself in anticipation. The evidence on the BVTL, it was decided, would be saved for trial.

Larry took a poll to determine what each considered being the Achilles heel of the defense's case. He told each of them to write it down and not let the others see. The ground rule for this parlor game was that each could only list one item.

When everyone had finished writing, Larry started around the table. The telephone calls and trip to Las Vegas, was the unanimous choice.

"It provided the motive," said Bodean.

"Easily explainable," said Jamie.

"Not so easy," said Larry and Gordie in unison.

"Now that we have established the number-one challenge," Larry said, "what are we going to do about it?"

It was Bodean who spoke first. "We need to contact Jamie's Uncle Matt and Cousin Patty. They will provide the alibi, so to speak."

"Have you spoken to either of them since the beginning of the ordeal?" Gordie asked Jamie.

"No," answered Jamie, and looking sheepish, he added, "I've been too embarrassed."

"Well, they helped get you into this predicament; they can help get you out of it!" Gordie said emphatically.

Larry interjected, "Even though we wouldn't call them to testify at the preliminary hearing, we need to contact them as soon as possible to ensure their availability and cooperation should we need them at trial." Turning to Bodean, Larry asked, "Bodean, can you do that before our conference on Wednesday?"

Bodean, who was taking notes, raised his head and asked Jamie if he had their addresses and telephone numbers. Jamie said he did and retrieved a small folded slip of paper from his wallet and handed it to Bodean. After copying the information Bodean returned the slip to Jamie.

"Wouldn't Coleman and the others like to have a copy of that?" Gordie asked, catching himself and adding, "Strike that, I'm sure they already have arranged for a sister agency in Las Vegas to interview Cousin Patty and Uncle Matt. That probably was the first information the police found and copied when they rifled through Jamie's wallet upon his arrest."

"That might have been what triggered the Las Vegas connection," Larry mused.

"Shouldn't we have Cousin Patty and Uncle Matt testify in my behalf at the preliminary hearing?" Jamie inquired.

"Not necessarily," Gordie responded. "The fact that you went to Las Vegas to bail Patty out of her predicament doesn't help our case at this point for a number of reasons. The first is the preliminary hearing is not a trial or even a mini trial. If there is a factual dispute, that will be for a jury to decide. A second reason is that it's immaterial what the money was used for. Whether to cover your gambling losses or Patty's, it was still the bank's money, at least according to the prosecution's slant, and you didn't have the bank's permission to take it. So, their testimony wouldn't benefit your cause—at least not at this juncture."

Bodean said he thought that the statements taken by their sister agency in Las Vegas would be skewed anyway. "All they wanted was to document your trip to Vegas," he said to Jamie. "They didn't know about it and Patty was not about to divulge her woes. They didn't ask; she didn't tell. So, all that Coleman's report indicates is that 'Patty Cooper confirmed that her cousin Jamie Cooper and his wife Jennie were in Las Vegas between the dates of June 23 and June 26, 1972.'"

"Well, doesn't Corbett need to fly them out here to testify at the preliminary hearing? Otherwise, isn't that hearsay?" asked Jamie.

"Good questions, both," Larry responded. "No, in answer to your first question and an equivocal yes in answer to your second question. It is hearsay when a person testifies as to what someone else told him or her. For Coleman to testify as to what Patty told the Las Vegas cop, who in turn told him, is double hearsay. Unfortunately, at preliminary hearings, the rules of evidence are relaxed, and hearsay is allowed at the sound discretion of the judge."

"Why couldn't Bodean interview Patty and Uncle Matt over the telephone and then relate at the preliminary hearing what they told him?" Jamie asked. "Wouldn't that only be firsthand hearsay and even more reliable than Coleman's double hearsay testimony?"

"Wow!" Gordie said. "I feel like I'm taking the bar exam all over again. That conceivably could be allowed. But what do you prove? All you do is corroborate the fact that you brought money into Vegas to support their local economy. It's still money and money that inferentially belonged to the bank."

"In law school, we called that a *Circulus Extracabulis*, which loosely translated means going around in circles," said Larry.

Jamie, still confused asked, "Does that mean that Coleman could be the only witness called by the prosecution at the preliminary hearing and could testify as to what the various witnesses told him?"

"That's also a possibility," answered Gordie. "Technically, Judge Dearborn has discretion to allow that. However, he would probably rule that the victim, here the bank through one of its officers, should establish the existence of the funds, their disappearance, Jamie's access, and more importantly, the finding of the one thousand dollars in Jamie's desk drawer."

"By the way," Bodean interjected, "the finding of the one thousand dollars in Jamie's desk drawer could have been a close second on my list of weaknesses in our case. If anyone is interested, I'll tell you why." Everyone nodded. "In theft cases, I found when I was in law enforcement that the jury required that the accused be caught with his hand in the proverbial cookie jar in order to convict.

Here, if we believe Alden, the 'cookies' were found in Jamie's lower desk drawer."

"I would second that," Gordie quickly added. "Although it might not make any difference at the preliminary hearing it might at trial where everything will hinge on Alden's credibility. If the jury questions Alden's credibility seriously enough to rise to the level of reasonable doubt, Jamie is home free. Otherwise, if they believe Alden, Jamie's goose may be cooked!"

"It's amazing," Larry exclaimed. "I almost put Alden's claim of discovery of the one thousand dollars in Jamie's desk drawer the number one concern. The only reason I didn't is because the one thousand dollars was never in Jamie's possession. The only person who had it in his possession was Alden. When the police arrived, it was not in Jamie's office or even on Jamie's desk until Alden, emerging from his own office, with cash in hand, threw the offending bills on Jamie's desk. That was witnessed by everyone including the officers who had bad intentions."

"Don't you think Alden's credibility is the number one prosecution concern?" Jamie asked Larry.

"Yes," Larry said without hesitation. "I think his credibility is the key to the whole case."

"My sentiments exactly," said Gordie.

"Mine too," echoed Bodean.

"I think, and I've thought about it long and hard," said Larry, "it was probably a spur of the moment thing for Alden. When he stumbled on the secret combination in his father's desk drawer the day before, he didn't think much of it. But after he went home and maybe while he was reclining in his favorite chair and replaying the day's events in his mind and pausing on the combination discovery, formulated his clandestine plan.

"After his wife was deep in slumber he snuck out of the house, drove over to the bank and finding that the secret combination worked, removed the thirty thousand. He then stashed one thousand in his desk drawer as Jamie's office was locked and he didn't want to take the time to hunt for the key. He then drove himself and the twenty-nine thousand home and after hiding the money, slipped unnoticed back into bed."

"Gosh, Larry," Gordie chided, "do you hire out for bedtime stories? My boys have tired of my mundane fables and anecdotes."

Ignoring Gordie because of deep concentration, Larry continued, "As I said, it could have been a spur of the moment thing, something totally impulsive, but I may be wrong. Alden may have been planning the frame-up for a number of years. With his father out of town, the opportunity presented itself and Alden acted upon it."

"With both of his parents out of town," Bodean speculated, "Alden could have placed the twenty-nine thousand temporarily in their home or outbuildings. They lived side by side and Alden undoubtedly had a key. That way, if his home were searched, he wouldn't be found to be in possession of the missing money."

"If Alden had been caught at the bank that evening," Gordie added, "he could have aborted his plan, at least for the evening and claimed he was attending to some unfinished business. He had a built-in excuse. All the cards, however, fell into place. Mission accomplished and not a trace!"

Larry then asked Jamie, "Do all the officers lock their offices? I guess I'm asking if Alden had a key to yours."

"There would have been a duplicate in Rita's desk drawer, but I don't think Alden had a key to mine and I know I didn't have a key to his," Jamie responded. "I think he was in a hurry the night before and didn't want to take the chance of being seen at the bank and therefore, didn't take the time to hunt for the key."

"I'm sure," Larry said, still deep in thought,

"that Alden figured he would be first to arrive at the bank the next morning and would have plenty of time to plant the one thousand in Jamie's office. Unable to find the right key and not expecting the bookkeeper's early arrival, Alden had to improvise. He was probably nervous about having the one thousand still in his possession and knowing he had to get rid of it, made his dramatic entrance into Jamie's office scattering the bills in his haste."

"How do we prove all that?" Jamie asked, looking in Larry's direction.

"It's just speculation and conjecture. It's not evidence. Just as the evidence surrounding you is circumstantial, so is Alden's in developing our alternate suspect defense. It's up to us to paint the picture and plant the seeds of doubt. Maybe we'll get lucky and Alden will make a mistake."

"Since it's just as likely that our version of events occurred as theirs," Gordie once again added, "the tie is required by law to be resolved in Jamie's favor!"

Bodean, not to be outdone chimed in, and looking at Jamie, said, "We don't have to prove anything. The defense never does. We don't have to prove a damn thing! We just need to raise reasonable doubt. If the prosecution doesn't prove their case beyond a reasonable doubt, the jury is required by law to return a not guilty verdict."

About that time the telephone rang. On the fourth ring, Larry looked at his watch and noticing it was after 7:00 and realizing that Verna and the rest of the staff had already left for the day, answered the telephone.

"Whittaker & Brownell," Larry responded. After a brief pause, he said, "Yes, he does… He's on his way. He's been unavoidably detained… I'll tell him to hurry!

"That was your wife," he told Gordie. When the phone rang again, he knew who it was and when he answered just said he was on his way home and hung up.

Jamie looked at his watch and cringed. "Anyone know a good divorce lawyer?"

"Hire me one, too," said Bodean as he gathered his work product and placed it in a folder.

Like a fire drill, the defense team raced out to their cars and headed home.

Larry yelled after them, "See you all at 8:00 on Wednesday. In the interim don't forget your assignments. Class dismissed!"

It was really only a recess as the ordeal would prove, and they were never very far from its grasp.

CHAPTER 13
CAUGHT IN THE CROSSFIRE

Early Tuesday morning Bodean dialed the numbers Jamie gave him for Jamie's Uncle Matt and Cousin Patty. The number for Patty had been disconnected. However, Bodean was able to reach Uncle Matt.

When he identified himself as Jamie's attorney, Uncle Matt was speechless. He appeared even more stunned when he was informed of the nature of the charge. "I thought that boy would be president some day," he said. Bodean assured him Jamie had been wrongfully charged and that everything would in all likelihood be resolved in Jamie's favor.

"I surely hope so," Uncle Matt replied, "I would trust that boy with my life."

Bodean explained that the authorities had misconstrued Jamie's Las Vegas telephone calls and trips. "They have alleged Jamie embezzled bank funds to pay gambling debts," Bodean informed him. "They have obtained copies of his airline tickets, hotel registration slips and receipts for the redemption of chits at Tampico Casino." Bodean then asked Uncle Matt what he knew but first wanted some information about him.

In response to questions from Bodean, Uncle Matt said his full name was Matthew Thomas Cooper and he was four years younger than Jamie's father, having just turned sixty in May. A widower for over two years, he had a daughter, Patty Ann Cooper, who was thirty-two. Patty was divorced and was a high school math teacher in Las Vegas. She'd been married for seven years but had her name changed back to Cooper when she divorced. She's lived in Las Vegas for approximately ten years and has had a drinking problem at least five of those years and a gambling addiction as well. She's well known on the Vegas strip and credit has been feely extended to her. Her compulsive gambling has resulted in her losing her teaching position, being evicted from her home, kiting checks, attempting to redeem various chits, defending lawsuits and on July 19, being arrested and charged with felony fraud by check. She's been unable to make bail and he's unable and unwilling to obtain a surety bond because of the high premium and the bondsman's requirement that the bond be secured by his home.

Bodean asked if Patty was currently represented by an attorney. Uncle Matt advised Bodean that the court had appointed the public defender to defend her and that they had been involved in plea negotiations that would require her to plead to one of the felony charges. In return, she would be granted probation and the remaining five felony counts would be dropped. She would also be required to perform one hundred hours of community service, be involved in an alcohol rehab program for a specified period of time and make restitution.

Uncle Matt stated that he had washed his hands of his daughter. She had placed him on the brink of bankruptcy, and he was on the hook for several notes he foolishly co-signed.

Bodean asked why Jamie had made the trip to Vegas in June. Uncle Matt told him it was to help him pay off a chit or marker that Tampico was hounding Patty to redeem. When asked if the chit was in any way related to Jamie's gambling, Uncle Matt said, "What gambling? That boy is as conservative as a preacher and as straight as an arrow. I'll do anything and everything I can to help him clear up this mess."

Bodean then asked if he knew where Jamie got the money to redeem the chit. "When I called my brother, Forrest, he volunteered Jamie to help since Jamie was a banker and knew what to do. Forrest said he would send Jamie with the money and pay Jamie's travel expenses. I assume that's what he did. I promised Forrest that once we got Patty out of the mess, I would pay him back."

When Bodean had asked if the authorities contacted him, he said he had several messages on his telephone a week or so back from the Steamboat Springs Police Department, but never returned the calls. He also was told by a neighbor that a Las Vegas police officer was looking for him, apparently needing to speak to him. He thought it might have to do with Patty, so he was avoiding them.

Bodean next asked if he knew whether Patty had been contacted by the Colorado authorities. Uncle Matt said he wasn't sure whether it was the Colorado or local authorities who talked to her, but she mentioned talking to an Officer Coleman and later to another police officer shortly before her arrest on July 17.

As soon as Bodean hung up the telephone, he tried unsuccessfully to reach Jamie at home and ultimately reached him at the Cooper Ranch.

"Did you reach the Las Vegas Coopers?" asked Jamie.

"Do you want the good news or the bad news first?"

"Tell me the good news first. I haven't had any in awhile."

"Well, I had a good chat with your Uncle Matt. He said he was willing to do anything he could to help you."

"Did he confirm the purpose of my trip and the bailout of Patty at Tampico?"

"Everything was consistent with what you told us—in every respect. Do you want the bad news?"

"Should I be seated?" Jamie asked Bodean.

"Patty was apparently contacted by Clinton Coleman the week of your arrest, presumably because of her name and Vegas telephone number having been found in your wallet. Anyway, Patty was caught in the crossfire and was arrested on June 17 on six felony fraud by check charges. Your Uncle Matt has refused to bail her out and she's sitting in the slammer as we speak."

Jamie was silent for a long moment and then slowly and sorrowfully moaned, "The sniper has taken aim and hit his mark once again. My cousin Patty absolutely was caught in the Hammerville crossfire, as you label it. There is no doubt in my mind now that the chief, bent on vindicating the dignity and restoring the reputation of his dear old dad, will stop at nothing to bring the Coopers to their knees. He wants complete annihilation."

"I remember you telling me that your father has experienced strange sightings at the Cooper Ranch since your arrest with strange cars and people snooping around. I don't think it's just trying to sniff out where you stashed the loot or looking for a stray to butcher or game to poach, but I think it's to find something to pin on your dad. What goes around comes around. Hammerville and friends are looking to return the favor."

"Bodean, you're right on. I don't think the chief is content to settle on a trade of one for one. I think he wants to topple the whole Cooper house of cards. And frankly, I think Alden is bent on the same mission."

"Wasn't there something in the Good Book about the generational thing you were discussing in reference to the comments in the *You Said It* column in the newspaper last week? Something about paying for the sins of the father. What was that?"

"Until my arrest, the term curse had no meaning. Now, I think someone is sticking pins in a Cooper voodoo doll because all the Coopers are starting to feel the pain and are vulnerable. Any sins there be were not of my father, but of me. I'm responsible for what has happened to the family, including Patty, and it's me and not them who should be punished. I just hope my children don't have to pay for the sins of their father."

Now it was Bodean's turn to be quiet, at least

for the moment. Not knowing quite what to say, he finally got up the courage to offer Jamie some brotherly advice. "They've dug a hole, a deep dark one, to put you in. The only way you're going to end up there is if you let them push you in. You're much too strong and determined to let that happen. You can't give up the good fight or even think about it. If there is a curse, it can be reversed. And I'm going to help you do it."

CHAPTER 14
DISPELLING
THE MYTH

"Never waive a preliminary hearing," Jamie, standing at Verna's desk, could hear Gordie say.

"What the hell did those ivory tower intellectual snobs disguised as law professors know anyway?" Jamie could hear Larry say.

"What's with them?" Jamie asked Verna in a hushed tone.

"They've been going at it ever since I arrived," she whispered back.

It was now 8:00 a.m. sharp and Larry came out of Gordie's office with an empty cup in each hand looking for refills. Seeing Jamie, he said, "Oh good, you're here. Grab a cup and one of Verna's cinnamon rolls."

About that time Bodean arrived and without being invited, helped himself to coffee and cinnamon rolls. Verna just rolled her eyes in mock disgust.

They all migrated to the conference room. Set up on a stand was a flip chart with a list of the purposes of the preliminary hearing. The purposes appeared in the following order: screening device;

serves as a fishing expedition particularly for the defense; pins down testimony; reveals prosecution's weaknesses; showcases the defense of the accused if the defense presents evidence which does not often happen; and if no probable cause established, case dismissed.

"Looks like someone's holding a seminar," Jamie commented, licking frosting from his lips.

"Call it whatever you want," Larry responded. "When last we met, we discussed the nebulous nature of the preliminary hearing and whether we gain anything by having one."

"Or by not having one," Gordie added.

"Before we do that," Larry said, "let's have Bodean brief us on the Las Vegas connection."

Bodean filled Larry and Gordie in on his telephone interview of Jamie's Uncle Matt and the precarious position in which cousin Patty had found herself.

"Chances are that she will be convicted of a felony by the time our case goes to trial if it goes that far," said Gordie. "That means she can be impeached with that felony if she testifies and the jury will be instructed that they can take the felony into account in assessing her credibility. In other words, under the law, if you are a convicted felon, you're presumed to be a liar."

"Wow," said Jamie. "That amounts to a nullification of the testimony of convicted felons. They'd be better off not testifying in the first place."

They all agreed the matter was moot at this point as they had no intention of calling Patty as a witness anyway, especially not at the preliminary hearing.

"A preliminary hearing or no preliminary hearing," Gordie said. "That is the question!"

Before making a decision, Jamie wanted to know what would happen if Judge Dearborn found probable cause. Larry and Gordie told him the judge would bind the case over to the district court. The county court would no longer have jurisdiction. All court appearances, hearings and trial would thereafter be in district court. Judge Dearborn would then set a first appearance date in district court. The good news was that Judge Dearborn would be replaced by District Judge Clayton Tibbits. The defense would request continuance of the bond in the present amount.

"Is it possible the judge could revoke my bond and I would have to post another?" Jamie asked anxiously.

"Possible, but not likely," Larry responded.

"A lot less likely if you waive the preliminary hearing," Gordie added.

"The preliminary hearing would be a spectacle; better than watching the barber give a haircut," said Bodean, finally having an opportunity to speak.

"A hearing and the judge finding probable cause is a lot more newsworthy than your waiving the preliminary hearing," Larry said to Jamie. "Getting the word out in advance will prevent a run on the courthouse and afford a little solitude."

And to Gordie, Larry said, "As much as I hate to admit it, with your persuasive abilities I have talked myself out of a preliminary hearing."

"Me too," Bodean conceded.

"You two finally got religion," Gordie joked.

"Don't want to agree with you too much," Larry joked back.

Turning to Jamie, Larry said, "Jamie, the decision is yours. You're going to have to sign a waiver acknowledging that this is a free and voluntary act on your part and that you're irrevocably committed, meaning you can't later change your mind. Is that what you want do?"

"Absolutely," Jamie replied without hesitation. "Sounds as though I don't have a choice anyway."

"While I have Verna type the waiver form for Jamie to sign, why don't the three of you figure out where we go from here. Speedy trial requires that trial be held no later than six months from the date of Jamie's entry of plea in district court." With that Larry left the room.

When he returned with the waiver form, Jamie signed it and it was then filed with the court.

• • •

Jamie was told he would still have to appear in court on Monday so that his first appearance date in district court could be set. Jamie wondered how his waiver would be interpreted by the public once it hit the local newspaper. He hoped it wouldn't be construed as an admission of guilt.

JUSTICE DENIED — CARROLL MULTZ

CHAPTER 15
A COMMUNITY DIVIDED

Hot off the press, Jamie was anxious to look at the following day's edition of the weekly rag. On page three, resembling a tombstone ad was the following:

PRELIMINARY HEARING VACATED

County Judge William Dearborn's clerk today announced that the preliminary hearing in the Jamie Cooper bank embezzlement case has been vacated.

Gloria Fitzsimmons, Judge Dearborn's clerk, stated that Cooper, 34, former employee of Steamboat Bank & Trust Co. had waived his preliminary hearing scheduled for Monday, July 31 at 9:00 a.m. His case will now be transferred to district court for trial.

Cooper will still be required to appear, according to Fitzsimmons, to schedule his first appearance before District Judge Clayton Tibbits. Cooper's attorneys refused to comment on the reason for Copper's waiver.

Skimming through the newspaper, Jamie turned to the editorial page. His eyes caught Eric Sweeney's editorial. The editorial read:

A COMMUNITY DIVIDED

Because of the derisive nature of the comments in the You Said It column regarding the Cooper embezzlement case, our editorial staff has elected not to print them. A community divided against itself cannot stand. Steamboat Springs is a respected community and its image is being tarnished by the campaigns being waged in the newspaper by the two camps.

The newspaper's editorial board feels it would be irresponsible to continue to print anonymous comments of this nature for a number of reasons, the least of which is the possibility that they might trigger a change of venue not only in the Cooper case but future cases as well.

Effective immediately, the newspaper is eliminating the You Said It column and reserving the right to reject any letters to the editor that do not contain a signature and an address. This editor and this newspaper refuse to be enablers and risk torpedoing an accused's right to a fair trial in Routt County.

Jamie thought the editorial was appropriate, especially the new policy. He had hoped, however, that Eric would have included language encouraging the citizenry to keep an open mind and not prejudge him. As Larry had said, "The charge was not evidence of guilt, only an accusation waiting to be proven."

· · ·

When Jamie first informed Jennie there wouldn't be a preliminary hearing and that he waived it, she appeared upset. "Why?" Jennie asked. "If you're innocent, why would you waive the preliminary hearing? Wasn't that the opportunity you were waiting for to get your side of the story out and get the charge dropped?"

Jamie said he told her that even if a preliminary hearing was held, he would not be testifying.

"What about Patty, wouldn't she testify?" Jennie wanted to know. "Nobody saw you take the money. None was ever found in your possession, for Pete's sake! Nobody has recovered the so-called missing money. How do we know the money is really missing? The vault was locked the night before by Alden and Rita, and Alden is the only one who was there when the vault was opened the next morning. Alden is the one who had the thousand dollars. How could they not connect the dots?"

It took Jamie a lot of patience explaining, but ultimately Jennie understood. She loved her husband unconditionally and was suffering for him. She knew he was innocent and was frustrated. She couldn't understand why anyone would believe he did what he was accused of doing. He was not capable of it. He needed to get his story out. She thought the preliminary hearing would have been the time and place to do so and that because of the scanty evidence, obviously contrived, the case would be dismissed. In her heart she felt the ordeal would then be over once and for all!

• • •

Jamie and his family spent the weekend at the Cooper Ranch. Bodean arrived with his wife, Natalie, and four-year-old daughter Katie. Katie rode Flossie, an old pony his father had when Max and Collette were Katie's age. Flossie was being spared being sent to the glue factory, thanks to Grandpa Cooper's sentimentality and doting attention.

Bodean had really come to interview Jamie's father, primarily to ask about the Las Vegas connection and the Hammerville incident. The two stories turned out to be just as Jamie had described. Now Jamie had corroboration.

• • •

When the Jamie Cooper family left the 11:00 a.m. service at the Hayden Congregational Church and said goodbye to Grandma and Grandpa Cooper, they stopped by the post office in Steamboat and picked up the mail that had been accumulating in their post office box since the previous week.

Jamie noticed a strange envelope addressed to him. *My name and address were typed by someone who should have taken typing lessons,* he thought. A lot of strikeouts and strikeovers and no attempt to erase mistakes. He looked for a return address on the front and back of the envelope. None. "I wonder who this is from?" Jamie queried.

"Open it up and see," Jennie replied.

Jamie slid his finger through the side of the flap and pulled the envelope open. Inside he found a three-fold slip of tablet paper with a frayed top. Typed on the paper, not respecting the lines and with strikeouts and strikeovers reminiscent of the envelope was the following (with mistakes omitted):

> *You robbed the bank. I saw you.*
> *For $5,000, I will keep my mouth shut.*
> *Otherwise I will tell the police.*
> *I will give you one week to pay.*
> *Wait for my next letter.*

Eyes wide, mouth ajar, hand trembling, Jamie sat numb.

"Well," said Jennie, "who's it from?"

Jamie handed Jennie the letter.

Stuttering and stammering through a torrent of tears, Jennie read the note aloud.

"Some cruel joke from some crank," Jamie said and took her hand in his. "Don't pay any attention to it. Here, give it back to me."

Noticing that Jennie was still shaken, Jamie pulled her close and holding onto each other tightly, Jamie comforted her as he wondered if the nightmare would ever end.

CHAPTER 16
THE MODERN-DAY COLISEUM

On this bright last day of July, Larry and Jamie arrived at the Routt County Courthouse early but were not the first to arrive. The spectators were scattered, busying themselves with gossip, speculation and conjecture concerning the Cooper case—no doubt the story of the year. Shortly after Larry and Jamie positioned themselves at the defense table, the Stillwell wolf pack arrived with the weasel in tow.

"Wouldn't miss it for the world," Alden was overheard telling the elderly couple seated behind the Stillwells.

"The courtroom is the modern-day version of the Coliseum," Larry said to Jamie in a low voice. "The righteous citizens have come to watch the Christians being fed to the lions. But no fight to the death struggle here! At least not this day."

"They'll all want refunds on their tickets," Jamie whispered to Larry. Both were surprised there were so many there and still filtering in, considering that the preliminary hearing had been vacated and the newspaper had so reported.

Corbett and his investigator, Dennis Harlow, swaggered into the courtroom with big broad smiles. Corbett was making the most of his election year presence known and managed to shake every spectator's hand, ingratiating himself even to the least friendly.

I can't imagine what it would be like if the preliminary hearing had gone as scheduled, Jamie thought. "I'm just glad my family isn't here," he told Larry. Gordie hadn't come because of the perfunctory nature of the proceedings. Besides, the conservative folk might think Jamie was being frivolous with his money, or more to the point, the bank's money. When Gordie entered the picture, both had assured Jamie they were not double billing. When the ordeal was over Jamie promised he would make it right.

• • •

The bailiff entered and announced, "The district court in and for the Fourteenth Judicial District is now in session, the Honorable Clayton Tibbits presiding."

Judge Tibbits looked and acted as one would expect a district judge to look and act. He stood six feet tall with chiseled features, a medium build and marshmallow- white hair that belied his fifty-two years. He was erudite and much respected by those members of the bar who appeared before him. He took more decisions under advisement than the average, which may have accounted for his extremely low rate of reversals. Polite to both sides, he referred to Bob as Mr. Corbett and to Larry as Mr. Whittaker. *No favoritism or perception of favoritism here*, a relieved Jamie thought, after having been exposed to Judge Dearborn's obvious display of prejudice.

"Quite a contrast between Tibbits and Dearborn," Larry wrote on his yellow pad for Jamie to see. Jamie nodded.

His first appearance or return date was over before it began. Jamie was re-advised of his rights, the nature of the charge and provided an outline of the court process that would follow. When Jamie was asked for his plea, standing erect and this time not sporting a broken nose and two black eyes, said, "I plead not guilty to the charge, Your Honor, and request a jury of twelve."

Judge Tibbits said, "Very well then, let's set a motions hearing date that is convenient for all."

Questioning Larry, the judge asked, "Counselor, I know it's way too early to tell, but what motions does the defense contemplate filing?"

"Judge, the defense has not received the entire discovery yet, but tentatively we can tell Your

Honor that we will be filing a motion for change of venue, and depending on the discovery, a motion for suppression of evidence and possibly statements. We will also be filing a motion for bill of particulars to ascertain the exact date and time of the alleged theft."

"I'm sure Mr. Corbett has anticipated your filing a motion for bill of particulars and realizes that under Colorado law, he is required to provide a bill of particulars upon your request inasmuch as this is a theft case. Is that correct, Mr. Corbett?"

Corbett stood and stated succinctly, "Yes, Your Honor."

"Very well, Counselor," Judge Tibbits replied. "The motions hearing date will be scheduled for September 15 commencing at 9:00 a.m. Defendant's bond will be continued to that day."

• • •

Gordie and Bodean were waiting in the conference room when Larry and Jamie returned from court. They were advised of the court setting. Jamie produced the envelope and letter he had received the day before; the one that had all the typing errors. After it had been passed around, Larry, Gordie, and Bodean sat poker faced. Jamie couldn't tell what they were thinking.

Jamie broke the ice by saying it was just some

crazy hoax by a bunch of kids not knowing what to do with themselves. Gordie said it was more than that; it was an extortion threat that needed to be taken seriously. Noticing the postmark, he pointed out that it had been mailed from Craig at 7:30 a.m. on Friday. The improper use of the mail was a federal offense. Also, state offenses had been committed in both Moffat and Routt counties.

Larry pulled a volume of the Colorado statutes from the credenza behind him. He then read the extortion statute which made it a felony to exact hush money.

"So, see," said Gordie, "it's more than kid stuff."

"Whoever typed it," Larry stated, "needs to retake Typing 101 and hire a good lawyer."

The dilemma now was what to do with it. They all agreed that they couldn't trust the police department because the chief was not there to help Jamie, but to bury him.

"In fact," Bodean said, "I wouldn't be surprised if this is the chief's doing. His mind has been so obsessed with vengeance he may think this is a way to sniff out the bank's money."

It was decided that Jamie would immediately notify Bodean of any future suspicious mail. They would not report it yet and maybe catch the culprit at the drop site which they expected would be specified in the next anticipated set of instructions.

• • •

The defense team hunkered down, realizing there was a lot to do before drafting the motions. Had Bodean come up with the name of a reliable polygrapher? A police-annexed polygrapher would be seeking to obtain a confession in his so-called quest for the truth. Or, he would claim deception where there was none. What were the options? A voice stress-test was not reliable, and Jamie surely wouldn't consent to the intrusive nature of injection of a truth serum. The others knew they wouldn't.

"Who was it that said polygraphs weren't even admissible in court because of their questionable scientific reliability?" Jamie asked.

"Anyone of us could have told you that," Larry responded, "but if you pass it, we'll try to get the results admitted or at the very least broadcast that you passed."

Bodean pulled an address card from his now famous battered brown leather briefcase. The card looked like it came from some sort of address spindle. He read the name Dr. Alphonso Lauderback, stating that the doctor was well respected in the law enforcement community and had a Ph.D. in sociology and criminal justice. He had moved from Colorado Springs to Denver and would not charge an arm and a leg. He had been employed as a polygrapher for the police department in Colorado Springs, but now was doing polygraphs on job applicants, both for the public as well as the private sectors. Bodean said he was familiar with Dr. Lauderback and his work when he was in law enforcement.

Both Larry and Gordie wanted a polygraph and Jamie was more than willing to submit. If Jamie passed, as was everyone's expectation, he or Gordie would prepare and file with the court a motion for acceptance of the polygraph results.

They brainstormed the types of motions that could and would be filed. Larry said he would pick up the additional five pages of discovery from the DA's office later that afternoon upon his return from court. They all acknowledged their assignments as well as the ticking clock. "Keep each other updated; we'll meet again soon." In the interim, Larry and Gordie would be preparing the motions and drafting the memorandum briefs in support thereof. So far, they were surviving the ordeal and attempting to minimize its sting.

CHAPTER 17
SO HELP ME GOD

Even though Larry hadn't sorted through the blizzard of paperwork starting to stack up on his desk as a result of his preoccupation with the Cooper case and was up to his eyeballs in research and drafting, he insisted on accompanying Jamie to Denver to be polygraphed by Dr. Lauderback.

Larry was gun-shy when it came to polygraphs. He recalled several would-be clients, bent upon saving a few bucks, declined representation and submitted to polygraphs administered by law enforcement personnel. They had proved to be disastrous and resulted in the poor misguided souls providing the pieces of the puzzle needed to ensure a conviction. In other words, they built the gallows for their own execution.

Jamie said he had been spending little time with Max, and with Max starting back to school soon, wondered if his son could accompany them on the round trip to Denver. Jamie was anxious for Larry to meet Max and vice-versa. Max was looking for yard work to supplement his allowance and this would be a good opportunity for Max to start lobbying.

Larry insisted on driving and at 7:30 a.m. on the first Friday of August, he arrived at Jamie's home in his station wagon. Larry was invited in and stayed just long enough to meet Jennie, Collette and Max. Jennie had prepared lunch for the travelers.

• • •

They arrived in Denver a little before noon, and after having scouted out Dr. Lauderback's office, stopped at a sporting goods store to browse. Larry purchased a baseball mitt Max had been ogling and an official baseball. Larry promised Max he would watch him play the next time Max had a Little League game. By coincidence, Larry had played second base also, from Little League through his second year in college. Max's jersey number was two and so was Larry's. Jamie was starting to feel like the odd man out. However, watching Larry, who had no children, and "Mr. Max" interact, generated a pleasure and contentment inside that defied description. Max looked and acted like Jamie. Every time Jamie looked at him it was like turning the clock back and staring at himself. Larry, in some ways, was providing a strength that not even a blood brother could have provided.

• • •

They arrived at the polygrapher's office a few minutes before 1:00 p.m. Dr. Lauderback was not as they had imagined. He was bald, overweight and walked with a shuffle. He presented a release/authorization form that he required Jamie to sign before he would proceed, and Jamie obliged.

Larry had prepped Jamie via the telephone when he realized Max would be joining them. Max's ears were too young and too sensitive to be exposed to the ordeal.

Larry and Al pretty much agreed on what questions would be asked. Of all the questions, Larry objected to only one. That was, "Do you know what happened to the money?" Jamie did know that $1,000 was in the hands of the bank, but he did not know what happened to the remaining $29,000. And since he could only answer yes or no, the question had to be rephrased and it was. Larry had instructed Jamie to take deep breaths before he answered, even with the control questions; otherwise it might detect deception even though there be none.

Larry was ushered out of the room but was allowed to watch from behind a two-way mirror where a speaker was set up so Larry could listen. Max sat in the waiting room reading.

After wires were attached across Jamie's chest and to his right index finger, Al began to ask questions and plot numbers and symbols at various intervals on a graph that simulated an electrocardiogram, only larger and encased in a tabletop console. Before they started, Jamie was once again instructed that he could only answer yes or no.

Jamie was then asked to look straight ahead and remain still and not move. Al then produced six playing cards from the same deck. As he held each card up and asked if each was the ace of diamonds, Jamie was required to answer yes. His lie pattern was then recorded with respect to the five cards that were not the ace of diamonds.

Jamie was then asked the following questions to which he replied yes: Is your name James Curtis Cooper? Is your nickname Jamie Cooper? Do you reside in Steamboat Springs, Colorado? Have you been charged with felony theft? Did you ever work at Steamboat Bank and Trust Co.? Is your wife's name Jennie? Do you have a son named Max? Do you have a daughter named Collette? Have you ever told a lie? Do you intend to tell me the complete truth?

Thereupon, Jamie was questioned regarding his criminal prosecution. To each of the following questions Jamie replied no. Did you take the money you were accused of taking? Did you ever take money from the bank without permission? On July

10, 1972, did you take any money from the bank vault without permission? On July 11, 1972, did you take any money from the bank vault without permission? From the time the bank vault was closed at 5:30 p.m. on July 10, 1972, until 7:30 a.m. the following day, did you enter the vault for any reason? Do you know for certain who took the money from the bank? Do you know where the missing $29,000 is? Was it you who placed the $1,000 in your desk drawer?

Al repeated the test two more times, varying the order of the questions and each time keeping track. After completion of the third test he unhooked Jamie and sent him out of the room. He then analyzed each of the three tests and in about thirty minutes joined Jamie, Max, and Larry.

Looking Larry straight in the eye, Al said, "I have found absolutely no deception. If any there be, I would have found it. This man, so help me God, did not steal the bank's money."

"No surprise!" Larry said, and smiled at Jamie.

Al said his findings and the process he followed in arriving at them would all be incorporated into a formal report, together with his ultimate opinion. Included would be the questions asked and answers given. As soon as it was finalized and typed it would be in the mail to Larry along with a billing statement.

With handshakes all around Larry, Jamie and Max left riding on the peak of that roller coaster ride they called the ordeal.

CHAPTER 18
CAUGHT RED-HANDED

In the mail at the post office on Saturday was a small package without a return address wrapped in brown paper containing heavy transparent tape. Jamie's name and address were in the same typed strikeout/strikeover format as the suspicious letter. The postmark displayed the following: *Craig, Colorado, July 31, 1972, 7:30 a.m.*

Lifting it by its corners and carefully sandwiching it between other mail, Jamie transported it home. Opening just one end, he coaxed the small box from its paper encasement. Careful not to obliterate any foreign prints, Jamie opened the box and found an unlocked combination padlock. The exposed hole was taped to prevent it from being accidently locked. The same notebook paper as the other containing the same careless and inept typing (with mistakes omitted) read:

> *In the back of Howard's Truck Stop in Craig*
> *near the men's restroom are six old lockers.*
> *Place $5,000 in the locker closest to the door*
> *and lock it with this lock. If the money is not*

there by 7:30 a.m. on Saturday, August 12, I will spill my guts.

. . .

With the rest of the weekend full of yard work, family time and dinner with his wife's sister and family on Sunday, Bodean rescheduled his meeting with Jamie until the following Monday at 9:00 a.m. at Larry's office. He had heard earlier about Jamie passing the polygraph and was ecstatic. He had already scheduled a meeting with Larry to go over the additional discovery and assist Larry in obtaining affidavits to attach to the motion for change of venue. That would be a good time to discuss how to foil the extortion plot. Larry's and Gordie's input would be helpful.

. . .

It was about 8:50 a.m. when Jamie arrived at Larry's office. Verna greeted him with "Congratulations! You know where the coffee and blueberry muffins are."

Barely a minute after Jamie arrived, Bodean strutted in. He greeted Jamie with a robust lumberjack handshake.

Glancing over his shoulder in Verna's direction, Bodean shouted, "Hello, good looking."

Without looking up from her work, she said, "I'm just great, how 'bout you?"

"Are you taking my medical history?" he responded, feigning indignation.

"We already know how you are psychologically. I was only asking how you were physiologically. Is that a crime?" she responded, mirroring his indignation. Then she added, "Forget it! I'm sorry I asked." Laughter from all three.

• • •

When Jamie and Bodean entered the conference room, with books and papers strewn around, Gordie arose and rushed at Jamie as if he were the prodigal son. Bodean then said, "Now I know how the son who stayed home helping his father felt. No fatted calf for me!" With the jubilation having subsided, each had a different idea of where to begin.

The most important were the motions, but first Larry wanted to distribute copies of the additional discovery, which consisted mainly of the Las Vegas connection, the telephone call to Cousin Patty and the local authorities. There was also an entry about the contact and conversation Clint Coleman had with the bank's insurance company. Apparently, the errors and omissions policy was going to cover the $30,000, minus the deductible and the $1,000 already recovered. Standard Casualty Insurance Company of Connecticut (SCICC) had already sent an adjuster to verify proof of loss and check the mechanism on the vault door. He was Joseph Michaels out of Hartford.

"Does that mean there won't be a civil action brought against me?" Jamie asked.

"It only means," Larry said, "that if the insurance company pays the loss, they will be the ones bringing the action if there is one. The customary subrogation clause in the insurance policy says that the bank claim is automatically assigned to SCICC upon payment of the loss."

"In other words," Gordie added, "SCICC stands in the shoes of SB&T Co. as far as the claim against you is concerned minus the deductible."

"What are the chances SCICC will file suit?" Jamie inquired.

"There's probably a pretty good chance that will occur, although now the suit will no doubt follow your criminal trial," Larry responded.

"Without the deductible looming," said Gordie, "the bank and the weasel figure they'll apply pressure and obtain valuable information from you with pretrial discovery and a trial that would help the state in your prosecution. They figure it's a win-win situation because even if you do invoke your Fifth Amendment rights against self-incrimination, they can basically win their case by default. The weasel is not smart enough to know that the court has the power to stay the proceedings pending the outcome of the criminal proceedings."

"Or, maybe," Bodean volunteered, "the bank had planned all along to let the prosecutors do their dirty work first and piggyback on their work product as SCICC will probably do."

"I think the weasel is more interested in billable hours and will probably be successful in convincing his blood-thirsty client to jump the gun and file the civil suit," said Jamie. "After all, the bank has the right to be reimbursed for the deductible."

Not much more to say about the Las Vegas connection, at least not for now, they all agreed.

Jamie now carefully opened the small brown paper bag he had sitting in front of him. He emptied the contents out onto the conference table revealing a brown wrapper bearing his typed name and address, the error-ridden folded typewritten note and the small box containing the combination padlock.

With Jamie seated, the rest of the defense team gathered around him and without touching anything examined the collection. All read the new extortion note with instructions and examined the address label and the postmark. They then examined the unlocked padlock, touching it only with the eraser end of a pencil to avoid obliterating any fingerprints.

"Same old strikeouts and strikeovers, no doubt with the same Underwood Standard typewriter and typist as with the suspicious letter we previously examined," Bodean surmised.

The latest in the saga of the extortion plot appeared now to be the most urgent. D-day had arrived. A decision and formulation of strategy could wait no longer. This was Bodean's territory and he was conscripted to carry the ball.

Bodean said, "I've been in touch with a PI in Craig by the name of Capp Farley. He thinks that to involve the police at either the Routt or Moffat County ends would be a mistake at this juncture because of the animosity towards Jamie. What he suggested was to set up a surveillance at the drop site starting at least an hour before the deadline drop time set by the extortionist. Capp has offered to assist."

"Whoever our extortionist is," said Larry, "is anxious for his money. He doesn't appear to be wasting any time."

"He's obviously an early riser as both postmarks are at seven thirty a.m.," said Gordie. "If it's like Steamboat, the post office opens at seven a.m. and the post office posts only on the half hour. This means that both the first suspicious letter and the latest were deposited between seven a.m. and seven thirty a.m. And the instructions with the lock have a drop deadline of seven thirty a.m."

"The package had the proper postage and a special postal service sticker on it, meaning that it, no doubt, was weighed at the post office by the clerk who ostensibly sold and affixed the proper postage thereto," Bodean said.

"That would mean that the clerk got a look at our extortionist," Jamie commented.

"Are you familiar with Howard's Truck Stop?" Larry asked Bodean. "It's a popular fueling spot for eighteen-wheelers, farm and ranch vehicles and delivery trucks. They do an unusually high volume of business and have the usual assortment of oil, common truck accessories, work gloves, some hats, clothing items and such. Actually, it's a typical convenience store, country friendly and open from five thirty a.m. until eleven thirty p.m. all week long. Howard's is the gathering spot during midmornings and midafternoons for those who don't wear suits and ties and like piping hot coffee. I forgot to mention they also sell a lot of smokes and chewing tobacco."

"Our extortionist must be a regular," Larry mused. "At least someone who is familiar with the layout and comfortable being there."

"Are there any buildings close by where you and Capp could conduct surveillance or a blind where your presence could go undetected?" Gordie asked Bodean.

"Yes," Bodean replied, "there's Cattlemen's Hardware Store right on the side alley separating the two businesses and some buildings across the back alley. I would have to scout out the area to be sure. I know where the restrooms are, but I don't remember any lockers. Could I use your telephone?" Before Larry could respond, Bodean asked if everyone was comfortable with using Capp for the job. All nodded and Bodean, after first calling his office for Capp's telephone number, called Capp.

Soon Capp was on aboard. Bodean would meet Capp at Capp's office in Craig at 4:00 p.m. They would scout out the area and stop off at Cattlemen's Hardware Store and meet with the owner, Capp's fellow Lions Club compatriot, Ross Jenkins. Then they would make arrangements to use the storeroom with the windows facing the restrooms and lockers at Howard's Truck Stop.

"Wow!" said Larry.

"Couldn't have done better myself," said Gordie.

• • •

Jamie was briefed by Larry and Gordie on the motions they would be preparing. Larry gave eight affidavits to Bodean to have signed before a notary public. They would be attached to the motion for change of venue. Since Bodean was a notary the process would be simple.

"What are the purposes of the affidavits?" asked Jamie.

"Basically," Larry responded, "we want to show that the pool from which your jury will be selected has been tainted by the excessive and widespread adverse pretrial publicity."

Retrieving one of the pre-drafted affidavits from the stack, Larry summarized, "Under oath, each affiant will swear that he or she possesses all the qualifications of a juror and could be called as a juror in your case. Then each will discuss his or her exposure to the pretrial publicity."

"I'm sure everyone has heard about all the sordid details about my case by now," Jamie interrupted.

"You can count on it," Gordie responded. "That's the whole basis of our motion."

"To continue," Larry said, "each affiant will attest to his or her familiarity with your case through exposure by way of the newspapers, radio accounts, and of course, television. As a result of that adverse publicity, he or she will state that he or she has formed the opinion that you embezzled funds from the bank where you worked."

"I'm not sure everyone believes I'm guilty," Jamie again interrupted.

"Of course not," Larry responded. "We'll be obtaining affidavits only from those who have been persuaded to the contrary. Anyway, the critical portions of the affidavit focus on the potential juror's inability to set aside his or her preconceptions. For example, he or she will state that it would be difficult, if not impossible, to change his or her opinion even if instructed by the judge to do so."

"Selected jurors are required to have an open mind as they embark upon their service as jurors," stated Gordie. "In other words, if they've already made up their minds, they obviously cannot be fair and impartial."

"The key here to having the place of trial changed to another county," Bodean said to Jamie, "is not only that a juror has been prejudiced but that he or she cannot set aside his or her bias and prejudice despite evidence to the contrary."

"Each affidavit will state that the affiant is prejudiced against you," Larry continued. "Also, he or she will state that he or she has conversed with others in the community who share the same opinion. Ultimately, he or she will state that it's his or her opinion that you cannot receive a fair, impartial and expeditious trial in Routt County."

"How could a judge find otherwise?" Jamie asked.

"Not without risking a reversal!" Gordie responded.

Bodean promised he would have the eight affidavits duly executed and returned to Larry by Wednesday. Larry and Gordie continued to work on the motions and tried to keep up with the demands of their other clients. Jamie and his family would spend the rest of the week at the Cooper Ranch helping Forrest and Bessie generate income that now was required to support two families.

· · ·

It was Saturday, August 12. Capp and Bodean had front row seats for a real-life drama that was about to unfold. Facing the six lockers, in remarkably good condition despite their exposure to the weather, Capp and Bodean riveted their attention on locker number one, the one closest to the men's restroom door. The lockers were used to store coats and other items by truckers while using the restroom to change clothes and wash away the day's grime.

Capp and Bodean had fashioned newspaper pages into the size and bulk of $5,000 in bills. These were placed into a small shoe box that had been modified to accommodate the simulated bills. The box in turn was wrapped in butcher paper and sealed with extra layers of opaque shipping tape. This was done to dissuade the extortionist from taking the time to inspect the contents at the pickup site and thus enhance discovery of the ruse. They wanted to catch the culprit red-handed with package in hand before he or she discarded it.

They had put the special package in locker number one, inserted the combination padlock into its mooring, and locked it.

With the furtive movements of foxes, they retreated to their place of concealment, waiting for their prey to take their bait. Sure enough, at approximately 7:45 a.m., they watched a tall, medium-built young man presumably in his late teens dressed in blue jeans and a white grease-stained T-shirt wearing well-worn western boots come traipsing around the corner and into the men's restroom. Within minutes Blue Jeans emerged, and after looking in all directions, obviously making sure no one was around, approached locker number one and began rotating the dial on the combination lock.

After a few unsuccessful tries, while Capp snapped photographs at various intervals, Blue Jeans, shaking his head in disgust, went back to the front of the truck stop and reappeared with a slip of paper to which he referred in dialing the proper combination. *Snap*, the lock opened, and Blue Jeans retrieved his pot of gold. In his haste and exuberance, he left the opened padlock dangling on the door.

Bodean was already making his way to the front of the hardware store and Ross Jenkins held it open as Bodean exited. Bodean ran to the edge of the building and peering around the corner observed that Blue Jeans had already claimed his prize and was walking with it to the front of the truck stop. While Bodean was exiting through the front, Capp exited through the back. Walking at first as if to go to Howard's, and not appearing to notice Blue Jeans, Bodean blocked the alley just long enough for Capp to grab Blue Jeans from behind.

On the way out the door Bodean had instructed Ross Jenkins to call the police. Minutes later two uniformed Craig police officers appeared on the scene and arrested Blue Jeans. The package he was carrying was taken from him and placed in evidence but not before Capp had captured the moment on camera. He had taken another photograph of the locker only this time with the door open and the padlock dangling. The padlock was carefully removed by one of the uniformed police officers. Blue Jeans was handcuffed, searched and transported to the police station along with his surprise package and padlock.

• • •

Capp and Bodean met the police officers at the station house. They brought with them the two extortion notes, envelope, box and wrapping. All were marked and placed in evidence envelopes. Capp and Bodean told them all they knew. They had another officer retrieve Blue Jeans' truck parked in front of Howard's Truck Stop. In searching Blue Jeans' truck, they found the notebook from which the paper containing the typewritten extortion messages had been torn. They also retrieved tape identical to the tape used on the packaging Jamie had received in the mail. The factory packaging for the combination lock lay on the floorboards of the passenger side of the truck. The price tag showed where it had been purchased: Cattlemen's Hardware Store. Those items were also marked and placed in evidence envelopes.

When Blue Jeans was arrested, he was searched and the factory combination to the padlock was taken from his left front pants pocket. In his left back pants pocket was his wallet which was not searched until he reached the police station. While in the cage in the back of the cruiser, Blue Jeans was read his rights. When he was booked, it was determined that his date of birth was May 24, 1954, and his name was Derrick Hammerville, the eighteen-year-old son of Jarred Hammerville, the chief of police of Steamboat Springs.

When Bodean saw the impounded pickup, he noticed that it matched the description of one of the suspicious vehicles Jamie's father reported seeing driving back and forth on the county road bordering the Cooper Ranch. It was an old, faded, light green pickup truck similar in color to those driven by the U.S. Forest Service with a faint logo still visible.

Blue Jeans, now known to be Derrick Hammerville, was released to the custody of his mother. One of the arresting officers said it was professional courtesy, inasmuch as the Steamboat Police Department was one of its sister agencies. Having been in law enforcement, Capp and Bodean understood this only too well. Derrick had also been allowed to call his employer, a local farmer for whom Derrick had been working the past summer, to let him know he would not be coming to work this day. He did not want to call his father just yet. He was allowed to retrieve his pickup and drive it home with his mother close behind.

Derrick had confessed to the extortion plot and

said it was all his idea and no one had put him up to it. *Sure*, Bodean thought. *Now that he's been caught red-handed, everyone will be distancing themselves from the foiled plot,* Bodean mused. *When you're riding high, everyone's your friend. When you stumble and fall, no one has ever heard of you. Just ask Jamie.*

CHAPTER 19
DISPARATE TREATMENT

"It's not what you know, it's who you know," Jamie said to Bodean.

"Especially if that someone is your father and the chief of police," Bodean replied.

Jamie and Bodean had been summoned to Larry's office to review the first drafts of the motions that Larry and Gordie proposed to file. It had been almost a week since Derrick Hammerville had been arrested for extortion. The only thing they knew was what they read in the Craig and Steamboat newspapers. Bodean had clippings of both. The one in the local press was buried in the middle of Thursday's issue.

TEEN ARRESTED IN SHAKEDOWN ATTEMPT

The Steamboat Police Department would neither confirm nor deny that a local teen had been arrested in an attempt to obtain hush money in the Jamie Cooper embezzlement case.

According to reliable sources, the shakedown was stymied before any money was paid. The newspaper has learned that the alleged scheme occurred in both Moffat and Routt Counties and authorities in both counties are investigating the matter.

The name of the teen was not released. Craig authorities have confirmed that the teen was released to the custody of his mother

"Sounds pretty innocuous," Jamie commented. "The Steamboat Police Department has made it sound like a juvenile was involved."

"At age eighteen he's an adult under the laws of our state but he's sure not being treated as one," Bodean said in agreement.

"The Craig paper didn't treat the incident much better," Verna said, joining the conversation. Bodean read aloud from the Craig account:

EXTORTION PLOT FOILED

The Craig Police Department today issued an official release on the local sting operation just completed.

According to local authorities, a teen had been arrested in the alley between Howard's Truck Stop and Cattlemen's Hardware Store. The teen was caught red-handed with what he thought was the extortion money he had demanded but later found to be fake money. The drop was a locker in the rear of the truck stop and surveillance had been set up in the storeroom of the hardware store. Sources said the incident was captured on film.

Detective Logan Anthony said as soon as the investigation was completed, the case would be turned over to the Routt County authorities for possible prosecution.

Our call to Steamboat Chief of Police Jarred Hammerville had not been returned by press time.

"They sure tweaked that one," said Jamie. "If that had been me, they would have had my name and my so-called alias plastered on all the billboards."

"But you're not related to the chief," Verna said sarcastically. "You need to change your name."

When Larry had finished his meeting with another client, he came out to greet the scalawags. "Come on back to the conference room," he said. Gordie had his door closed and was still tied up with a client.

They could hear the clock on the City Hall chime ten times. "We're getting a later start than usual," said Larry.

Before they even sat down, Larry told them about the latest gossip. "The Steamboat Springs Police Department has lost the evidence connected with the extortion plot."

"They what?" Jamie asked incredulously.

"Apparently," Larry continued, "late yesterday afternoon, Clinton Coleman drove to Craig to pick up the tagged evidence. While driving back with it, he handled a disturbance call at a bar on the outskirts of Steamboat. He apparently left the car unlocked and when he returned, due to either carelessness or lassitude or both, he found that the evidence had disappeared. Apparently, he was working a double shift. Anyway, according to him, someone stole the whole shootin' match while he was inside the bar."

"Sure, and we're supposed to believe that ridiculous story! And without any evidence, there's no case against Coleman's boss's son!" Bodean sighed in resignation.

"Not so fast," Jamie said, "We still have the smoking gun; something the prosecution doesn't have in my case. You have eye-witness accounts. Capp and Bodean witnessed the whole event. You have incriminating photographs and a confession. Again, things you don't have in my case. Larry kept copies of the extortion notes. You have Jennie and me. Ross Jenkins may even remember selling the combo lock to Derrick, a lock with Derrick's fingerprints," Jamie reminded them, rolling his eyes and shaking his head.

"We have a client who makes Sherlock Holmes

look like a rookie," Gordie said with glee as he entered the conference room.

"Thank God for the backup," Larry said with a broad smile.

Gordie went on to relate that the word was out that the teen extortionist was the chief's son.

"It would be interesting to know who leaked it," Larry commented.

"It sure wasn't the chief," Gordie exclaimed. "The client I just finished with said that while at breakfast at the Sundowner, he overheard the chief, who was seated at the table next to him, say that it was just a harmless childish prank, no doubt referring to his son's misguided caper."

Bodean said he had talked to Capp earlier in the morning and Capp related what happened when he took a set of the photographs he had developed and was waiting for the detectives at the Craig Police Department. Apparently, an elderly hulk of a man with a withered hand walked out of the chief's office bellowing, "My grandson was only trying to do his civic duty in attempting to recover the bank's stolen money, you goons! He should have been given a medal instead of a scolding." Still shaking his fist, he added, "That's why nobody has any respect for you guys."

"Guess who?" Larry asked.

If they all hadn't been so sickened about the whole thing, they would have laughed. But it wasn't funny. They all knew of the double standard that marked one of the shortcomings of the criminal justice system and even though this was a fact of life, they believed it was not something society should condone.

"Should we turn it over to the feds?" Bodean asked.

"Not right now," Gordie responded. "Had we known there would be no state prosecution, we would have considered that alternative at the outset."

•••

Everyone was provided copies of the motions and memorandum briefs. The first on the stack was a motion for bill of particulars. It requested that the prosecution specify the exact date and time of the alleged offense, the precise manner in which the offense was alleged to have occurred and the name and address of each person present at the scene of the alleged offense at or about the time the offense was allegedly committed. This would allow the defense to specify where Jamie was during that critical period which they presumed would be 7:00 p.m. on July 10 to 7:00 a.m. the following day.

The next was the motion for change of venue, which stated that Jamie could not receive a fair, impartial and expeditious trial in Routt County, and that the citizens thereof had been prejudiced because of the adverse, massive and pervasive pretrial publicity. The pretrial publicity consisting mainly of newspaper articles, editorials, letters to the editor, comments in the *You Said It* column, and the transcript of Zoren's television broadcast, were attached to the motion along with the eight affidavits.

Next was the motion to suppress statements and evidence. It targeted any incriminating statements Jamie may have made and evidence seized at or after his arrest from his person, vehicle and effects. This would include the slip of paper with Uncle Matt's and Cousin Patty's names, addresses and telephone numbers taken from his wallet without his consent and any evidence derived therefrom, including the whole Las Vegas connection. Since all were the result of an unlawful arrest and thus an unlawful search, they should be suppressed.

"That means if they are suppressed, they can't be introduced into evidence at trial," Bodean explained to Jamie.

"We may want to reconsider suppression of Jamie's statements," Larry said, "considering they were exculpatory in nature and not incriminating in the least."

"Basically, all I said was, I didn't do it," Jamie exclaimed.

It was quickly decided that Larry would have Verna retype the motion to delete all the portions seeking to suppress Jamie's statements. It would only be a motion to suppress evidence.

The most problematic of all the motions was the motion to admit polygraph results. There was a 99.9 % chance this one wouldn't fly.

"Polygraph results are not deemed to be reliable evidence; they're not scientifically recognized," said Gordie.

"We still need to raise the flag and see if Judge Tibbits salutes it," Larry suggested.

Of lesser note was a motion to strike. This was aimed at Jamie's alias.

"Including Jamie's nickname in the caption of the case had no purpose other than to alienate and inflame the minds of the jury," said Gordie. "Defendants with aliases are usually considered sinister," he added mockingly.

"Been with me since birth," Jamie replied.

The motion labeled the alias as immaterial, impertinent and scandalous. It was not a life or death motion by any means but one they all agreed needed to be made.

The legal authority for the granting of the

various motions was included in the respective motions. The motions were filed later that day.

Corbett filed his bill of particulars indicating exactly what the defense team had anticipated. Pursuant to Corbett's disclosure, Larry filed the notice of alibi, specifying where Jamie was and what he was doing on the aforesaid dates and times. Witnesses included Jamie, his family and his fellow chamber members.

Corbett opposed the remaining defense motions challenging the facts and legal authority and offering countervailing facts and legal authority of his own. At the motions hearing on September 15, all that each side had to do was to convince Judge Tibbits that he should rule in their favor.

JUSTICE DENIED — CARROLL MULTZ

CHAPTER 20
A SEA OF DISCONTENT

On Friday, August 18, while the family was preparing to head for the Cooper Ranch, there was a knock at the door. When Jamie answered he saw a uniformed Routt County Sheriff's deputy standing there with official looking documents in hand. "Are you James Curtis Cooper?" the deputy politely asked.

"I am," Jamie replied.

"I have some papers to serve on you." With that the deputy handed Jamie a civil summons and complaint.

Jennie emerged from the kitchen to see who had come to the door. Standing by Jamie's side in the open doorway they both read the court documents. The complaint listed the bank (SB&T Co.) and its insurance carrier Standard Causality Insurance Company of Connecticut (SCICC) as plaintiffs and Jamie as the defendant. The missing portion of the $30,000 ($29,000) was sought by way of damages ($24,000 by SCICC; the $5,000 deductible by SB&T Co.). It was signed by J. Henry Ross, Attorney for SB&T Co. and Richard D. Colquist, Attorney for SCICC.

"Better call Larry," Jennie suggested, and her voice cracked with emotion.

Jamie closed the door and immediately picked up the phone and dialed Larry's number. When Verna heard Jamie's reason for calling, she insisted on interrupting Larry, who was with a client. Larry groaned when Jamie filled him in on the latest development and requested that Jamie come by his office with the summons and complaint before the Cooper family left for the Cooper Ranch.

Larry's client was just leaving when Jamie arrived. Jamie handed Larry the summons and complaint that he had just been served. They seemed simple enough. Larry just shrugged his shoulders. "I guess we anticipated these," he said. "However, I thought for sure they would wait to see what happened in the criminal trial."

"Greed," Jamie retorted. "Alden is just interested in money. Jennie calls him a shylock and she's pretty damn accurate. We think he's been that way all his life. I guess the whole family has been that way going back to Wellington D. Stillwell."

"It's obvious that Alden is getting some fiendish delight in all this and that may be the motivation more than the money," Larry commented.

"I feel as though I'm adrift in a sea of discontent with the water pouring in on all sides and no life raft," said Jamie.

"When it rains it pours," Larry said peering over his glasses. "What do you think of including a counterclaim for a groundless and frivolous action in our answer? That way maybe we can collect attorney fees and court costs if we succeed."

"Including a counterclaim sounds like a good idea," Jamie responded. "Maybe we can make them sweat a little. Speaking of attorney fees, my father has another check that I'll bring in on Monday."

"Don't worry about it. Your credit is good here. I only wish all our clients were as conscientious," said Larry.

"Not all your clients keep you as busy as I do. You should be paid for what you do. Besides, I don't want you to put my case on the back burner. We now have wars on two fronts!"

When Gordie emerged from his office, Larry handed him the civil paperwork. "Here, look these over," Larry said.

Gordie reviewed the latest in the saga of the ordeal. He thought the timing strange as well and wondered if it would be to the defense's benefit in the criminal case to have a civil trial first. They had some Fifth Amendment concerns, but felt Jamie had nothing to hide and the sooner they let the air out of the public's perception balloon the better.

"A verdict in favor of Jamie in a civil case would sure dispel the myth of Jamie's culpability and take some wind out of their sails," Gordie said as he departed. "I need to get back to work."

Larry had another appointment waiting. It was decided that Jamie and the rest of the defense team would meet at 10:00 the following morning.

Returning home, Jamie picked up the rest of the family and they departed for the Cooper Ranch. Another hurdle to overcome, but just another challenge in a series of strands interwoven in the web of the ordeal.

CHAPTER 21
LITTLE CAUSE TO CELEBRATE

It was a cool overcast August Monday, the twenty-first, the day defense motions were due to be filed. Fortunately, that had been done the week before. Now the defense team could concentrate on the civil case, at least for the moment.

Copies of the summons, complaint, answer, and counterclaim were positioned at the two places expected to be occupied by Jamie and Bodean. Larry and Gordie already had their copies and were looking them over and discussing the advisability of having the civil case precede the criminal case when Jamie and Bodean arrived. Jamie and Bodean were quickly integrated into the discussion. If only there was some way for Jamie to be able to go to trial on the civil case without providing fodder for the criminal case. If SCICC was as eager to go to trial as SB&T Co. and didn't want a stay until after the criminal trial and lengthy appeals, then there might be some wiggle room. All agreed that it would be legal suicide for Jamie to submit to discovery in the civil case since his statements could be used in the criminal case. A stay in the civil case would prevent that from happening.

"Surely, they don't think that Jamie's refusal to submit to discovery would trigger a default judgment in the civil case, do they?" Gordie asked Larry.

"I'm sure the SCICC attorney, at least, is sophisticated enough to know that the Constitution trumps every other law and that to punish a defendant for invoking his Fifth Amendment rights would be doing indirectly what can't be done directly. In other words, any conflict between the result dictated by law and the result dictated by the Constitution will always be resolved in favor of the Constitution."

"Well spoken, Justice Whittaker," said Gordie. "And for what it's worth, I agree with you."

"Maybe SCICC, since they're the biggest stakeholder on the plaintiffs' side, would be willing to forego discovery," suggested Larry, "and convince SB&T Co. to do the same. That would save them a lot of time and expense especially since they already know what our side is going to say."

"I can't imagine," said Gordie, "that they would agree to a unilateral waiver of discovery. But I think you're right on track. It's likely they would consider a mutual waiver."

"It depends on how desperate they are, doesn't

it?" said Bodean, more as a statement than a question.

"Interest doesn't begin to run on the twenty-nine thousand dollars until the day of judgment," Larry said. "The longer they wait, the longer it takes before they get that interest clock ticking. And you know how bankers and insurance companies are. They are tortured by idle funds."

Larry agreed to call SCICC's attorney, Richard Colquist, and discuss the situation. Otherwise, the civil case would sit in limbo for six months if there were no appeals in the criminal case, and perhaps years if there were. All agreed that Colquist was the end they should start with, although the weasel might be motivated, depending on what his income was for the month, to agree to waive discovery. And if Alden thought Jamie would be dissipating all his assets in defense of the criminal prosecution and that there may not be a pot of gold at the end of the rainbow, the bank might be motivated to waive discovery so that the civil case could proceed first.

Gordie, noticing the perplexed look on Jamie's face, said, "Let me see if I can put this in context for Jamie." Larry nodded and gestured for Gordie to proceed.

"The civil suit ordinarily in a case such as this would not have been filed until after the criminal trial so as to get a feel for the strengths and weaknesses of the case," Gordie began. "In other words, get the state to do their dirty work.

"Because of the long statute of limitations, there would be no rush for either the bank or the insurance company to file. The only urgency would be if they felt you would dissipate all your assets in fighting the criminal case before a judgment could be rendered in the civil case. You can't be forced to waive your right against self-incrimination and invocation of that right can't result in you being punished for having done so. In all likelihood then, the civil case would be stayed or held in abeyance until the criminal prosecution ran its course, and only then, would you lose your Fifth Amendment rights.

"At the civil trial, you would have to testify or risk losing the case. If you testified, you would be subjected to cross-examination. Since the burden of proof in the civil case is only the greater weight of the evidence, the plaintiffs have a lesser burden than the prosecution in a criminal case where Corbett, for example, will have to prove your guilt beyond a reasonable doubt. So if you win the civil case, not only do you escape paying the twenty-nine thousand dollars, but you send a message to the DA that if the weasel and the rest can't win the civil case with a lower standard of proof, he better dismiss the criminal prosecution to avoid embarrassment, especially during his election year."

"I don't see where Jamie has anything to lose by testifying or going to trial in the civil case," Larry said with a frown. "It gives us a chance to see how Jamie would hold up in the criminal case and also gives us a chance to evaluate the prosecution's witnesses."

Seemingly, pleased with the explanations, Jamie inquired, "Who would the plaintiffs call beside Alden and Rita Baker?"

"Maybe Horace Green, the head bookkeeper and custodian of the records at Tampico," Bodean speculated, "to place in evidence the receipt showing payment of the chit."

"We're going to have to make sure Green also produces the chit itself," added Gordie. "That will prove that it was Patty's and not Jamie's."

"We need to have Bodean talk to him ASAP. His telephone number is in the discovery documents," said Larry.

Bodean promised he would.

They discussed which witnesses would testify in Jamie's behalf at the civil trial. Jamie, Jamie's father, Uncle Matt, maybe one of the Skylers, Ursula Russell, and Jennie headed the list. The defense could call Alden and Rita Baker as well depending on the type of testimony needed. Hopefully, the defense would be able to elicit the needed testimony on cross-examination and wouldn't have to call them in the defense's case-in- chief.

"What about one of the arresting officers who could testify that it was Alden who brought the $1,000 into Jamie's office?" Bodean asked.

"Depends on what Alden testifies to," Larry responded. "It would be good to corroborate Jamie's testimony on that point."

"I suppose Dr. Lauderback's testimony is inadmissible in the civil trial because of the lack of reliability of the polygraph and its lack of scientific recognition," Jamie postulated.

"True," replied Gordie. "Maybe we should waive a jury trial in the civil case, and have it tried before a judge. After the motions hearing, Judge Tibbits will already have been made aware that Jamie passed the polygraph."

"I have a feeling Judge Tibbits will be recusing or disqualifying himself from the civil case since he will be presiding over the criminal case," Larry offered. "Otherwise he may hear evidence in the civil case that might not otherwise be admissible in the criminal case. Once he's heard it, even if he can segregate it, it can't help but influence his decisions and rulings. But then again, who knows?"

• • •

On August 25, Verna buzzed Larry announcing that Richard Colquist was on the telephone calling on the Cooper civil case. Verna didn't have to bring in the file; Larry had it sitting in front of him.

Richard D. Colquist, who said he preferred to be called RD, seemed pleasant enough. They soon determined they had two important things in common other than being attorneys and liking the outdoors. Both had been members of the same social fraternity and both had been members of the same legal fraternity. It was unfortunate they were now on opposite sides. It was understood, however, that they could disagree without being disagreeable.

"I received a copy of your answer," said RD. "The counterclaim bothered me, but I assume you know what you're doing."

"You don't know Jamie like I do," Larry quipped. "He comes from a fine family and has been unjustly accused. I don't doubt money is missing, but Jamie didn't take it. If you would like a copy of his polygraph results, I would be glad to send it."

"Do that, even though polygraph results are not admissible in court. I nonetheless find them helpful," RD replied. "I was a deputy district attorney in Boston for a short period following my graduation from law school. Polygraph results can often be a valuable tool in determining guilt or innocence."

Umm, Larry thought, *that's refreshing. RD is just the opposite of the weasel.*

"Are you still there?" RD asked.

"Just thumbing through the file," Larry replied. "Sorry about that."

"I see you requested a jury trial," RD said.

"Yes, usually do on cases like this. I wondered why you didn't request one."

"I didn't want to get home-towned, although I've found the juries in Colorado to be more tolerant and fairer than most."

"With regard to the Cooper case, let me lay it on the line," Larry said sharply. "The civil case is an obstacle we would like to overcome. There doesn't seem to be any room for negotiation. The bank is convinced Jamie did it. Jamie is adamant about his innocence, which is borne out by the polygraph results and his clean record. I don't have any trouble putting him on the stand, but I wouldn't be much of a lawyer if I fed him to the lions by allowing pretrial discovery in the companion civil case. If you will waive pretrial discovery, I will do the same. Then we won't have to get a court order to freeze the proceedings in the civil case and wait months and maybe even years to have a civil trial."

"I have complete authority in this case, but I will need at least the weekend to consider your proposal," RD replied. "I'll be frank with you as well. SCICC is afraid that if we wait too long to go to trial, and even if we win, there won't be anything left to collect. We understand that your client is now unemployed, and I can only imagine the legal fees he's incurring. The people I'm responsible for want us to get what we can as quickly as we can. With the Colorado homestead exemption and other exemptions afforded to a judgment debtor, there may not be anything left to execute upon."

"Do you have any idea how the bank will react?" Larry asked. "They may be the fly in the ointment."

"Our insurance contract gives us the right to make all trial decisions although we like to respect the bank's wishes as well. However, since we have paid the bulk of the loss, the bank would be hard pressed to be heard to complain. I have spoken with a Mr. Ross, who has already, on behalf of the bank, given us the green light to proceed in any manner we deem best."

Larry, sensing RD was of the same mind, said, "I think through stipulations mutually beneficial to both sides, we can cut down on expensive travel costs for witnesses. I for one am not good at games and am anxious to have this matter resolved in a fair and expeditious manner."

"I agree and always opt for the high road. I look forward to working with you and apologize for not having given you advance notice of my call," said RD.

"No apologies necessary. I was contemplating calling you today anyway. I'll await your call on Monday, or is that rushing you?"

"That would be more than ample time. Even though I know what my decision will be, I had better sleep on it. I'll call you at, say, eleven a.m. your time if that's convenient."

"It is. Talk to you on Monday."

After hanging up, Larry felt relieved. Although there may be little cause to celebrate, Larry felt in his heart that to go forward with the civil trial would be the right thing to do—especially with the concessions RD appeared willing to make. Victory in the civil case would certainly set the tone for the criminal prosecution and ultimately change the mood of the community.

• • •

RD, true to his word, telephoned Larry on Monday, August 26, with his decision. The two agreed that there would be no pretrial discovery between the parties; that is, no depositions, interrogatories or requests for admissions and denials. RD agreed to draft a stipulation. After all parties signed off, the original would be filed with the court.

• • •

Judge Tibbits, as expected, disqualified himself because of his involvement in the criminal case. Judge Cole Black was appointed in his place and trial was scheduled for the week of October 16.

So, the first of the two trials that would mark the ordeal was fixed and the defense was poised to do battle. It was referred to by Bodean as World War I.

JUSTICE DENIED — CARROLL MULTZ

CHAPTER 22
VIEW THE SCENE

With permission of RD and the weasel, Dustin and Bodean were allowed to view the scene so to speak. It was one thing to view photographs and still another to examine firsthand the bank vault and the bank premises.

Dustin Davies, the banker from Kalamazoo, a self-proclaimed expert on bank vault time lock (BVTL) antiques, surprised Bodean with a telephone call from Denver. He was there for a banking seminar and he and his wife had rented a car, he stated, to take a banter or frolic into the mountains of Colorado. Was it okay to spend the weekend in Steamboat? Stay with us Bodean insisted.

Bodean convinced Dustin to play hooky from the seminar and drive up early on Friday, September 1. That way they would have longer to visit, and anyway, he wanted Dustin to examine the time lock mechanism on the bank vault he had spoken to him about. Brandon Stillwell said 1:30 that afternoon would be convenient.

• • •

Steamboat was nudging autumn and the air was a little crisper than in Denver and much welcomed by the longtime strangers to the western slope. Dustin and wife, Sherri, arrived at approximately 11:30 a.m. and called from a service station on the edge of town. He was told to drive to the other end of town and meet Bodean and Natalie at Riverbend for lunch.

Bodean and Dustin had much to catch up on, reminiscing about the good old college days while their wives embarked on a conversational journey of their own. With 1:30 quickly approaching and not wanting to be late for their appointment to view the scene, the two old buddies left in Dustin's rental car. The women would be driving home in Bodean's Mustang.

• • •

Bodean and Dustin arrived on time at the historic Steamboat Bank & Trust Co. It was a stately and stylistic building, bold in its imposing large blocks of granite.

Bodean and Dustin were greeted by Brandon, who turned the tour over to Alden. Alden appeared gracious, showing the two men the various offices including his, with its annex containing his grandfather's old roll top desk, which he proudly pointed out, as well as the vacant office next to him that was formerly Jamie's. After obtaining Alden's permission, Bodean proceeded to take photographs.

Alden shadowed every move Bodean and Dustin made, especially when they approached the vault and examined the door and time lock.

Dustin asked Alden if the bank ever had any trouble with the vault time lock, and Alden replied, "Not that I know of." Pressing his luck, he asked Alden if the bank could bypass or override the time lock. Alden gave the same answer.

Bodean was shown the cash drawer in the vault that had allegedly contained the missing money. He noticed the cash was stacked to the front of the drawer just as Jamie had indicated was the bank's custom.

Dustin and Bodean had found out everything they needed to know and thanking Alden, departed for Larry and Gordie's office. Larry was in court, but Dustin was introduced to Gordie and Gordie was briefed on what the view of the scene revealed. Dustin was not only another witness to Alden's statements but a potential expert witness as well.

CHAPTER 23
EXCURSION INTO
THE UNKNOWN

It was the fifteenth day of the month, the date scheduled for the motions hearing in the criminal case.

At 7:45 a.m., the defense team was almost last to arrive at the courthouse. Corbett was already seated, with his investigator beside him. The coliseum had about the same number of spectators as the last two court appearances—virtually the same faces, with a few new ones. The Stillwells, together with the weasel, were seated in the front row. The editor and the two couples Larry subpoenaed were finally spotted.

At 8:00 a.m. sharp, the court was called to order with the Honorable Clayton Tibbits presiding. Predictably, Judge Tibbits denied the motion to strike, stating that it wasn't prejudicial to list the legal and nicknames of individuals in the pleadings as almost everyone had a nickname. And just as predictably, Judge Tibbits denied Jamie's motion to admit polygraph results after first inquiring if Corbett had received a copy of the polygraph results. In denying the motion, the judge said the polygraph was not recognized as being *reliable scientific evidence.*

Larry asked if he could briefly be heard on the issue. Judge Tibbits replied, "Briefly!"

"Your Honor, I know that there is still skepticism about the accuracy of polygraph results. I know we can't unscrew the top of someone's head or look into their heart to determine whether or not they're telling the truth. The polygraph is the closest thing we have, and if it weren't accurate, then why are so many law enforcement agencies and employers using it? Jamie has taken and passed the polygraph. Isn't that worth something?"

Corbett rose to counter but was motioned by Judge Tibbits to sit down. "Mr. Whittaker, you make some good points. However, until a higher court mandates me to do so, I will deny your motion."

"Thank you, Your Honor," Corbett said with a glint in his eyes.

"Mr. Corbett, I see where you have complied with Mr. Whittaker's request for a bill of particulars and that the defense has filed a notice of alibi pursuant thereto. Mr. Whittaker, are you satisfied with the district attorney's specification?"

"Judge," Larry began, "Mr. Corbett has indicated that the offense occurred sometime within a twelve-hour span. That doesn't really pinpoint it and defeats the purpose of the bill of particulars."

Turning to Corbett, Judge Tibbits said, "Mr. Corbett, can't you pinpoint the time of the theft or at least establish some shorter range?"

"No, Your Honor," Corbett replied. "Alden Stillwell and another employee of the bank counted the money and set the vault time lock for seven a.m. the following day. With people in the bank until seven p.m. on the tenth and people in the bank at seven a.m. the following morning, the theft could only have occurred sometime within that period. We don't have anything more definitive than that."

"Sorry, Mr. Whittaker," Judge Tibbits said. "You're going to have to live with it. Any other problems with the bill of particulars?"

"No, Your Honor. Nothing other than that."

"Very well, the next matter we will take up is the motion to suppress. Mr. Whittaker or Mr. Brownell, you may proceed."

"Your Honor," Gordie began, "Mr. Cooper's arrest was made without a warrant. There were no exigent circumstances to eliminate the requirement to obtain a warrant. Two judges were available on the date to issue a warrant, yet the officers didn't obtain one. The arrest being illegal, the search was illegal. The search being illegal, the evidence obtained as a result thereof was likewise illegal and should be suppressed."

Corbett countered, "Mr. Stillwell had already made a citizens arrest. The officers were effectuating the arrest. Officers are allowed to conduct a search incident to a lawful arrest. The search being legal, seizure of evidence and everything derived therefrom was likewise legal. Therefore, the motion to suppress should be denied."

Judge Tibbits took the matter under advisement and announced he would render his decision by Wednesday of the following week.

Now for the all-important change of venue motion. Larry asked the judge to take judicial notice of the attachments to the motion—affidavits from Eric Sweeney, the editor of the newspaper, and the four witnesses from rural Routt County to establish that the adverse pretrial publicity was massive and pervasive to such an extent that Jamie could not receive a fair trial in Routt County. Larry then made an offer of proof that the witnesses would testify in accordance with their affidavits.

"No need to call them as witnesses, Your Honor," Corbett said. "I will stipulate as to the testimony without conceding that the motion should be granted."

"Admitted for that limited purpose," Judge

Tibbits ruled.

Larry argued that the pretrial publicity was so massive and pervasive that it prevented Jamie from receiving a fair trial in Routt County. He argued, "The community is so small that the effect is even more pronounced here than it would be in a larger locality. The intensive publicity and misinformation have swayed public opinion against Jamie already as indicated by the affidavits filed with the court. Jamie hasn't even told his side of the story and yet has already been tried in the press and been convicted. It's been a trial by media, not by jury.

"To proceed to trial in Routt County would deprive Jamie of his Sixth Amendment right to a fair trial. The picture of guilt is so indelibly etched in the minds of the prospective jurors that it can't be erased, no matter the quantum or quality of the evidence to the contrary. Justice cries out for a change in the location of trial. It's the only viable option the court has to prevent a manifest abuse of justice."

Corbett opposed the motion for change of venue because a relocation of the trial would mean all the participants, including the judge, defense attorneys, defendant, witnesses, and prosecutor would need to be transplanted. The jury would be selected from the new venue. A change of venue would be costly to the citizens of Routt County. All the transplants must be transported, housed and fed in some distant community. Corbett argued, "I have greater faith in the citizens of Routt County to do the right thing than to leave it to strangers who have no vested interest."

Corbett further argued that even if the impact of the pretrial publicity was as bleak as that painted by the defense, it could be mitigated or lessened by less drastic alternatives. *Voir dire* (jury selection) would weed out those whose minds were already made up. Corbett continued, "Then there is change of veniremen where Routt County could import jurors from another county, but then that too would be expensive, although not as expensive as a change of venue. Your Honor could delay or continue the trial until the dust settles, but then critical witnesses might become scattered and lost. Your Honor is familiar with the other options, none of which accomplish what the defense is looking for—jurors who are deaf, dumb, and blind—and I would contend that doesn't describe the citizens of our county nor the type of jurors who should sit on a complex case such as the one now before the court."

The spectators applauded. After banging his gavel, Judge Tibbits announced, "Any further outbursts and I'll have the bailiff clear the courtroom."

Then looking at Larry, Judge Tibbits asked, "Any rebuttal, Mr. Whittaker?"

"Thank you, Your Honor," Larry said as he walked to the podium. "We have a lot of confidence in the jurors in Routt County as well. Jamie is a third-generation resident of this fine community and *is* one of them. However, we respect the fine citizens of Routt County to the extent that we don't wish to place them in a compromising situation or position. They shouldn't have to walk a tightrope, nor do I think they especially want to pass judgment on one of their own. I know I wouldn't want to sit on the jury in this case, and I have not lived in Routt County as long as have many of them. I'm sorry, but the inconvenience claimed by the prosecution by a change of venue is not a violation of the United States Constitution but not changing the place of trial would deprive Mr. Cooper of his Sixth Amendment right to a fair trial and *would* be a violation of the very constitution Mr. Corbett swore to uphold!"

There were audible chuckles.

Judge Tibbits again banged his gavel. "This is the last time I warn you. This hearing is not a spectacle, and if you want to observe, you'll have to do so in a respectful and dignified fashion." Judge Tibbits then said to the attorneys, "I've heard enough argument. I will take this matter under advisement, and as with the previous motion, will notify you of my decision by Wednesday of next week. In the interim, I'll continue Mr. Cooper's bond until that date. Since this covers all the defense motions and none have been filed by the prosecution, this court will stand adjourned."

• • •

At 9:00 a.m. on Wednesday, September 20, true to his word, Judge Tibbits announced his rulings on the defense's pending motions. Only about half of the usual spectators showed. The Stillwells, with the weasel, were sitting in the first row in Sunday attire, missing only their hymnals.

Not optimistic, the defense team was not overly surprised or disappointed when the rulings were announced. They all had butterflies in their stomachs as Judge Tibbits announced his rulings. He denied both motions. The motion for suppression of evidence was denied because the arrest was based on a citizen's complaint and probable cause was established on the basis of the substantial amount of missing money, some of it having been found in the possession of the defendant. The motion for change of venue was denied on the grounds that any prejudice there be could be mitigated by *voir dire*, admonition to the jury, or sequestration of the jury, or perhaps all three. Change of venue was a drastic remedy for an anecdotal defense claim that, even if true, could be cured by less drastic measures. After a brief pause, Judge Tibbits concluded by stating, "Granting a change of venue might be perceived as impugning the integrity of the fine citizens I serve."

The defense team was not as upset by the ruling as much as the rationale. Larry would later tell Verna that it was a stupefying display of innocuous legal gibberish. While everyone was there, Judge Tibbits said he wanted to set the matter for trial. Jamie's criminal case was set for a jury trial the week of February 12, 1973.

Jamie asked Larry if he knew for whom the bell tolls, referring, of course, to the outcome of his criminal case. Larry, also being familiar with Hemmingway as well as John Donne, replied, "I hope it tolls *not* for thee!" Jamie was not as sure of the outcome as he had been in the recent past. His hope was fading into the sunset as the darkness of the ordeal was setting in on a community torn apart.

JUSTICE DENIED — CARROLL MULTZ

CHAPTER 24
THE CIVIL TRIAL

With the motions hearing in the criminal case behind them and the criminal jury trial not scheduled until February 12, 1973, the defense team was now concentrating their efforts on the civil jury trial scheduled for October 16, 1972.

The defense team had pretty much settled on who they would call and what exhibits they would introduce. That was a no-brainer. They also speculated as to what witnesses the bank and insurance company would call in their behalf. That was also a no- brainer.

The defense team had met frequently over the past several weeks and now felt confident that they had a chance to win the civil case. They didn't feel their hunch was a false reading. They predicted the unfavorable outcome in the motions hearing; now they were predicting a favorable outcome in the civil trial.

It was Friday the thirteenth, so far not an unlucky day and hopefully not a bad omen, at least not for the defense. The civil jury trial was only a couple of days away. The leaves on the Aspen and Cottonwoods formed a kaleidoscopic pattern of yellows, golds, oranges, pinks and reds that glistened in the sun and shimmered in the hastening breeze. It would not be long before the leaves would be gone, and the snows would bring the hoards to the ski slopes and money into the cash registers of the local businesses.

The defense team assembled around the conference table in optimistic anticipation.

"Not the flip chart again," Bodean chided as Larry assumed his professorial role with a newly purchased pointer. Larry ignored the comment. What they were about to discuss was of extreme importance to the case. Their attention was drawn to the list of potential witnesses for the plaintiffs. They included: Brandon Stillwell, Alden Stillwell, Rita Baker, one or both of the arresting officers, Matthew Cooper, Horace Green, a bookkeeper from United Airlines, Forrest Cooper, and possibly Jennie. Their potential testimony was then discussed as well as who would be cross-examining the witnesses and what questions would be asked.

Larry flipped to the page listing all the defense witnesses and the defense team discussed their possible testimony. They were soon trial-ready.

• • •

RD had arrived in town the previous day. He

had called Larry and the two, together with the weasel, met at the weasel's office and negotiated a tentative agreement.

The stipulation, in essence, read that the parties agreed that the certified exhibits could be introduced into evidence without objection and without the necessity of laying a proper foundation or calling witnesses. This included the contract between the bank and the insurance company whereby SCICC was subrogated in the amount of $24,000 paid to SB&T Co. and SB&T Co.'s $5,000 deductible.

• • •

Jamie and Bodean met with Larry and Gordie at the latters' law office at 7:00 a.m. on Monday, October 16. After they arrived, they were quickly ushered into the conference room where Larry and Gordie were buried in work. Larry and Gordie were in the process of reviewing the list of potential jurors who had been summoned in the case. Jamie and Bodean were asked to review the list to see who they knew, who they wanted and who they didn't want. Proper notations were made to reflect their comments.

Larry and Gordie estimated that it would take at least three and maybe four hours to pick a jury. They would be meeting with Judge Black promptly at 8:00 a.m. along with RD and the weasel to take care of last-minute items, such as sequestration of witnesses. Larry and Gordie had already decided not to have Bodean sit at the defense table; otherwise, with two attorneys, it would look like they were ganging up on the poor plaintiffs and had money to burn.

• • •

When they reached the courthouse a little before 8:00 a.m., they were beginning to experience a little stage fright. A lot was riding on this case, not just the civil ramifications, but the effect the outcome would have on the criminal case.

The prospective jurors were already seated in court, quiet and reserved. All sixty of them! Maybe some of them were experiencing stage fright as well. After all, this was not the average run-of-the-mill case.

When they entered the courtroom to organize their books, papers, trial notebook, pleadings and legal pads, they noticed that the Stillwells, who had been relegated to the back of the courtroom to make room for the general venire, were comingling and ingratiating themselves with the prospective jurors. They were shaking hands, patting each other on the back and emitting nervous laughter. All such action, of course, was totally improper. Larry reported this to RD. RD turned and whispered something to the weasel, who in turn reigned in his clients.

"The Judge will see you now," the bailiff announced. Larry inquired as to whether he wanted the clients as well, and the bailiff said, "No, just the attorneys."

When they entered the judge's chambers, Judge Cole Black stood and greeted them. The judge was fairly nondescript. His most distinguishing features, however, were his piercing blue eyes and an aura that reflected someone of stature. He radiated a magnetism and mystique that one felt when in the presence of a celebrity or a high-ranking official.

"Judge Black was very accommodating," Gordie would later say. "Instead of feeling you were his servant, he made you feel as though he was yours. Even with the black robe he was a human just like the rest of us." His manner, knowledge and eloquence would soon earn the respect his person and position deserved.

He asked if his proposed trial schedule was agreeable, as well as the proposed midmorning and midafternoon recesses. He suggested that court commence at 8:00 a.m. and adjourn at 5:00 p.m. once the jury was selected. That was agreeable to all. He asked if the parties were requesting a sequestration of witnesses and both sides indicated that they were. He stated that the clients, even though they might be witnesses, were allowed to sit with counsel at trial.

Judge Black said since the defendant had two attorneys, he would have to restrict tandem or double presentment. In other words, the two attorneys could not split opening statements; only one per side. The same thing was true for final arguments. And only one attorney would be allowed per witness. The plaintiffs would not be so constrained because each counsel represented a different plaintiff. RD told the judge that since their interests were merged, more or less, that they would abide by the same restrictions as those imposed on defense counsel.

Since this was a jury trial, he said he would follow the usual civil process. He then asked how long they estimated the trial would take and was told between three and four days.

"I see from the court file that there are certain stipulations that you have made. I compliment you for making the effort to expedite the proceedings. Are there any other stipulations that I need to be made aware of before we start?"

"No, Your Honor," both sides responded.

"If it looks as though we are taking longer than necessary to pick a jury, I will have to limit your *voir dire*. Try not to be redundant and direct as many questions as you can to the panel as a whole."

With the rules of the game pretty well understood, the attorneys retreated to their respective tables. Brandon Stillwell was already seated at plaintiffs' table; Jamie at defendant's.

Six potential jurors were called to the box. Judge Black asked general questions to illicit background information. The attorneys, starting with the plaintiffs, asked the usual questions in an effort to make sure the prospective jurors would not be prejudiced against their side. None of the jurors evinced bias or prejudice and none were challenged for cause. All were customers of SB&T Co., which was expected, since SB&T Co. was the only bank in town. That was not grounds for disqualification Judge Black had previously ruled.

After the jury was selected, the attorneys made opening statements. Since the plaintiffs had the burden of proof, they went first and would do so throughout the trial.

RD made the opening statement for the plaintiffs.

"Ladies and gentlemen of the jury, my name is Richard Colquist. I represent Standard Casualty Insurance Company of Connecticut in this action. My co-counsel is Henry Ross. He represents Steamboat Bank and Trust Company. I will be making an opening statement for both plaintiffs.

"The evidence will show that James Curtis Cooper was an employee of Steamboat Bank and Trust Company and had been for a number of years. On the morning of June 11, 1972, Alden Stillwell, the son of the owner of the bank and an employee of the bank, while looking for a file, discovered one thousand dollars in one of the desk drawers of another of the bank's employees, Jamie Curtis Cooper, the defendant in this case. Upon opening the bank vault, he discovered that thirty thousand dollars was missing. He confiscated the one thousand dollars he found in Mr. Cooper's desk drawer and called the police. The police subsequently responded and arrested Mr. Cooper for theft.

"The evidence will show that Mr. Cooper was working at the bank the evening before the money was found missing. When Alden arrived at work the next morning, Mr. Cooper's car was in the outermost portion of the bank's parking lot. But there was no sign of Mr. Cooper. In fact, he didn't appear at the bank until eight a.m.

"The evidence will show that Mr. Cooper had a gambling addiction. A secret not even his co-workers or closest friends knew. We will be presenting toll records of numerous telephone calls

Mr. Cooper made and a trip he took to Las Vegas in the weeks preceding the discovery of the missing money. To prove our claim, we will be placing in evidence a receipt from Tampico Casino in Las Vegas showing that during Mr. Cooper's visit to Las Vegas, he redeemed a gambling chit for twelve hundred dollars. To prove the trip, we will produce a printout of his roundtrip airline ticket.

"When all the evidence is in, you will be convinced by a preponderance of the evidence that Mr. Cooper allowed his gambling propensity to take over his better judgment, resulting in him dipping into his employer's till to the tune of thirty thousand dollars. At the end of our presentation we'll be asking you to return a verdict in favor of the plaintiffs in the amounts requested."

After RD made his opening statement, the weasel passed a note to RD via Brandon, the plaintiffs' advisory witness, who was seated between the two attorneys. RD looking at the note and leaning past Brandon mouthed "thank you" and smiled at the weasel.

"Thank you, Mr. Colquist," the judge said. "The defense may now make its opening statement."

Larry then began, "Ladies and gentlemen of the jury, Mr. Brownell and I represent the defendant in this action. First, I want to introduce you to a man who is thirty-four years of age. His lifetime ambition has been to be a banker. It started the summer after his senior year in high school culminating in thirteen years of outstanding service to that same bank, the Steamboat Bank and Trust Company. So stellar was his performance that he rose to the level of first vice-president, hop-scotching or leapfrogging over everyone at the bank, including the owner's son, Alden Stillwell.

"The man that I want you to meet is a third generation Routt County resident and the president-elect of the Steamboat Chamber of Commerce. This man excelled in sports and was the valedictorian of his high school class. He was a business major and graduated with honors from the University of Colorado. He is married and has two children Max, age twelve, and Collette, age ten.

"On the evening of June 10, 1972, this man was working late as was his custom. He loved his job and had great responsibilities. He was loyal to his boss, Brandon Stillwell, and wanted to do everything he could to repay Mr. Stillwell for the faith Mr. Stillwell reposed in him. This man left the bank at six fifteen p.m. on the evening of June 10, leaving only the Skyler Cleaning Service owners, Ron and Betty Skyler, in the bank.

"There was a vault time lock that did not

permit admittance to the vault from the time of closing of the bank until seven the following morning. The closing of the vault and setting of the time required what was called dual control which meant two persons, namely Rita Baker and Alden Stillwell to count the money, follow a checklist that Alden was required to initial upon completion of each step, trigger the timer and lock the vault door. This procedure was followed on the evening in question. At least that's the statement the bank provided the police.

"When the time expired and the vault could be opened with the regular combination having been dialed, guess who dialed the combination? Alden Stillwell. Guess who opened the vault door when the time expired at seven a.m. on June 11? Alden Stillwell. Guess who was alone in the bank after the vault door was open? Alden Stillwell. Guess who discovered the so-called missing money? Alden Stillwell. Guess who had the thousand dollars of so-called recovered money in his hands when the police arrived? Alden Stillwell. Guess whose office Alden Stillwell came out of with the thousand dollars? Alden Stillwell's.

"Guess who didn't take the so-called missing money or any part thereof? The answer is the man I now want you to meet." With that, Larry went over to the chair where Jamie was sitting, and placing his hand on Jamie's shoulder said, "This is the man! His name is Jamie Cooper."

After Larry made his opening statement, there was a deafening hush that pervaded the courtroom. Even Judge Black seemed to be caught up in a moment of reflection. Could it be that the pendulum was swinging back in the right direction? Hopefully, the jury and everyone else were asking, "Why are we here?" Jamie was certainly asking himself that question. No note from the weasel to RD this time!

Judge Black looking at his watch said, "It's twelve oh five. This is a good place for our noon break." He admonished the jury not to talk about the case among themselves, not to read any newspaper accounts, watch any television, or listen to any radio accounts of the case. He declared the court adjourned until 1:30 p.m.

• • •

Verna had lunch waiting when the defense team, including Bodean, returned to the office. Everyone seemed to have an appetite, but the conversation centered mostly around the proposed cross-examination of Alden Stillwell and Clinton Coleman. They were the key witnesses and the two who appeared to have an axe to grind. Larry was set to cross-examine Alden and Gordie was set to cross-examine Coleman.

Jamie sat there in careful reflection. He could see that RD was not a stranger to the courtroom and knew how to go for the jugular. But Larry had impressed him the most. RD was obvious about what he was trying to do, and Jamie remembered from his logic's class in college a Latin phrase that described RD's approach: *non sequitur*, meaning a conclusion that does not follow from the facts. Hopefully the jury could see through it. Larry on the other hand was subtle and appealed to logic and common sense. Rhetoric alone wouldn't cut it.

• • •

Almost by the time they left for lunch it was time to return to court. There seemed to be a different tone permeating the courtroom now. Even many of the spectators were looking in Jamie's direction. Some of the scowls were turning into smiles. Even the Stillwell strut was becoming more of a shuffle.

Brandon was indeed the first witness called by the plaintiffs. After he was sworn in the weasel questioned him on direct. He testified to basically what the defense had anticipated. Gordie did a good job neutralizing his testimony and eliciting some evidence supporting Jamie's defense.

Cross-examining Brandon, Gordie asked,

"Now, Mr. Stillwell, you were gone the whole week of June tenth, is that not true?"

"Yes."

"When you were gone, you said your private office was locked. Who had access, if anyone?"

"My son, Alden."

"Did anyone else have access?"

"No."

"When the vault time lock was set for the night, that is from seven p.m. until seven a.m. the following morning, could it be overridden or bypassed?"

"No."

"Do you ever know of a time when the vault time lock was overridden or bypassed?"

"I remember a dozen years ago or so we had trouble with the vault time lock and had to call the manufacturer. It seems we were provided with some kind of combination to gain access."

"You don't know if Jamie ever had that combination, do you?"

"No."

"Now, you testified that the cash drawers in the vault were accessed by a key, is that correct?"

"Yes."

"During business hours, were the drawers kept locked?"

"They were required to be locked at all times."

"How many keys did the drawers require in order to gain access?"

"Because they were the old style, they only required one."

"Who had keys to those drawers?"

"Rita Baker, Alden, Jamie, and myself."

"Who normally unlocked the cash drawers?"

"My son, Alden."

"How did you find out that money was missing from the bank?"

"Alden told me."

"By the way, I assume you fired Jamie?"

"Yes."

"Who replaced Jamie as first vice-president of Steamboat Bank and Trust Company?"

"My son, Alden."

"No further questions."

"Very well, Mr. Colquist or Mr. Ross, if you have no re-direct you may call your next witness," Judge Black said.

It was only fitting that the weasel would examine Alden. Alden was sworn in and testified just as the defense anticipated. It was not as if the defense was clairvoyant. After all, they had Alden's statements from the discovery in the criminal case. It would be difficult for him to change his testimony now. It had already been etched in stone. Though tedious, Gordie thought the weasel had done a decent job in examining Alden.

It was time for the midafternoon recess. When the court resumed it was time for Larry to demonstrate his cross-examination skills.

Larry asked, "Mr. Stillwell, you're certain the vault door could not be accessed or overridden from seven p.m. on June tenth until seven a.m. on June eleventh, aren't you?"

"Yes."

"Is that because you personally tested the vault door to see if it worked?"

"Yes. Oftentimes after the timer has been set and the door has been closed, I will try the combination just to double check. I did test it that night as I did every night Dad was gone. I didn't want anything to happen during my watch."

"If you and Rita Baker closed the vault door and the timing device was working as you testified and you were there at seven the following morning when the timer expired, how do you explain how Jamie or anyone else could have accessed the vault during that time period?"

"You'll have to ask Jamie. I don't know. The money was there when we closed the vault door and it was gone when I got there at seven a.m. on the eleventh."

"Now, if your father had testified that the vault time lock couldn't be bypassed from seven p.m. the evening before until seven the next morning, would his testimony have been correct?"

"Yes."

"To your knowledge, has the vault time lock ever been bypassed or overridden?"

"No, not to my knowledge."

"The one thousand dollars that you testified you found in Jamie's drawer, where was it when the police arrived?"

"After I confiscated it from Jamie's desk, I put it in my office for safekeeping until the police arrived."

"Was Jamie's office locked when you arrived that morning?"

"Yes, because I had to get Rita's key to unlock the door."

"And where was the key?"

"In Rita's desk drawer."

"Wasn't her desk drawer locked?"

"Yes, but I had a key."

"Was Jamie's office the only one you searched?"

"Yes, at that time. We searched the rest of the bank later."

"Aren't there three offices in a row perpendicular

to the vault? In other words, wasn't Jamie's office sandwiched between yours and Nan Morris'?"

"Nan Morris retired but her husband Gene still does our appraisals. Annette Carrie took Nan's place and she's now in Nan's old office."

"Did you search Annette's office?"

"No."

"Why not?"

"She had customers in with her and we didn't want to disturb them."

"After the police left, did you search Jamie's office more thoroughly?"

"Yes."

"Did you find any other cash or anything you thought suspicious?"

"No."

"Did anyone ever search your office?"

"No, why would they?"

"My question is, did anyone ever search your office, yes or no?"

"No."

"No further questions."

Judge Black asked the weasel if he had any redirect and he answered "No."

Judge Black, then looking at his watch, said that it was getting late and that this would be a good place to break for the day. The jury was admonished once again not to talk about the case with anyone or among themselves and not read any newspaper accounts, watch television, or listen to any radio accounts of the case and that they were to be in the jury room no later than 7:45 the next morning.

• • •

Larry, Gordie and Jamie met up with Bodean, who had been sitting in the hall reviewing case documents and going through the discovery provided in the criminal case and making notes. The defense team headed back to Larry and Gordie's office.

They critiqued the days events, re-evaluated the jury and prepared Jamie and Bodean for direct and cross-examination. They were careful, however, in not discussing Brandon's and Alden's testimony in front of Bodean because Bodean might be called as a witness. They could not and did not violate the sequestration rule and the judge's orders—either directly or indirectly. They all had a long day, and each needed some quiet time alone.

• • •

They met the next day promptly at 7:30 a.m. and readied themselves for the second day of trial.

Everyone appeared to be more relaxed and many of the jurors made eye contact with members of the defense team and smiled. The Stillwells resumed their official seating in the front row of the courtroom on plaintiffs' side. Brandon and Alden, having been excused as witnesses, were among them.

Judge Black called the court to order, and determining that both sides were ready to proceed, asked Colquist and Ross to call their next witness.

Plaintiffs then called Rita Baker. She took the usual oath to tell the truth, and in response to questions by the weasel, said that she was the head teller and part of the dual control team Alden had described. She had been working at the bank about the same length of time as Jamie. She was certain all the cash was accounted for the night the bank's vault door was closed and locked and that it couldn't be breached or accessed until 7:00 a.m. the next morning. She, Brandon, Alden and Jamie all had the regular combination to the vault and keys to the cash drawers.

The weasel then had Rita identify the bank closing checklist and the vault balancing journal for the dates in question. The weasel then offered the items in evidence.

After the weasel announced he had no further questions, it was Gordie's turn to cross-examine.

"Ms. Baker, you stated on direct that you, Brandon, Alden, and Jamie all had the regular combination to the vault. Now, my question is this, did the regular combination when dialed allow any of the four of you access to the vault between the hours of seven p.m. and seven a.m. the following day?"

"No."

"And you are certain of that?"

"Absolutely."

"So, even with the knowledge of the regular combination, Jamie couldn't have possibly gained access to the cash in the bank's vault from seven p.m. on July 10 to seven a.m. on July 11. Is that your testimony?"

"Yes, actually the timer was set to begin when we closed and locked the vault door and that was at five thirty p.m. when the bank closed."

"Then let me understand, Ms. Baker, that regardless of whatever time you and Alden may have completed your count and closed and locked the vault door, the timer was triggered and the vault couldn't be accessed until seven a.m. the following morning. Is that your testimony?"

"Yes."

"When you arrived at the bank at seven fifteen a.m. on July 11 who, if anyone, was present?"

"Alden Stillwell."

"Who dialed the combination and opened the

door of the vault that morning?"

"Alden said he did."

"Did Alden tell you that he had some of the so-called missing money?"

"Yes, he told me that. He said he had found one thousand dollars in one of Jamie's desk drawers."

"Did you see the one thousand dollars?"

"No, not until after the police arrived."

"When was the first time you saw the money?"

"When Alden brought it from his office and threw it on Jamie's desk."

"When you say his are you referring to Alden's office?"

"Yes."

"You did not mean to suggest that the one thousand dollars Alden produced came from Jamie's office, did you?"

"No."

"Did you assist in the search of the bank for the rest of the missing thirty thousand dollars?"

"Yes, we all did."

"Did you search or see anyone else search Alden's office?"

"No."

"Did you see the police search Jamie's car?"

"Yes."

"Could you tell if they found any of the missing

money in Jamie's car?"

"No, not while I was watching."

"Did you ever see the police or anyone else search Alden's car?"

"No."

"Then you don't know whether the so-called missing money may have been in Alden's office or Alden's car at the time, do you?"

"No."

"What happened to all of Jamie's personal belongings that were left in his office, if you know?"

"Alden had me box them up and bring them to him."

"Was Jamie's door then left unlocked?"

"Yes."

"By the way, Ms. Baker, whose office was closest to the vault?"

"Alden Stillwell's."

"No further questions."

The weasel was asked if he had any redirect. He had none.

RD then called Officer Clinton Coleman to the stand. After he was sworn to tell the truth, he testified about Jamie's arrest and Alden claiming to have found the one thousand dollars in Jamie's desk drawer. The one thousand dollars was then offered into evidence.

Larry asked if he could question the witness with regard to the proffered exhibit. The request was granted, and he asked Coleman:

"Officer Coleman, was the one thousand dollars handed to you by Jamie Cooper?"

"No, I received it from Alden Stillwell."

"Was the one thousand dollars in Jamie's office when you and the other officers arrived at the bank?"

"No. It was brought into Mr. Cooper's office by Alden Stillwell after we arrived."

"Your Honor, we object to the introduction of plaintiffs' tendered exhibit on the grounds that it is irrelevant, immaterial and incompetent," Larry interjected. "There is no nexus to Mr. Cooper. There is a nexus to Alden Stillwell but not to Mr. Cooper."

"Overruled. Ladies and gentlemen of the jury, you are instructed that the evidence is offered only to show that it was given to the officers at the time of the arrest by Alden Stillwell, not that it was in the possession of Mr. Cooper. Anything else, Mr. Colquist?"

"No, Your Honor, we have no other questions of Officer Coleman."

The judge announced that the defense could cross-examine.

Larry began by asking, "Officer Coleman, did you or your fellow officers, if you know, remove any money from Jamie Cooper?"

"We removed some currency from his wallet. As I recall it was thirty-eight dollars. We also removed some change he had in his pants pocket. Other than that, no."

"Did you have occasion to search Mr. Cooper's vehicle that was parked in the employee section of the bank parking lot?"

"Yes. Officer Michael Heath was in charge of that."

"To your knowledge did Officer Heath or anyone find any currency or any items that would tie Mr. Cooper to the alleged theft from the bank?"

"Not to my knowledge."

"Did you or any of the officers ever search Alden Stillwell's vehicle or office?"

"No, we didn't."

"Did you or any other officer search any other employee's vehicle?"

"No, not to my knowledge."

"How do you know that the one thousand dollars was found in Jamie Cooper's office?"

"Because Alden Stillwell told us it was."

"But you didn't see the money in Mr. Cooper's office until after it was brought in there by Alden

Stillwell, did you?"

"No." Coleman then glanced in Alden's direction.

"No further cross, Your Honor."

"Any redirect Mr. Colquist."

"No, Your Honor."

"Call your next witness."

"Judge, may we have a moment?" RD asked.

"Yes, but just a moment."

The plaintiffs' team then huddled obviously preparing for their next play. In a surprise move, RD announced, "The plaintiffs rest their case-in-chief."

When Gordie looked at Larry and frowned, Larry just shrugged. "An early Christmas present," Larry whispered to Jamie.

Gordie stood and announced, "Your Honor, we have a motion to make outside the ears of the jury."

"Very well. Ladies and gentlemen, the bailiff will escort you to the jury room while the court takes up a matter out of your presence."

The jury was excused and Gordie moved for a directed verdict on plaintiffs' claim in favor of the defendant on the grounds that the quality and quantum of evidence was not sufficient to allow the case to be placed in the hands of the jury. "Because of the groundless nature of the plaintiffs' claim," Gordie argued, "a judgment should also be entered in favor of the defendant on defendant's counterclaim."

Gordie didn't even flinch when, without asking counsel for the plaintiffs to respond, Judge Black said, "Denied." He cited as rationale the testimony of Alden Stillwell to the effect that money was missing and that $1,000 had been recovered from the defendant's desk. "That raised an inference that supports plaintiffs' claim," Judge Black ruled, "and depending on defendant's evidence, would be a credibility issue for the jury to decide." The motion for directed verdict on the counterclaim was denied on the same basis. The defense team expected as much and showed no reaction to the denial.

Judge Black announced that he had some other pressing court matters that he had to attend to by telephone and asked if counsel had any objection to releasing the jury until 1:30. That would give the defense time to line up their witnesses. Neither side objected. The bailiff was instructed to so inform the jurors, which he did.

• • •

Back in the courtroom at 1:30, the defense was ready to call their first witness: Jamie Cooper. With the criminal case looming, Larry and Gordie were nervous about having Jamie testify. If the strategy of going forward with the civil trial backfired, it would be their fault.

Jamie was prepared and appeared to be relaxed when he took the stand. He lived up to their expectations and beyond. Afterwards, they would award him a perfect ten. When asked about the Las Vegas connection, Jamie testified he was not a gambler. He stated that he indeed made the seven telephone calls in June and the five telephone calls in July to Las Vegas. He also stated that he travelled to Las Vegas to pay off the chit posted by his cousin, Patty Cooper, in the amount of $1,200. *This testimony is as straight forward as you can get. No deception here,* Larry thought.

Jamie testified as to the purposes of the dozen telephone calls and the trip to Las Vegas and noted from whom he had obtained the $1,200 and travel expenses. He said the airline tickets testified to were paid by his father.

At that point Jamie identified the copy of the chit as well as the receipt from the Tomahawk Café establishing alibi and the United Airline purchase receipt. All three were admitted in evidence.

Larry announced he had no further questions. It was a relief when the weasel rose to cross-examine Jamie. RD would have been much more formidable. The Stillwells obviously thought they picked the right attorney to conduct the punishing cross-examination; the *coup de grace* needed to ensure victory for the plaintiffs.

Many of the weasel's questions were caustic, demeaning and condescending. All of Larry's objections were sustained. *Thank God for a fair and impartial judge like Judge Black,* Larry thought. The weasel was argumentative and succeeded only in reinforcing Jamie's position and in alienating the jury. Several times Larry was on the verge of asking for a mistrial but felt that Judge Black's admonitions to the weasel and the jurors' awareness of the weasel's cheap shots were more than ample. Gordie, whispering in Larry's ear, asked, "Do we have to split our fees with the weasel since he's done such a great job for our cause?"

"No redirect," Larry announced without being asked.

The weasel had taken so long it was time for the midafternoon break. Judge Black announced that the jury would reconvene at 3:15.

As the jury filed out of the box, none looked in the direction of the plaintiffs' table and noticeably avoided eye contact with the gallery of Stillwells reminiscent of a flock of vultures. Newfound confidence was swelling as the trial progressed.

At break, Larry told Gordie and Jamie, "It's

strange how cases either come together or fall apart during trial. This one is coming together!"

• • •

The court reconvened at 3:15. Larry called G. Forrest Cooper to the stand. He testified about all of Patty's gambling woes and having conscripted Jamie to deliver the $1,200 to Tampico to stave off a civil suit and criminal prosecution. The funds he provided to Jamie came from the sale of eggs, chickens and beef. He told the jury how sorry he was that he got his son involved in the mix.

As hard as RD tried on cross-examination, he was unable to shake the patriarch of the Cooper clan. Not wanting to bury the plaintiffs completely, RD announced that he had no further questions and tried unsuccessfully to mask his displeasure as he retreated to his seat.

Jennie was the next defense witness. She corroborated everything that her husband and father-in-law had testified to. Since it would have been like cross-examining Mother Teresa, RD and the weasel opted not to cross-examine her.

Betty Skyler from Skyler Cleaning Service was called as Jamie's next witness. She confirmed that she and her husband were cleaning at the bank on the evening in question; Jamie's presence when they arrived and his departure while they were still there; their unlocking the outside door for Jamie upon his exit; and that when Jamie left he didn't appear nervous and wasn't carrying anything because, if he was, they would have noticed.

RD and the weasel again chose not to cross-examine.

Ursula Russell was the defendant's next witness. She testified that on the morning of July 11, 1972, she observed Jamie drive into the parking lot of the bank; watched as he parked and walked in the direction of the Tomahawk Café; shortly thereafter she observed Alden Stillwell park in the bank parking lot and go inside. She thought that strange because he usually didn't arrive at the bank that early.

RD was getting nowhere with cross-examination, and being the good trial lawyer he was, aborted midway.

Gordie presented the next two witnesses, Jackie Stiles and Charlie Blankenship. Jackie was a waitress at the Tomahawk Café. She confirmed the times Jamie was at the chamber meeting on the date in question. Charlie also corroborated Jamie's alibi.

RD and the weasel wisely chose not to cross-examine, and the defense rested their case. The plaintiffs then announced they had no rebuttal so the jury was excused until the following day when they would be instructed on the law and hear final arguments.

Even though it was after 5:00 p.m., Judge Black pressed on. He instructed the attorneys on both sides to meet in chambers to finalize jury instructions. The task was completed in record time.

It was almost 7:00 p.m. when the defense team exited the courthouse. Tired but buoyed, they looked forward to the next day.

• • •

It was Wednesday, October 18, the third day of trial. The attorneys and their clients were seated, poised for final arguments. Jamie remarked, as they awaited Judge Black's arrival, that they should probably tip the weasel for his contribution to the anticipated outcome of the case. Larry cautioned Jamie not to be over-confident.

"Remember the Alamo," Gordie admonished referring to the motions hearing.

The usual spectators were in attendance. However, their mood was more somber. The only one who seemed confident was the weasel. It was apparent that he was oblivious to the fact that there was a real possibility that the jury would return a verdict in Jamie's favor and that he, the weasel, would become the scapegoat.

The plaintiffs had already cleared it through Judge Black that RD and the weasel would divide final argument. The weasel would give the opening and RD would give the closing. After the jury was instructed on the law, the weasel literally strutted to the podium.

Looking smug and self-assured, he began: "Thank you, ladies and gentlemen, for your time and service." Then looking back over his shoulder toward the defense table, said, "What we have here is a case of a banker gone wild in an attempt to cover a gambling addiction fueled by greed. Thirty thousand dollars is a lot of money. Handling money every day has a desensitizing effect. Obviously, the defendant didn't consider, or worse yet, didn't care about the effect his actions would have on his family, friends, employer and the poor depositors who entrusted him and the bank with their hard-earned money.

"Over the last few days you've heard testimony to the effect that Alden Stillwell discovered that thirty thousand dollars was missing from a cash drawer in the vault of Steamboat Bank and Trust, Company, and searching defendant's office found one thousand of it—"

"Objection!" Gordie shouted.

"On what grounds?" Judge Black asked with

irritation in his voice.

"There's no evidence that the one thousand dollars was part of the missing money and we object to counsel assuming a fact not in evidence."

Judge Black overruled the objection saying, "This is final argument and I will give counsel some leeway in recounting the evidence. The jury will determine whether or not Mr. Ross' recollection is correct."

The weasel smirked and appeared to be even more confident now that Gordie's objection had been overruled. He continued, "Defendant was caught with his hand in the proverbial cookie jar. If it weren't for Alden Stillwell finding the one thousand dollars in defendant's desk drawer and Officer Coleman uncovering the Las Vegas connection, we wouldn't be here. Fortunately, a leopard can't hide its spots—at least not for very long.

"Defendant had the means, motive and opportunity to take the money. Even he can't argue that the money belonged to him or that he had it coming or that he took it by mistake. He hasn't asserted any of those defenses. If he did, I didn't hear it, and I've sat here throughout the whole trial.

"Of course, the defendant is going to come into court and say he didn't take the money. I would have thought more of him, and so would you, ladies and gentlemen, if he had come into court like a man and admitted his mistake. I see no remorse for what he's done to those who trusted him. He's coming in here with hat in hand, begging you to believe him and disbelieve everyone else and to rule in his favor because he's the president-elect of the Chamber of Commerce. All I can say is the chamber has been duped like the Steamboat Bank and Trust Company has been duped and like he would like to have you duped. Don't be fooled by that all-American façade. Beware of wolves dressed in sheep's clothing.

"Sympathy should not be a factor in your decision. All of us feel sorry for Mr. Cooper. A promising banking career out the window. The adverse spinoff effect on his family. And the tarnishing of the Cooper name and reputation. Decide the case on its merits and not on emotion. And if you do that you will find that you have no choice but to rule in the plaintiffs' favor on their claims and against defendant on his counterclaim."

The weasel winked at Brandon as he resumed his seat.

"Thank you, Mr. Ross, and now for the defendant's final argument," Judge Black announced.

Gordie knew the plaintiffs would have two cracks at final argument one on opening and the other on closing. That was because they carried the burden of proof, at least on their claim. The defendant would be given only one chance and it better be good! The pressure was on.

"Ladies and gentlemen, on behalf of my co-council Larry Whittaker, the defendant Jamie Cooper and myself, I would like to thank you for your taking time to sit as jurors in this case. Jury duty is not easy, and I would rather be slotted in my role as a defense attorney than yours as a decision maker, especially in a few minutes when the case is handed over to you ladies and gentlemen to render that all-important verdict.

"Mr. Ross asked that you not be guided by sympathy or emotion and yet he made an emotional appeal—one that is not based on the evidence presented. To begin with, it's always difficult to prove a negative. How do you prove you didn't do what you've been accused of doing? Normally all you can say is you didn't do it. Without a solid alibi it's your word against the accuser's word. Then you are judged on the basis of the likelihood that you did or didn't do it. Jamie has told you under oath that he didn't do it. What's the likelihood that he did or didn't based on what you learned in this trial?

"Mr. Ross used the cookie jar analogy, one that is used in virtually every case of this kind. If there are cookies missing, then let's trace the cookie trail in this case. One thing both sides agree on, it's all about the cookies! Let's allocate a cookie for every piece of the puzzle dealing with the disappearance of the thirty thousand dollars.

"By everyone's account all the money was accounted for when the vault door was closed and locked, triggering the running of the vault time lock clock. It couldn't be opened even with a combination until the time on the clock expired and that was at seven a.m. the following morning. The evidence by all was to the effect that the vault time lock couldn't be bypassed or overridden while the timer was running.

"I'm going to use this flip chart and I'm going to list all the categories and assign a cookie under either Jamie's column or Alden's column indicating to which one it applies. I will use a black circular sticker with a sad face to represent the cookie."

With that Gordie asked each question in the following order and then placed a cookie under whichever column the answer applied.

	Alden	Jamie
Who was there when the time lock expired?	🙁	
Who opened the vault door?	🙁	
Who was there when Rita arrived at seven fifteen a.m.?	🙁	
Who set the time lock after work the night before?	🙁	
Who had access to the cash drawers when no one else was at the bank?	🙁	
Who unlocked the cash drawers?	🙁	
Who claimed to discover the money missing?	🙁	
Who claimed they found one thousand dollars in Jamie's office?	🙁	
Who was the only person, other than Brandon, who had access to Brandon's office and could have found some secret combination, if any, to override or bypass the vault time lock?	🙁	

	Alden	Jamie
Who had the thousand dollars in his possession when the police arrived?	🙁	
Whose office was not searched?	🙁	
Whose desk was not searched?	🙁	
Whose vehicle was not searched?	🙁	
Whose person was not searched?	🙁	
Who searched Jamie's office?	🙁	
Who claimed Jamie stole the money?	🙁	
Who called the police and had Jamie arrested?	🙁	
Who is the only one who had a fifteen-minute window to have taken the thirty thousand dollars?	🙁	
Who stood to gain the most by Jamie's arrest?	🙁	
Who replaced Jamie as the bank's First Vice-President?	🙁	

"If my addition is correct, that's twenty cookies that were taken from Mr. Ross' imaginary cookie jar. Guess who took all twenty of them? Guess who didn't take any? Mr. Ross is correct in one respect. The person who stole the cookies most likely is the thief who stole the thirty thousand dollars—but that person was not Jamie! Why the frame-up? You'll have to ask Alden. He's the only one who benefited from the ruse.

"The plaintiffs introduced a receipt in evidence issued to Jamie showing payment of a chit or a marker in the amount of twelve hundred dollars to Tampico Casino in Las Vegas. But they told you only part of the story—a misleading one at that. It took the defense to unravel the rest of the story. The actual chit or marker Jamie redeemed, with money provided by his father, was incurred by Jamie's cousin, Patty. The gambler was Patty—not Jamie. If the plaintiffs were fair and honest, they would've told you that the Las Vegas connection, as Mr. Ross terms it, is only a figment of their imagination. It never existed, and it doesn't exist. Try as they might, there are no dots to connect—at least not to Jamie.

"It's difficult to defend a case like this. As I said, how do you prove a negative? I only hope Mr. Whittaker and I effectively convinced you of

Jamie's lack of culpability in seeking justice for him. But our duty at this point is over and we're placing Jamie's fate in your hands—to seek and administer justice. In doing so, we trust you'll rule in Jamie's favor on plaintiffs' claim for relief because plaintiffs have wholly failed to meet their burden of proof by a preponderance of the evidence. We also hope you'll rule in Jamie's favor on the counterclaim because he has met his burden. Thank you."

After Gordie resumed his seat, the judge said, "The court will take a short midmorning break to allow the jury to stretch. The court is in recess for fifteen minutes."

When court reconvened, RD was already standing at the podium ready for plaintiffs' rebuttal argument.

"Ladies and gentlemen, I, too, thank you for your service and attention. I will be brief. Mr. Ross has already outlined the evidence, but there are a few impressions I need to dispel in Mr. Brownell's recollection of the facts and his interpretation thereof.

"First, despite whether Mr. Cooper paid for Cousin Patty's gambling debts or his own is immaterial. He used cash to redeem the one chit and we don't know how many others —"

"Objection, Your Honor," Gordie exploded. "That calls for speculation. There's no evidence whatsoever that there were other chits."

"Overruled! Mr. Colquist, you may proceed."

"Regardless, we do know that all the expenses of that trip were paid by cash. It's Plaintiffs' contention that the money belonged to the bank and was taken without authorization.

"Second, Mr. Brownell in his eloquent illustration connecting the cookies forgot about a misplaced cookie, a cookie larger than all the rest. That jumbo cookie, the dot that connects Mr. Cooper, is the fact that one thousand of the missing thirty thousand dollars was found in his office in a drawer in his desk. I refer your attention to the evidence consisting of the Federal Reserve band and the twenty fifty-dollar bills. That is the smoking gun in this case.

"Third, and final, the defendant wants you to believe that it was Alden Stillwell who was responsible for taking the thirty thousand dollars. My only question to you is this: Why would Alden take the money? It would be like stealing from himself since he was the sole heir of his father's estate."

"Objection, Your Honor." Gordie once again was livid. "There is absolutely no evidence that

Alden was the sole heir. We object on the grounds that Mr. Colquist is assuming a fact not in evidence. Furthermore, the money didn't belong to Alden Stillwell's father, it belonged to the depositors and shareholders of Steamboat Bank and Trust Company."

"Sustained. The jury will be instructed to disregard the sole heir reference. Mr. Colquist, please refrain from any such further references."

"I apologize. Thank you, Your Honor. Ladies and gentlemen, I appeal to your logic and not your emotions in asking you to return a verdict in favor of the plaintiffs as to both plaintiffs' claims and defendant's counterclaim. We, too, ask that you dispense justice. Justice is marking a simple x in the box opposite plaintiffs in both verdict forms. Thank you."

"Thank you, Mr. Colquist," Judge Black said. "Ladies and gentlemen of the jury, the bailiff will now escort you to the jury room along with the written jury instructions and exhibits. The rest of you please remain standing until the jury has left the courtroom."

Judge Black asked that the attorneys let his clerk know where they could be reached in the event the jury had a question or were ready to return a verdict.

...

Back at Larry and Gordie's office the defense replayed the mental trial tape recounting the key testimony mainly for Bodean's benefit since the exclusion of witness rule prevented him from being in the courtroom. They also did it for their own benefit because they wanted to bask in the sunshine of their anticipated victory.

Jamie complemented and thanked them all for the superb job of representing him in the civil trial. He asked if any of them would, in retrospect, have done anything differently. After careful reflection, they all said, "No, not a thing!" They also complemented him on *his* great job on the witness stand.

"Again," he said, "it's easy when you're telling the truth."

Bodean said the defense team had been working together too long; they were beginning to think alike. They all felt Jamie would prevail on the main claim but that the counterclaim was in jeopardy. Larry reminded everyone that the counterclaim had been included more for the psychological impact than anything. He said that even though he felt the plaintiffs' claims were frivolous, he didn't think the jury would rule in their favor.

Gordie said he agreed and thought jurors liked

compromise verdicts. "They like giving something to each side."

"I would certainly trade losing the counterclaim for winning the main claim," said Larry. They all agreed.

They speculated that if the jury went back to the jury room at twelve thirty, had lunch until one thirty, reviewed jury instructions until two and deliberated for four hours, they would come back with a verdict around six thirty. "If they stall long enough, they'll get a free dinner at one of the restaurants, usually the Crazy Cat down in the next block," said Gordie. "When my wife had jury duty that's where they were taken."

Because they didn't know when the jury would return, they all thought they should stick around. Larry and Gordie went to their respective offices to sort through their mail. Bodean ran an errand. Jamie called his wife and browsed in the firm's law library.

The hours were going by slowly and Verna was kept busy answering, "Have you heard anything yet?" When the clock on the town hall chimed five, five thirty, and then six, the defense team was beginning to feel the jitters, as Bodean would later say. Bodean ran over to the courthouse and confirmed that the jury had indeed been taken to dinner at the Crazy Cat. They left about six fifteen. The defense team went to the Tomahawk Café, returning to the office about seven fifteen. At about eight thirty, they received a telephone call from the bailiff announcing that the jury had reached a verdict and that the judge wanted them back in the courtroom ASAP.

The defense team arrived first. RD and the weasel arrived next with Brandon, Alden and the rest of the Stillwell clan close behind. Apparently, the plaintiffs had a different read on the outcome of the trial. They were all gloating. The defense team was now rethinking their strategy and wondering what they could have done differently and what they were missing. They were in an anomalous situation. Panic was trying to assert itself and each took a turn in trying to dispel it.

"I see the weasel is his usual inimitable self," Larry said to Jamie and Gordie.

"You knock him down and he keeps getting up asking for more," Gordie replied.

"I wonder how he'll feel after the verdict is read," Jamie quipped.

Less than half of the usual onlookers showed up. Hardly a fitting tribute for the story of the year. The vultures must have found other prey, Larry thought. Just then the jury came in escorted by the bailiff.

Judge Black entered and called the court to order. "You may be seated. Mr. Foreman, have you reached a verdict?"

"We have, Your Honor," the foreman said and then handed the verdict forms to the bailiff who in turn handed them to the judge.

Judge Black looked at the first verdict form and then the second and nodded. He then read the verdict forms aloud. "We the jury, duly impaneled and sworn in the above entitled cause as to plaintiffs' claim for relief do find for... defendant." Those in the court room let out a collective "Ooh!" Turning to the second verdict form, he read, "We, the jury, duly impaneled and sworn in the above entitled cause as to defendant's counterclaim do find for... plaintiffs." Not much reaction.

"Was and are these your verdicts, Mr. Foreman?"

"They are, Your Honor."

"So say all you ladies and gentlemen of the jury?"

"We do," they all responded.

"We have a motion to make outside the ears of the jury," RD announced.

"Ladies and gentlemen," said Judge Black, "we have a matter to take up outside your presence. We thank you for your valuable service. You can wait in the hall or leave if you wish. You can say as much or as little as you want to the attorneys or nothing at all. Should they or anyone criticize you for your verdicts, please report it to me. You're now excused with the thanks of the court."

As the jurors filed out, they all made eye contact with Jamie. RD made a motion for a directed verdict notwithstanding the juries' verdict in favor of Jamie. Larry made the same motion with respect to the defendant's counterclaim. Both motions were denied on the grounds that the jury had spoken and there was sufficient evidence, if believed, to support the verdicts.

This was not the place to celebrate but the defense team, having been joined by Bodean and Verna exchanged handshakes, hugs and whispers of congratulations. "I knew it," they said and to Jamie, "You deserved to win, and we've been praying for you."

RD came over to the defense table and shook everyone's hand, including Jamie's. The weasel did not join in the congratulatory ceremony but instead went to where the Stillwells were standing and commiserated with them in somber resignation over what they must have considered the *incredulous* verdict.

The jurors were all waiting in the corridor when the defense team left the courtroom. They greeted Jamie with handshakes and smiles. They said they had reached a verdict on the plaintiffs' claim on the very first vote but had trouble reaching a decision with respect to defendant's counterclaim because of the way the instructions were worded.

When RD exited the courtroom, he shook hands with and thanked the jurors. None of the others from the plaintiffs' table or side of the courtroom did. Judge Black came out into the hall after shedding his robe and visiting briefly with everyone before riding off into the sunset. His part in the ordeal had been fulfilled.

• • •

When they returned to Larry and Gordie's office, they found that the conference room had been decorated with crepe paper and had the trappings of a New Year's party. A large cake with "Congratulations Jamie" was in the middle of the table along with several bottles of bubbly in ice buckets and a large punch bowl. There were two trays of cold cuts and assorted cheeses, diced fruit, and breads and crackers of all sizes, shapes, and kinds.

The defense team was greeted by relatives, friends and well-wishers. Jennie, Max and Collette were the first to greet the victorious defendant. Next were Jamie's mom and dad, Forrest and Bessie. With the clan hanging, hugging and holding, the others had to fight just to touch him. Many of Jamie's church families were there, along with the pastor, Rev. Joseph Langley, and even Eric Sweeney, the newspaper editor.

The law offices were filled beyond capacity. "I just hope the fire department doesn't take a head count," Bodean was heard to say.

Larry whispered to Verna, "Thank you for planning this magnificent celebration, but didn't you take a calculated risk? How did you know Jamie was going to prevail?"

"I just did!" With her hands pressed together in prayerful pose and while looking heavenward said, "Didn't we?"

In the next day's edition of the newspaper was a front-page article with a headline that read, *Verdict Favors Cooper!* Although the defense didn't notice a reporter present, all twenty of the cookie points Gordie made in his final argument, together with the sad-faced cookies were printed in graphic form. The paper quoted Gordie extensively, including where the cookie trail led. The editorial with the caption *The Cream Always Rises to the Top* was the only one the Coopers would clip out and save.

Just as Judge Cole Black rode off into the sunset, so did the civil trial phase of the ordeal.

JUSTICE DENIED — CARROLL MULTZ

CHAPTER 25
MY FAIR LADY

Christmas 1972 was a special one in the Cooper household. The Chamber gala Christmas celebration was held in the banquet room of the Broken-Bow Hotel, an old but elegant hotel in Steamboat. It was at this event that the outgoing president would turn the presidential reins over to president-elect Jamie Cooper.

For a Christmas present, Larry's wife, Bonnie, had given Jennie what Bonnie, for lack of a better description, called a French, sea-blue satin party dress, which the Whittaker's had brought back from their Paris trip. Bonnie had obtained Jennie's size before leaving for Paris hoping to find just such a dress. With Jennie in it, Bonnie thought it was even more stunning. So did everyone else.

Jennie had just turned thirty-four in September, but she had the looks and shape of a twenty-four-year-old. She had penetrating blue eyes about the color of the dress. She had a peach complexion and facial features of a China doll. Her hair was a natural golden blond reflecting the Nordic side of the family. White perfect teeth were always on display even during these difficult times. Shoulders straight, she still graced the streets of Steamboat and made heads turn in the grocery stores.

Jennie, much to her embarrassment, was described by her parents as a perfect child and they were not just speaking about the outside, but the inside as well. An accomplished pianist, she had taken classical piano lessons since she was five years of age.

She was an honor student in high school as well as college. She had spent a semester abroad when she was a junior in college and loved to travel. She spoke French and Spanish fluently and a little German. She had been a cheerleader and captain of her squad both her senior year in high school as well as college. She also ran track in both high school and college.

• • •

Jennie and Jamie had been in love for as long as they could remember. Described as the perfect couple, they treated each other with the utmost respect and love that each needed and deserved. They were very family-oriented, and their adult lives were centered around Max and Collette. All four grandparents were very much a part of their lives as well. Jamie's parents had been almost as much a part of her life as her biological parents, them having known her for as long as she had known Jamie. Forrest and Bessie loved Jennie as much as she loved them.

Things had been difficult since Jamie had been arrested. Jennie had been shunned by many she thought were her friends but not, as it turned out, by what Jamie called her real friends. She had resigned from several boards and organizations because she felt ostracized by some and barely tolerated by others. She still was active in her Bible study group and church activities and she believed she couldn't have made it without their love, prayers, support and understanding. She and Jamie also had started having financial problems because he had been the sole provider. Both sets of parents had been helping and Jamie was receiving some income by working at the Cooper Ranch.

The spinoff of the ordeal was also having a deleterious effect on Max and Collette. Although they were not whiners, when Collette was overheard crying on occasion, that hurt worse than anything. Max and Collette were treated by some of their classmates and a few teachers as if they had leprosy, the way Max had described it. Max was able to express his feelings and emotions. Collette, on the other hand, was keeping it for the most part inside and refused to talk about it.

Collette became so withdrawn that it was

not long before she was under the care of a child psychologist. She was diagnosed as agoraphobic (fear of being in public places), anhedonic (unable to express pleasure), and psychotic (losing contact with reality). No one in the family, except Collette, would know how cruel her classmates had been.

The verdict in favor of Jamie in the civil jury trial had eased the situation somewhat, but with the shadow of the criminal jury trial looming over them, it was obvious that both children were still experiencing anxiety and depression.

Whether the district attorney would dismiss the criminal case was something they could only pray for. With Chief Hammerville, the driving force in his personal quest for revenge, the DA, they speculated, might be more determined than ever to obtain a conviction. So far, the prosecution was not bending. For now, the Coopers must try to live their lives as if the ordeal was nothing more than just a bad dream.

・・・

It was the day of the Chamber Christmas party and it had been snowing since early morning. Jamie showered in the guest room and put on the starched white shirt Jennie had laid out for him and the dark suit she had earlier pressed. While he was getting ready, Jennie was fitting herself into her new party dress in the master bedroom. Jamie finished dressing first and was reading the previous day's edition of the newspaper when, what he described as an angelic vision, appeared in the room. Jennie indeed looked like an angel in her sea-blue satin dress, with her blond hair in a tight bun exposing the full lines of her fine face, a gold necklace and earrings to match, and blue Cinderella high heels. *What a vision to behold, and she's mine*, Jamie thought.

"Am I dreaming, or did I die and go to heaven? Did God send you to meet me? You look absolutely stunning!" Jamie exclaimed.

"You look pretty handsome yourself. I'm going to hang onto you, so the young ones don't get their hands on you." Jennie smiled broadly as the two slid into each other's arms, holding each other so tight that neither could breathe.

"I love you," Jennie said softly.

"I love you, too," Jamie replied. Neither wanted to let go.

. . .

When they walked into the banquet hall everything seemed to stop. Even the orchestra quit playing for that brief moment. It wasn't just Cinderella shoes that walked into the banquet hall, it was Cinderella herself! Every eye was also riveted on the handsome prince leading Cinderella into their midst.

"Don't leave after midnight, otherwise your carriage may turn into a pumpkin," Charlie Blankenship, the Chamber president, chided.

"And your horses into mice," an unidentified voice added.

After the rare prime rib and roasted chicken had been consumed, the pastries relished and the dishes cleared, Charlie called the annual meeting to order. It was brief and the slate of officers was unanimously approved for the coming year. Charlie presented Jamie with the gavel and Jamie in turn presented Charlie with a plaque acknowledging Charlie's valuable service to the Chamber as outgoing president. As his first order of business, Jamie declared the meeting adjourned. "Let the dancing begin," he proclaimed.

As was the custom, the newly elected president and the first lady were to dance a few bars and then be joined by the other members and their spouses. Tonight, was different. Those who were watching became mesmerized by the magic of this Steamboat Camelot. The music ran out before the men could ask their partners to dance. The name of the song: *The Impossible Dream.*

Jennie was the belle of the ball. The Chamber

group was as cordial and caring as their church group. It was as if a moratorium had been declared and if anyone had the power to declare so, tonight it would be for the Steamboat Springs Chamber of Commerce Christmas party. The armistice was a welcome respite, especially during the blessed Christmas season and in the wake of the absolution brought about by the verdict in the civil case.

Jamie and Jennie danced well into the night. Caught up in the fairy tale themselves, the ordeal lost its stranglehold, at least for those few precious hours. Max and Collette stayed at the Whittakers' until the next day. Jamie and Jennie could continue to be lost in the deep throes of love and ecstasy until the star-filled sky was interrupted by the day's dawn and before long, the noonday's sun.

CHAPTER 26
THE PASSING OF
THE SEASONS

Seasons come and go as do good times and bad. The ordeal had been like a tennis match. First in one court and then in another. It was match point and Jamie was not serving.

Corbett, no doubt because of Hammerville's influence and pressure, refused to dismiss the criminal case. Both Larry and Gordie had tried to persuade Corbett to take another look at the case and if Corbett wanted Jamie to take another polygraph, he would do so. Corbett didn't believe in polygraphs. If Jamie prevailed in a case where the burden of proof was less than in the criminal case, how did Corbett expect to obtain a conviction? "Different jury—different issues," said Corbett.

On January 12, 1973, Corbett deposited an additional page of discovery into Whittaker & Brownell's drop box at the courthouse. It was a follow-up report of Officer Clinton Coleman dated January 10, 1973, and a bombshell. The report read:

> *This reporting officer received a telephone call from Alden Stillwell, first vice-president of SB&T Co., regarding the James Cooper*

theft case. On January 10, 1973, at ten hundred hours. Stillwell reported that while sorting through some of Cooper's personal effects that had been boxed up and stored in Cooper's old office since Cooper's arrest, he found a vault combination slip in his father's handwriting that did not match the current combination to the main vault. When he checked with his father, his father confirmed that the numbers and letters were in his handwriting.

Stillwell reported that his father then went on to relate that approximately twelve years ago, about the time Cooper first came to work at the bank, the bank had trouble with its time lock and had to call the manufacturer to get the bypass combination. The combination on the slip was tested by Stillwell and his father after the time lock had been set and it was found to be the bypass combination. That meant that Cooper must have returned to the bank at some time between nineteen hundred hours on June 10 and seven hundred hours on June 11, 1972, when no one was there, and using the bypass combination, overrode the bank vault time lock and stole the $30,000.

For obvious reasons the bank refused to release the combination. However, this reporting officer did confirm with Brandon Stillwell that everything his son had reported was accurate.

When Verna brought the additional discovery into Larry's office, along with other court documents, Larry read in utter disbelief. "I wondered when the other shoe was going to drop," he said dejectedly.

The usual imperturbable Gordie was flabbergasted when he read Coleman's report. Shaking his head, he uttered, "This could be the smoking gun the prosecution has been looking for."

They both wondered if the Cooper curse was indeed more than just a fable.

Larry asked Verna to call and set up an appointment with Jamie and Bodean. They were scheduled for 1:30 that afternoon.

When they assembled in the conference room, each was reminded of the victory celebration that took place there following the verdict in the civil case back in October. That was now becoming a faded memory in light of the so-called newly discovered evidence. Although they had taken one giant step forward it now appeared, they had taken two giant steps backward.

For the most part, the defense team had prepared for the criminal trial when they prepared for the civil trial. Now a whole new challenge faced them. How could they contend with this new devastating twist and were there other dragons out there that would be rearing their ugly heads?

It was decided they couldn't take Alden's word for it. They had to confirm that the so-called override combo was legitimate. Did it indeed override the bank vault time lock? When was the override combo written? Was it of recent vintage and thus contrived? Or was it written as suggested twelve or thirteen years ago? Was it found in Jamie's personal belongings as claimed or was it planted there by Alden? Was that how Alden accessed the vault? Had he found it in his father's desk when he was looking for something else? Or was it father-son collusion and contrived?

The defense team knew the answers to these questions were key to Jamie's defense. But who would be allowed to inspect the override combo and try it? The entrustment of the override combo just to anyone would be a breach of bank security and an invitation for the unsavory.

It was decided that Larry or Gordie would immediately contact Corbett and arrange for an independent determination. They knew that the bank wouldn't allow Bodean or anyone of the defense's choosing to perform the task. It was Larry, the one closest to the conference room telephone, who called Corbett. Corbett was sympathetic to Larry's concern and after some discussion, it was decided that a local locksmith and antique dealer by the name of Kaiser Elliott, who was bonded and a third-generation Steamboat resident, would be a likely candidate. Plus, he was a member of the sheriff's posse and would be trusted by law enforcement. Corbett agreed to contact Brandon Stillwell and get the green light. He would call right back, one way or the other.

Within minutes, Corbett was on the phone saying Brandon wanted to check with the insurance company first, and if they were in agreement, the bank would be also. Corbett agreed to call Larry as soon as he heard back from Brandon. In less than half an hour the defense's request was granted. Corbett would contact Kaiser Elliott and the two would meet with either Brandon or Alden and detail the assignment.

At 3:30 p.m. Larry, Gordie and Bodean met at Corbett's office, joined shortly thereafter by Kaiser Elliott. Kaiser would arrange that day, if possible, to inspect the paper on which the override combo was written to determine its antiquity and test the combo to see if the bank vault time lock could be bypassed. Kaiser would then contact both Corbett and either Larry or Gordie and report his findings. Kaiser also agreed to record his findings and provide Corbett and Larry or Gordie with signed copies of his report. Even though Kaiser wasn't an expert, the defense had faith in him.

• • •

The next day Gordie called Jamie and then Bodean with the bad news. He had Kaiser's report sitting on his desk. Kaiser had met Brandon and Alden at the bank at approximately 7:30 the previous evening. In his presence while confirming the numbers, turns and directions on the dial with those on Brandon's slip of paper, the bank vault time lock was overridden. His report indicated the timer was activated at the time. In his opinion, because of the condition of the paper and faded ink, it was at least a dozen years old. Kaiser, however, had made it clear when he spoke with Gordie that he was not an expert in document dating.

• • •

Dennis Harlow, Corbett's longtime investigator and sounding board, had sat in on the civil trial and had recorded much of the testimony and final arguments. He was known as a thorough note taker. When asked for his recommendation, he advised

Corbett that the prosecution would be ill-advised to pursue the Las Vegas connection in the criminal case. As a result, Corbett decided not to pursue the Las Vegas connection.

He told Larry that he had made the decision based on his concern that because of the bogus nature of the so-called gambling motive, which the defense would negate, the jury would end up throwing the good evidence out with the bad, much like what he surmised happened in the civil case. He said he didn't want the jury in the criminal case "to throw the baby out with the bathwater."

He also noted that he had won many a trial where the defense shot-gunned the jury, throwing everything in their arsenal at them with the result that the valid defenses got lost with the bogus. Corbett believed there was also the ethical or moral issue. The district attorney's office had conducted a thorough investigation and found absolutely no evidence of gambling on Jamie's part. Also, his office was convinced that Forrest Cooper was telling the truth when he testified the cash used in Las Vegas came from him.

Corbett was asked to and did provide Larry with a letter to that effect. The defense was now free of the worry over the Las Vegas connection. Larry and Gordie felt that was a wise strategy decision on Corbett's part. And they also respected him for his ethics. Besides, with the so-called newly discovered evidence Corbett didn't need to take any cheap shots.

• • •

It was a sunny Monday, February fifth, a good day to test the slopes. There was a foot of fresh powder on the top of the hill and the Ski Steamboat Corporation's reduced Monday fare was beckoning them. It was not to be, at least not this day. The defense team was snuggled in for their long winter trial prep. With the Las Vegas connection no longer a part of the equation, it would be a shootout at the O.K. Corral between Alden and Jamie. It would boil down to whom the jury would believe—Alden or Jamie. Alden was the prosecution's lynchpin.

All agreed it would be a simple, straightforward trial. The prosecution would call Brandon Stillwell, Alden Stillwell, Rita Baker, Kaiser Elliott and Officer Clinton Coleman. The only exhibits they would introduce would be the bill strap with the Federal Reserve stamp and the twenty fifty-dollar bills. They couldn't introduce the slip of paper with the override combo because of the security risk. However, they could still refer to it in their case-in-chief.

The defense would call the same witnesses as

in the civil trial. Their only possible exhibit would be the receipt from the Tomahawk Café on July 10.

Larry summarized the evidence of the prosecution; Gordie summarized the evidence of the defense.

Jamie seemed to be holding up pretty well in light of the latest setback. He said that the outcome of the civil case had accomplished a number of things. Other than the obvious, it had let the air out of the Stillwell balloon, had changed the public mood somewhat and had resulted in elimination of the Las Vegas connection. The drawback, he speculated, was that since the plaintiffs' feathers had been ruffled by the adverse verdict, the Stillwells had to come up with some way to stack the deck. The resurrection of the override combo was their answer.

Bodean surmised that Alden accidentally found the override combo in his father's desk drawer while his father was away. Curious, he tried it after hours and found it worked. On the night of July 10, he removed the $30,000, and as an afterthought, decided to plant part of it in Jamie's office so as to divert attention away from him. The rest he took home and squirreled away.

Larry suggested Alden might have had a dual reason for taking the money. The first was to enrich himself knowing the loss would be covered by insurance. The second was to frame Jamie to even the score for all those years Jamie had cheated him out of his perceived just desserts.

Gordie speculated that Alden, having stumbled on the override combination and finding it worked, impulsively removed the $30,000 and stuck it in his desk. Afraid he might be implicated and not wanting to part with all the money, conceived of the ruse to plant $1,000 in Jamie's office but ran out of time. Making it appear that he had confiscated the $1,000 from Jamie's office, he dramatically scattered the currency on Jamie's desk when the authorities arrived. The remaining $29,000, in all probability, remained hidden in Alden's office until he could safely remove it. Regardless, he was $29,000 richer but couldn't spend it without arousing suspicion. He was in one heck of a predicament.

The jury list they surmised wouldn't be provided by the court clerk until Thursday or Friday. The profile of the ideal juror had to be along the same lines as the jurors in the civil trial, Gordie proffered. Young and preferably women. No schoolteachers—they were too technical and strict. No senior citizens—they were too judgmental and inflexible. No middle aged or older men because they were unsympathetic. No businessmen who had been victims of embezzlement or theft. No bankers or ex-bankers.

"That doesn't leave very many from which to choose, does it?" Larry said more as a statement than a question.

All agreed it was just the luck of the draw in the civil case. Even the rejected jurors were not bad and would probably have come up with the same results. Leaving Jamie's fate in the hands of chance didn't seem to be the proper way of dispensing justice. Jury selection was like a lottery; one never knew whose number might come up or whose name might be drawn. In the civil case, Jamie had been accused of gambling and in the criminal case, he would be risking his future on the gaming tables of the judicial system.

CHAPTER 27
THE CRIMINAL TRIAL

The day that was the center of Jamie's nightmares since his July arrest and a day that he had dreaded was now at hand. The drab gloomy day of reckoning, Monday, February 12, 1973, would wait no more.

Jamie was again seated in the courtroom whose every inch had been scoured and indelibly etched in his memory. He was seated between his guardian angels, Larry on his left and Gordie on his right. Bodean, who was designated as defendant's advisory witness, was seated to Gordie's right. That meant that even though the advisory witness rule was in effect, Bodean could still testify, even if he sat through the whole trial. The same thing would be true of the prosecution's advisory witness.

Across from Larry was the prosecution's table, formerly occupied by the plaintiff's team, RD, Brandon and the weasel. Only this time, Corbett sat in the chair to the right and his investigator, Dennis Harlow, sat in the chair to the left. The chair formerly occupied by Brandon had been removed. Dennis was designated as the prosecution's advisory witness.

"What a difference a season makes!" Jamie

commented to his guardian angels. During the civil trial, there were warm autumn days, windows open and the rustling of the crisp leaves vibrating in the breeze. Today, the windows were tightly closed against their frames, frost covering the outsides and some even on the insides. The riveting action of the old-fashioned hot water radiators announcing their functioning held the attention of several of the prospective jurors. They were trying to warm their frozen hands but were careful not to touch the piping-hot, silver-colored radiators. Some of the prospective jurors were still wearing their heavy winter coats and scarves, others were shedding their snow boots and shaking off the snow from their mittens and still others were just sitting there with red noses and faces—all obviously in nervous anticipation.

"Didn't the county pay the heat bill?" Bodean asked Gordie.

"Don't know, but they must have turned the heat on just before we arrived," Gordie complained.

"Things will heat up soon enough," Jamie muttered.

Conspicuous from their absence in the courtroom were the Stillwells. Corbett must have warned them to stay away, at least during *voir dire*. No cajoling and insincere handshakes here.

No ingratiating smiles or winks of endearment or platitudes. Why risk a mistrial or reversal in event of a conviction?

Ron Scott, the bailiff, banged the gavel commanding all to stand, as Judge Tibbits entered.

Plopping down in his swivel chair, the judge said, "Call the case of *People of the State of Colorado, versus James Curtis Cooper also known as Jamie Cooper, Defendant.*"

Apparently ascertaining that everyone was ready and greeting the prospective jurors, Judge Tibbits had them stand, raise their right hands, and take the oath to truthfully answer all questions proposed by the court or counsel.

Twelve prospective jurors were called to the box. The judge asked the same general questions of the panel as a whole.

When asked if they had read, seen, or heard anything through the print or electronic media regarding the case, all raised their hands. Without telling what they read, saw, or heard, had they made up their minds as to the innocence or guilt of the accused? If they said yes, they promised they would set aside their preconceived notions and judge the case solely on the evidence presented. Their answers were postured in such a way that there could be no challenge for cause. However, the defense team noted who said yes as well as who admitted to knowing various prosecution witnesses. It was difficult to determine which way the prospective jurors were leaning. They masked their biases, if any they had, remarkably well.

When it was time for the attorneys to *voir dire*, Corbett went first. That was because the prosecution had the burden of proof. Corbett was most ingratiating. He said he just wanted to make sure the laws of the state of Colorado were being enforced. He acknowledged that the prosecution had the burden of proving Jamie guilty beyond a reasonable doubt but pointed out that did not mean proof beyond *all* doubt as that would be an impossible burden.

Corbett made sure that they understood that if the prosecution met its burden and proved Jamie's guilt beyond a reasonable doubt, they were bound by law to return a guilty verdict. And if the prosecution was to prove each and every one of the elements of the crime charged, could they find Jamie guilty?

He also asked if any of the jurors banked at SB&T Co. All raised their hands. Since the bank was the named victim in the case, he asked whether that would in any way affect their verdict. All said no. This was the same question Corbett was to ask all replacement jurors.

Gordie turned to Bodean and remarked, "Corbett's pretty foxy. Knowing we would be asking the question, he beat us to the punch."

"Just taking the wind out of our sails," Bodean replied. "Besides, he wants the jury to marvel at his fairness."

Overhearing their conversation, Larry whispered, "I call it gilding the lily!"

Corbett concluded by asking them whether there was anything that he should have asked and didn't that might indicate bias or prejudice on their part one way or the other. All shook their heads and answered no. Corbett then passed the jurors for cause, which meant he had no legal basis for disqualification.

It was Larry's turn to *voir dire*. He walked to the podium without a list of the jurors' names and no notes of any kind. He had memorized their names—all twelve—during Corbett's *voir dire*.

Larry told the jurors that this was the opportunity for the attorneys to ask questions in an effort to ascertain whether they could be fair, not just to one side or the other, but to both sides. He remembered the jurors who had raised their hands, acknowledging prior jury service, knowing a witness, or being exposed to pretrial publicity, and asked each by name the follow-up questions. Do you realize there are two sides to every story? That you haven't heard Jamie's side yet? Would you keep an open mind and not judge the case until you've heard all the evidence?

Corbett had postured the questions concerning presumption of innocence, burden of proof and reasonable doubt to suit the prosecution. Now it was Larry's turn to posture but in a vein favorable to the defense. Since these concepts were the essence of a criminal prosecution, and the attorneys could only ask questions and not make statements, Larry was cautious and deliberate.

Do you realize that every person charged with a crime is presumed to be innocent? Do you realize that the presumption of innocence remains with the defendant in an American court throughout the whole trial and should be given effect by you unless and until, after considering all of the evidence, you are then convinced that the defendant is guilty beyond a reasonable doubt?

Do you realize that the burden of proof is upon the prosecution to prove to your satisfaction beyond a reasonable doubt the existence of all of the elements necessary to constitute the crime charged? Do you realize that Jamie doesn't have to prove anything, that's the prosecution's job? Do you realize that Jamie doesn't have to testify and that if he doesn't it can't be held against him?

Do you realize that the gauge in this case is not whether Jamie is guilty or innocent but whether he is guilty or not guilty? In other words, whether Jamie is innocent is irrelevant in the eyes of the law and if the prosecution fails to prove any one or more of the elements of the crime charged, then you are bound by law to return a not guilty verdict. Do you understand that?

Do you realize that the proof in a criminal case differs from the proof in a civil case? In a civil case, it's just the greater weight of the evidence, which means that the side to which the scale of justice tips, even slightly, wins. In a criminal case, on the other hand, the burden of proof imposed on the prosecution is greater. The burden of proof is proof beyond a reasonable doubt. Do you understand that? If the prosecution fails to meet its burden of proof, what would your verdict be?

Larry concluded, "Mr. Corbett has attempted to give you his definition of reasonable doubt. Do you realize that the court will instruct you that reasonable doubt means a doubt based on reason and common sense that arises from a fair and rational consideration of all of the evidence, or the lack of evidence in the case? It is a doubt that is not a vague, speculative, or imaginary doubt, but such a doubt as would cause reasonable people to hesitate to act in matters of importance to themselves. If you were given such an instruction, would you follow it?"

No challenges were exercised by either side for cause. Corbett exercised all of his peremptory challenges; Larry exercised all but one of his. Both ultimately said they accepted the panel as presently impaneled and constituted. With that, the jury that would decide Jamie's fate had been selected.

They had taken the usual midmorning recess in between selection of jurors and now it was noon. The jurors who had not been called to the box were excused. Those who were selected were released with instructions to return again at 2:00 p.m. Upon discharge they were given the same admonitions that Judge Black had given the jurors in the civil case.

The defense was not happy with the jury that was selected. It seemed as though the replacement jurors were less desirable than the ones who had been challenged and excused. Larry and Gordie held back the last peremptory challenge just in case they needed it. They were skeptical of Casey Rawles, but were afraid if they used their last challenge on him they might end up with someone far worse. It was not the perfect jury they had hoped for and certainly not like the one they had in the civil case. Worry spread as Gordie said he observed one juror Irene Stapleton, nod and smile at Corbett as the jurors filed out of the courtroom.

· · ·

After lunch and back in the courtroom with familiar faces in the gallery, Judge Tibbits instructed Corbett to give his opening statement.

Corbett strutted to the podium and began by recounting the facts leading to Jamie's arrest. He then stated:

"Defendant, of course, was discharged from the bank and his personal effects were boxed and stored. In preparation for this trial, Alden Stillwell went through the defendant's personal belongings and found a suspicious-looking paper with Alden's father's handwriting that appeared to have a vault combination number written on it. After the discovery and closing that night and after the bank vault timer was set, Alden tried it. Bingo! The vault door opened. It was the combination bypass that could override the time lock. No one knew or at least remembered that anyone at the bank had the override combo. Come to find out, it was in defendant's possession the whole time!

"Brandon Stillwell will testify that he vaguely

remembered a problem with the time lock some years back when defendant had first come to work at the bank and that the manufacturer had provided some type of bypass combination which allowed access to rectify the problem. He recognized his handwriting on the slip of paper his son found in defendant's belongings but will testify that he doesn't know where it has been all these years.

"When the evidence is all in, we trust you will be convinced beyond a reasonable doubt that defendant is guilty of the theft with which he has been charged. We will, therefore, be asking you to return a guilty verdict. Thank you."

The defense attorneys in a criminal case have three options with respect to opening statements. They can either give their opening statement now, wait until the prosecution has completed its case-in-chief, or they can waive it altogether. The timing depends on a number of factors. There was some school of thought that if you give it now, you alerted the prosecution of your theory and allowed them to counter it in their case-in-chief, thus nullifying the sting. Another theory was to let the jury know there was another side to the story as early as possible so that they don't make up their minds until after they have heard all the evidence. Jamie's defense attorneys opted to give their opening statement now. It was delivered by Larry.

After advising the jury that even though the defense was not required to present evidence and the defendant was not required to testify, Larry stated that the defense would nonetheless be presenting evidence to refute the charge and that Jamie would in fact be testifying in his own behalf.

Larry thereupon gave an opening statement similar to the one he gave in the civil case. Concentrating on the so-called newly discovered evidence, he stated:

"Jamie will testify that the first he had heard of the override combo was when, months after his arrest, Alden Stillwell claimed he found it in Jamie's belongings left at the bank. Jamie will testify he never had it in his possession or ever saw the slip of paper on which the override combo was written. He will state that even as of yet, he has not seen or had in his possession the override combo."

Larry then concluded by saying, "If the evidence presented in this case is as the defense anticipates, we'll have no hesitancy whatsoever at the close of all the evidence in asking you to return a *not guilty* verdict."

• • •

The first witness called by the prosecution was Brandon Stillwell. His testimony was similar to that in the civil trial. The only difference was with respect to the slip of paper on which was written the override combo. He identified his handwriting. He vaguely remembered the incident involving the vault malfunction that occurred about the time Jamie had first been hired.

On cross-examination, Gordie established that Brandon didn't know where the override combo slip was found, other than what Alden had told him. He said he didn't know where it had been stored all these years and had no knowledge that it had ever been in Jamie's possession. He admitted that Alden could have made up the story about where he found the override combo but didn't think Alden would do such a thing. When asked who had replaced Jamie as first vice-president of SB&T Co., he responded that his son, Alden, had taken over.

It was time for the midafternoon break. After the break, Alden Stillwell was the prosecution's second witness. He testified in the manner and fashion as in the civil trial but was more prepared. With regard to the slip of paper containing the override combo in his father's handwriting, he testified that he stumbled on it totally by accident while preparing for trial and reexamining Jamie's personal belongings that had been stored in a box Rita had brought to his office after Jamie's arrest.

He knew it was the override combo because he tried it when the timer was on and it worked.

On cross-examination, Gordie realized that the dress rehearsal of the civil trial had been of benefit not only to the defense but the prosecution as well. Alden was now a formidable force to be reckoned with. Gordie followed almost identically his cross in the civil case. Regarding the override combo slip, Gordie concentrated on Alden's credibility and the unlikelihood that the slip was in Jamie's possession and more likely something Alden had planted in an effort to frame Jamie.

Rita Baker was sworn in and also testified as she had in the civil trial with the additional testimony regarding the override combo slip. She testified that she was there when the locksmith, Kaiser Elliott, performed the experiment. She said, even though she did not read the slip, she watched Kaiser gain access by the use of the slip Alden provided.

Cross-examination mirrored the cross-examination in the civil trial with the exception of the adjustment now required by the override combo testimony. Rita admitted she had never seen or heard about the existence of the override combo slip until Alden produced it. She had never seen it in Jamie's possession or ever heard him talk about it. She had not inspected Jamie's belongings at or during the time she boxed them up or at any time since. Certainly, it could have been placed there by someone other than Jamie and maybe even planted there by Alden but didn't think so.

Kaiser Elliott was sworn in and testified that he was a locksmith. He had done maintenance work on the mechanisms on the vault door including the timer for the bank on various occasions. He had tried the override combo when the timer was on and it worked.

On cross-examination by Gordie, he admitted he didn't know where Alden had obtained the override combo slip. It was always in Alden's hands. He never saw Jamie or anyone else with it.

It was time to break for the day. The jury was excused until 8:00 a.m. the following morning.

• • •

Promptly at 8:00 a.m. on February 13, the criminal case of *People v. Cooper* entered its second day. There were a few less spectators than the previous day. Corbett called Officer Clinton Coleman as his last witness.

Officer Coleman was unabashed in relating his police training, years with the Steamboat Police Department, his certifications and re-certifications. He testified as he had in the civil trial, with the exception of the evidence relative to the Las Vegas connection and the new evidence regarding Alden's discovery of the override combo. In fact, none of the witnesses made any reference to the Las Vegas connection.

Gordie on cross-examination followed his previous script with the exception of the modifications dictated by the direct examination. Coleman admitted that all he knew was what he had been told by Alden Stillwell. He neither saw the belongings from whence the override combo slip came nor was he present when it was discovered. Until Alden called him seven months after Jamie's arrest, he had no idea that such lock combination existed and to his knowledge neither did any of his fellow officers.

Corbett rested the prosecution's case-in-chief.

After the jury was excused to take up matters outside their presence, Larry made a motion for judgment of acquittal.

"If Your Honor please, the defendant moves the court for an order entering a judgment of acquittal of the offense charged on the grounds that the evidence is insufficient to sustain a conviction."

Corbett argued that the evidence was more than ample to allow the case to be submitted to the jury, and to grant such a motion would be to contravene the province of the jury and a complete nullification of the role of the jury in our whole justice system.

Judge Tibbits summarily denied the motion and removing his glasses, asked, "Do you intend to call witnesses, Mr. Whittaker?"

"We do, Your Honor."

"Very well. Be prepared to call your first witness after the break. The court is in recess for fifteen minutes."

After the break and after the court reconvened, Larry announced, "The defense calls the defendant Jamie Cooper to the stand."

Jamie couldn't have been more effective or impressive. He certainly came off as a man's man. There was quite a contrast between Jamie and his nemesis. Alden had never been competition and today was no different. In comparing the two it was obvious why Alden was no match. Unless one had blinders on it was easy to tell which one was telling the truth, and which one had an axe to grind.

Excluding the testimony regarding the Las Vegas connection, one couldn't tell the difference between Jamie's testimony in the civil trial and this trial. With regard to the override combo slip, Jamie testified he had never seen it; didn't know it even existed. As far as he knew, it wasn't included in the items taken from his office and was certainly not among the items that belonged to him. He testified that he had inherited certain files and folders from the retired loan officer who had occupied his office before him, and he never had occasion to sort through those files. The slip could very well have been in one of those files, but he said he doubted it. He never accessed the vault as Alden had suggested, never took the missing money or any part thereof, and never put the $1,000 in his desk drawer. The first time he saw the money was when Alden threw it on his desk.

When it was Corbett's turn to cross-examine, Corbett committed the unpardonable sin. He asked one or maybe two too many questions, "Do you know who placed the one thousand dollars in your desk drawer?"

"Yes."

"Who?"

"Alden Stillwell."

It was obvious that even Judge Tibbits had difficulty trying to keep from bursting into laughter. It was indeed hilarious. Corbett needed to go wash his mouth out with soap and water.

"With so much riding on the line and this being an election year, how could Corbett have been so stupid?" Gordie whispered to Larry as Corbett announced, "I have no further questions."

Jennie was sworn in as the second defense

witness. It indeed was Cinderella, but this was not make-believe; it was part of a drama that could change her life and the life of her family forever. Jennie was radiant despite the occasion. She was articulate and straightforward. When she answered she looked at the jurors, each and every one, in the eye. No deception here.

Jennie testified that Jamie had come home his usual time which was about 6:15 or 6:20 p.m. on Monday, July 10. Dinner was waiting and after dinner, while she washed the dishes, Jamie played with Max, Collette and Maya, their pet. They were playing catch with an old football of Jamie's and the kids were joined by two neighbor boys as well as one of Collette's girlfriends. When Jennie had finished the dishes, she joined in the fun. She remembered because Jamie was arrested the following day and that was the last time they had a day and night free of worry.

She testified they lived in the middle of town several blocks from SB&T Co. She was not a sound sleeper and hadn't been since Max and Collette had been born. If Jamie had arose in the middle of the night and left the house, she would have heard him. The cars were in the garage adjoining the house and if Jamie had used one of them, she again would have heard him. She related Jamie left home at approximately 6:25 the next morning to attend a Chamber meeting and from there to work.

She further testified that she saw no extra cash and that Jamie had not acted suspiciously. Jamie loved his job at SB&T Co. and would have done nothing to jeopardize it. He took pride in his position as first vice-president and was loyal to his boss, Brandon Stillwell. She believed there was no way Jamie could or would have taken even a dime from the bank.

Although Corbett was reeling from his previous cross-examination, he was still going to give it the law school try.

"Mrs. Cooper, you love your husband, don't you?"

"Yes."

"And would do anything to help him, wouldn't you?"

"If you're inferring that I would lie for him, the answer is no. I love him and respect the system too much to do that."

Corbett flinched and managed a barely audible, "No further questions."

This was probably an ideal place to break. Corbett was not about to object. He needed a hole to crawl into. The jury was excused with the usual admonitions. Court was adjourned until 8:00 the following morning, February fourteenth.

• • •

It was Valentine's Day. The timing was uncanny. Jamie said they would go out to dinner when he returned from court. The hiatus in the middle of trial was just what the doctor ordered. It would give them time to put everything on hold and just focus on each other. Jamie had smuggled in heart-shaped boxes of chocolates for Jennie, Max and Collette. It was now only a matter of days before the bad memories would fade away and the ordeal would be no more. At least, that's what they hoped and prayed.

• • •

After the trial resumed, Betty Skyler testified as to the events on the night of July 10. Same direct as in the civil trial. Cross-examination, however, was more accusatory and caustic. She was asked, "You don't know what defendant put in his pockets, do you?" and "You don't know what he might have put in his car before you arrived, do you?"

Ursula Russell testified as per the civil trial script. Same ineffective cross- examination.

Jackie Stiles and Charlie Blankenship confirmed Jamie's alibi. Cross-examination was crass. "You don't know what defendant did before the meeting or what he did afterwards, do you?"

Great try but totally ineffective! the defense team thought.

Larry announced that the defense rested. Corbett said the prosecution had no rebuttal witnesses. Larry said he had a motion to make outside the ears of the jury. The jury was excused and ordered to return at 1:45.

Outside the presence of the jury Larry renewed the defense's motion for judgment of acquittal. Without argument the judge denied it, stating there was sufficient evidence to go to the jury and any factual issues there be were for the jury's consideration, and not his.

The attorneys went back in chambers with Judge Tibbits and worked on the instructions. After a little wrangling, the instructions to be given to the jury were agreed upon.

• • •

After the court reconvened, and the jury had been brought in, Judge Tibbits instructed them as to the law that they were required to follow. The jury was also given a verdict form on which they were to check either not guilty or guilty and have it signed by the foreperson.

After the instructions were read, the attorneys were called upon to give their final arguments. Since the prosecution had the burden of proof,

Corbett would go first and last.

In his opening argument, Corbett compared what he said the prosecution would prove in their opening statement with what he alleged the prosecution ultimately proved. "The prosecution kept its word," Corbett argued. "Alden Stillwell while searching for a file found bank money in defendant's desk drawer. Alden Stillwell became suspicious and checked the cash drawer in the vault and found thirty thousand dollars missing. When Alden and Rita Baker had left the bank the night before, they counted the money and set the timer on the vault door so that it couldn't be opened until seven the following morning.

"If the money was in the vault when the timer was set and couldn't be accessed until the timer expired by the regular combination, then how did the thief gain access? I didn't hear any testimony that it had been blown open, did you? The only way that the thief could have had access was knowledge of the manufacture's override combo. The mystery was solved when Alden found the override combo in defendant's belongings he had left at the bank.

"It's clear that the road of guilt leads to the defendant. No matter how you slice it, it was defendant who took the money. The only one who had the ability to access the vault while the timer was running was defendant. Because the evidence and therefore the road of guilt leads to Jamie Cooper, we're asking you to return a verdict of guilty to the charge. Thank you."

Gordie was facing a daunting task. Corbett's argument had been persuasive. One plus one equals two. Corbett's cookie trail led to Jamie, at least by Corbett's assessment.

"Ladies and gentlemen of the jury," Gordie began. "Thank you for your unselfish service. Mr. Corbett has put everything in a nice neat little package and tied it with a bow and now wants you to buy it. If you follow his directions, you'll get lost. The road of guilt doesn't lead to Jamie. It leads to someone else. When Mr. Corbett says one thousand dollars of the missing funds was found in Jamie's desk drawer, he forgot to remind you that was what Alden claimed. If Jamie took the thirty thousand dollars, why would he put one thousand dollars in his desk drawer where it would likely be discovered? It just doesn't make sense! Conspicuous, is the absence once again of any corroborating testimony. When Mr. Corbett says the override combo was found in Jamie's belongings, he forgot again to remind you there was nothing to corroborate Alden's claim. He didn't mention in his final argument that the override combo was not in Jamie's handwriting but in Brandon Stillwell's handwriting. Nor did he mention that Jamie didn't have access to Brandon's office and desk, but that Brandon's son, Alden, who replaced Jamie in the number two position at the bank did. And didn't you find it odd that the override combo was not discovered by the investigating officers when they searched Jamie's office looking for the missing funds?"

After hesitating a few moments, Gordie continued. "The likelihood is greater that Brandon's handwritten slip came from Brandon's desk rather than Jamie's belongings that supposedly sat idle in Alden's office seven months before it was allegedly discovered by Alden. What are the odds that such a critical piece of evidence would magically appear at the eleventh hour? How fortunate for the prosecution! By Mr. Corbett's calculations, one and one doesn't equal two. They equal four or maybe six or eight by his assessment. What kind of fuzzy math is that?"

Gordie then asked the twenty rhetorical questions he had asked the jury in the civil case, plus one more: "Who claims they found the override combo in Jamie's belongings some seven months after Jamie's arrest?"

Gordie then pointing at the easel, pressed: "If you

answered Alden Stillwell to all twenty-one of these questions, then the road of guilt leads to someone other than Jamie. Not only has the prosecution failed to prove Jamie's guilt beyond a reasonable doubt, but the defense has done something we're not required to do and that is to prove that Jamie is not the one who committed the theft in this case. In fact, the evidence points the finger of guilt at the most likely suspect, the one who stood to gain the most from Jamie's prosecution—Alden Stillwell, Jamie's accuser.

"After three days of trial, everything boils down as to who to believe: Jamie or Alden Stillwell. It also boils down to motive. Who had the most to gain by eliminating Jamie? It would have been suicide for Jamie to have done it. Jamie's becoming a bank officer was the realization of a dream that started when he first worked for SB&T Co. while still in high school. Alden Stillwell, on the other hand, couldn't stand to be in third place behind a non-Stillwell. With Jamie out of the picture guess who became the bank's first vice-president? The man who staged the theft and framed Jamie—Alden Stillwell!

"During defense's opening statement we promised that if the evidence produced at trial was as we anticipated, we would have no hesitancy at the end of the trial in asking you to return a *not guilty* verdict. We're keeping *our* promise. We're not asking you to find Jamie *innocent* even though he is; we're just asking you to find him *not guilty* because the prosecution has wholly failed to meet its burden of proving Jamie's guilt beyond a reasonable doubt.

"It's not easy for an attorney to represent someone where you have to prove a negative—where you have to prove your client didn't do it. Keep in mind a defendant never has to prove anything. However, Mr. Whittaker's job and mine in seeing that justice is rendered is complete at this stage. And now, ladies and gentlemen of the jury, we're placing Jamie's fate in your hands to ensure that justice is properly administered. And in doing so, we request that you follow the trail the evidence leads and return a verdict of *not guilty*. Thank you."

Corbett now had the last opportunity to sway the jurors. Theoretically, he could only respond to the defendant's final argument.

Corbett began, "I'll be brief. The defense had the opportunity to attempt to refute my opening argument. Now I have the opportunity to return the favor.

"To attempt to imply that Alden Stilwell stole the thirty thousand dollars, and not Jamie, defies all logic. To deflect guilt away from his own client is one thing, but for Mr. Brownell to suggest that Alden would in essence steal from himself is to insult the intelligence of all you good ladies and gentlemen. I've heard the saying that a sucker is born every minute, but I have greater faith that you will not fall for the defense's sleight of hand trick. He who commits theft, or any crime, must be prepared to pay the price. Don't let defendant off because Mr. Brownell says you should. Return a guilty verdict because defendant *is* guilty. Thank you."

Judge Tibbits, turning to the jury, said, "Ladies and gentlemen, the bailiff will now escort you to the jury room for your deliberation. Let the bailiff, who will be positioned outside the jury room, know when you reach a verdict."

After the jury departed, the attorneys were instructed to leave their telephone numbers with Judge Tibbits' clerk so that they could be reached if and when a verdict was rendered, or they were otherwise needed.

• • •

The defense team went their separate ways. Larry and Gordie said they thought it would be a long night. Little did they know that a verdict would not be rendered until late Friday.

On that Thursday afternoon at five thirty when

the jury still had not been able to reach a decision, Judge Tibbits gave them a modified version of what trial attorneys refer to as the Allen Charge. Simply, it instructs the jury to go back and try and try again to reach a decision. The instruction Judge Tibbits gave the jury read in part, "It is your duty as jurors to consult with one another and to deliberate with a view of reaching a verdict, if you can do so without violence to individual judgment. Each of you must judge the case for yourself but do so only after impartial consideration of the evidence with your fellow jurors."

The jurors were not locked up for the night or kept together. Each was allowed to go home and return the next day. Judge Tibbits told the attorneys that if the jury had not reached a verdict by 5:00 p.m. Friday, he would be declaring a mistrial and there would be a retrial with a different jury.

Larry had advised Jamie that, if Jamie was convicted, his father would be required to agree to continue the bond or Jamie would be incarcerated. So, Forrest and Bessie stayed in town Thursday night with Jamie and Jennie and were prepared to do so again on Friday if necessary. In the event of a conviction Jamie would be sentenced at a later date. They would be asking for a bond pending an appeal because certainly they would appeal any conviction.

Jamie said to Larry, "Things don't seem to be too promising, do they?"

"I can't read this jury," Larry responded, "but we need to prepare for the worst— just in case!"

• • •

It was colder than usual on that February Friday, and at 4:00 p.m., the cloak of darkness was beginning to assert itself. Everyone would rather be home with family in front of a warm crackling fire, snuggled in their favorite comforter. But that was not meant to be for those cast in various roles in the Cooper criminal jury trial.

The Stillwells were in their usual place on the prosecution side behind the railing that separated the participants from the spectators awaiting the much-anticipated verdict. So were the usual dedicated group of curious.

For the first time, seated in the front row on the defense side, were Jennie, Forrest and Bessie. They were hoping for a favorable verdict but were prepared in case the verdict was unfavorable. Max and Collette stayed behind with Larry's wife, Bonnie.

It was fingernail-biting time and although the jury had been brought in, Judge Tibbits had not yet made his appearance. Gordie asked Larry if he noticed who had the verdict form in hand. Larry nodded. Casey Rawles, the juror they worried about but had to keep, was the foreman. A bad omen. Two of the female jurors were wiping tears from their eyes and another sat shaking his head with his eyes fixed on the floor. Larry and Gordie didn't like what they saw.

While they were waiting, Jamie prayed quietly, *Heart of love, I place my trust in You. Though I fear all things from my weakness, I hope all things from Your goodness.*

"Judge Tibbits is taking his sweet time," Gordie whispered to Larry.

"Wonder why the delay?" Larry whispered back. The longer Judge Tibbits delayed, the greater the suspense and anxiety being experienced by the defense team, especially Jamie. Clutched in Jamie's hand was a note passed to him by Jennie when she arrived in court. It read:

Dearest Jamie,

Regardless of the verdict, you are innocent Whatever they do to you they do to me. Wherever you go I will be there also. Trust in God and his plan for you. Continue to give him glory regardless of the outcome Question not his wisdom. Know you are in my heart and soul and will always be.

Love,

Jennie

From the moment Judge Tibbits entered the courtroom there was an eerie silence. Even for Larry and Gordie it was gut-wrenching time. They were representing an innocent client who had placed his future and the future of his family in their hands. They only hoped they had created enough reasonable doubt to produce a not guilty verdict. They were asking the jury to return only a *not guilty* verdict, not a verdict of *innocence*—even though the latter was warranted.

Larry's hands were clammy, and he could feel beads of sweat collecting under his armpits. He couldn't have been more nervous even if he had been the one on trial. Trial attorneys were supposed to be dispassionate but not this time—not for him and not for Gordie—especially not for a defendant like Jamie. He wondered if he was the only one who could hear the pounding of his heart. If he felt that way, what about poor Jamie and Jamie's wife and parents? What must they be feeling?

When Judge Tibbits called the court to order and asked if the jury had reached a verdict, Casey Rowles stood and announced they had. The jury foreman was then instructed to hand the verdict form to the bailiff and he immediately complied. The bailiff, in turn, delivered it to Judge Tibbits who then asked Jamie to stand. After a longer pause than usual, Judge Tibbits read the verdict form.

"We the jury duly empaneled and sworn in the above entitled cause do find defendant, James Curtis Cooper, a.k.a. Jamie Cooper...*guilty* of felony theft, to-wit: embezzlement of bank funds."

When the word *guilty* was announced, Jamie sagged, and it was as if life left him at that very moment. Larry could still hear the sting of the word *guilty*. A word no defense counsel wants to hear. Still vivid was Jamie and his family's reaction when the verdict was announced.

• • •

As strong as Jamie had been throughout the whole ordeal, the guilty verdict was more than even he could bear. Jamie and his family were now on a collision course with destiny.

• • •

Except for the Stillwells and their faithful, those who remained in the courtroom sat in stunned silence. Even Eric Sweeney sat shaking his head in disbelief.

The only Stillwell not taking a curtain call was Debbie, Alden's wife. She sat as still as stone as the other Stillwells congratulated each other. The Stillwells had set out to bury Jamie and at long last had succeeded.

Although the outcome was somewhat

predictable, it was still a tremendous blow. Even when things looked dismal there was always that glimmer of hope that against all odds, Jamie would emerge victorious.

Later, when Bodean interviewed several of the jurors, he was told that even though Alden had something to gain, they thought it unlikely that he would steal from his own father and ultimately himself. They thought if he had taken the money, the money most likely would have magically reappeared. The claim of the $1,000 was not as important as the finding of the override combo in Jamie's belongings. Without that, one juror said, they probably would have acquitted.

"Convicting an innocent man is not something the criminal justice system was designed to do," Larry later told Gordie. "I guess it happens sometimes but why in Jamie's case where the evidence was so scanty?" Both wondered if it all was just a bad dream.

• • •

At the sentencing, despite Larry's plea for probation and the probation department's recommendation of probation and no opposition from Corbett, Jamie was still sentenced to ten years of imprisonment and a fine of $5,000. Because of the ruling in the civil case, no restitution was ordered. However, Jamie was still required to pay the costs of prosecution. Judge Tibbits did agree to stay execution of the sentence pending appeal and also agreed to Jamie continuing to stay out on bond.

CHAPTER 28
IN THE WAKE OF UTTER DISASTER: UTTER DESPAIR

From the time of Jamie's arrest, the Cooper's lives had been turned upside down. Nothing would ever be the same, but they hadn't realized just how much.

They were already in the throes of financial ruin and to pay a $5,000 fine plus the costs of prosecution meant they would have to sell their home. Ultimately, that's what they did and moved in with Jamie's parents until they could renovate the house that had formerly been occupied by his grandparents. Max and Collette, being closer to the Hayden school system, transferred there. One good thing, at least, they were closer to their church whose members had not abandoned them.

Jamie resigned his chamber post before he was asked to do so. The house sold quickly. The snows had melted somewhat but moving was still a hassle, especially when they left the county road and turned into the Cooper Ranch. They had a lot of help that last weekend in March with the rest of the defense team and their wives, Charlie Blankenship, Eric Sweeney and their church friends. Life could have been worse, but Jamie and Jennie didn't know how.

The appeal took about ten months and Jamie's conviction was affirmed by the Colorado Court of Appeals the Friday after Christmas, December 28, 1973. The Colorado Supreme Court refused to hear the case. Jamie turned himself in to the Routt County Jail and was delivered to the Colorado State Penitentiary in Canon City to begin his ten-year sentence on January 4, 1974. With good time/earned time, Jamie would be released in about five years and could be eligible for parole even sooner. Whittaker & Brownell even tried to get Jamie's case heard before the United States Supreme Court because of the constitutional issues, but the high court declined to issue a writ of review.

• • •

Outwardly, he appeared very brave as he said his goodbyes to Jennie, Max, Collette and his parents and told them that time would go by quickly and they would all be back together soon. Inwardly, he felt as though his heart and soul had been snatched from him. He felt hollow inside. Unable to sleep at all the previous night, he was still haunted by the thought of his conviction and having to leave his family behind.

As he was led from the sheriff's office to the

unmarked cruiser that would transport him across the broad expanse of Colorado to the Colorado State Penitentiary he took one last look at Jennie, Max, Collette and his parents, and he also caught his last glimpse of freedom. Coming to grips with uncertainties, he would learn, would become a daunting task—a struggle he hoped he could endure.

• • •

Jamie was determined to better himself during his prison sentence. He took whatever educational courses they offered. He even became the Assistant Chaplain and helped his fellow prisoners cope with their birdcage existence and having nothing but time on their hands. He read incessantly and started writing poetry. He was helping inmates draft *habeas corpus* petitions and told Larry during one of Larry's visits to get an office ready for him because he would be ready to practice law when he was released.

• • •

Jennie was frantic without her Jamie. Forrest and Bessie started to suspect she was sampling the sauce. Max and Collette were coping but that was about all. Even after they moved into the renovated Cooper cottage, they still missed their home and their friends. Nothing was the same without their daddy. Even Maya tired of running to the door whenever she heard a car drive into the Cooper Ranch. One day she just disappeared and never came back.

• • •

Jamie was a model prisoner. His goal was to be so impeccable that the parole board would have no choice but to grant him early release. He was looked up to, and being Assistant Chaplin, was sought out for counseling and despite his own distress, never lost his compassion for his fellow inmates.

Tragedy, however, struck when he had barely served two and a half years in the Colorado State Penitentiary. While trying to break up a fight in the prison's exercise yard, Jamie was stabbed in the chest with a homemade knife. The knife pierced one of his major organs, and being told Jamie was not expected to live, Jennie, Max and Collette, accompanied by Larry and Bonnie, were soon at his side in the prison infirmary.

Jamie, holding Max's hand in his, told Max to go to law school like Uncle Larry and Uncle Gordie and fight for all those poor innocent souls who had no one to fight for them.

Now holding both of their hands, he told Max and Collette, "I had all these great things I was going to tell you, now I can't remember them.

When I see you, all I can think of is how much I love you and I thank God for putting the two of you in my life. I can't imagine how empty it will be without you. But I won't be that far away, and I'll be watching you every day. When you look at the sky, smile and never frown, otherwise I will think you're upset with me. When you think you're alone, God will be on one side of you and I will be on the other. Please promise me that you will live your life in such a way that we all end up together in heaven someday. I don't want to spend eternity without the two of you."

Wearing the religious medal and chain that Larry had given him at the start of his legal journey and with his two hands extended and holding Larry's two hands in one and Bonnie's two hands in another, Jamie said, "Take care of these three like you took care of me." Looking into Larry's eyes, he said, "See you in the big court in the sky."

Even though his injury theoretically had prevented him from sitting up, he sat erect and reaching for Jennie said, "Hey! What are you doing up here? I didn't know they would let you wear that sea-blue satin dress up here. You look gorgeous, *My Fair Lady*." Pulling her close, their blue eyes reflecting their undying love for each other, Jamie went to be with the Lord. Jennie's heart went with him.

• • •

Life was pretty difficult without a husband, a father, and a son, but somehow Jennie, Max, Collette and Jamie's parents survived. Max and then Collette finished high school. Max went onto college. But just before Collette's high school graduation, Max received a letter from Larry saying that Collette had run away. That was May of 1981 when Collette was eighteen years old. Max had not heard from his mother in quite some time and depended upon Larry, Bonnie and his grandparents for news from home.

• • •

With both Max and Collette gone and having been bombarded with one tragedy after another, Jennie began to console herself with alcohol. The bottle became her constant companion. In short order, Jennie was fighting acute alcoholism and in and out of rehab. A DUI conviction resulted in her losing her privilege to drive and she ultimately was forced to sell her car to pay for her daily supply of coping power.

Although his grandparents were reluctant to tell Max, they felt he had a right to know that his mother was frequenting the local cowboy bars and bringing a cowboy home now and then. The news from his grandparents was so distressing that Max started throwing away their letters without reading them.

• • •

Max worked the summers in Boulder and very seldom visited Steamboat. Steamboat had ceased to become home after his father's conviction. Steamboat no longer was considered home. Friends and acquaintances were few and far between and he felt like a stranger in his own hometown.

The year Max graduated law school, he received word from his grandparents that his mother had passed away. That was on September 16, 1985, the day after her forty-seventh birthday. The death certificate recorded the cause of death as acute alcoholism and heart failure. Jamie's parents told the county coroner that the cause was not heart failure but a broken heart.

A few years later Max's grandfather and grandmother died just a few months apart. The Cooper Ranch was sold. One-half of the proceeds went to Max and the other half was put in trust for Collette, if and when she returned.

• • •

The ordeal had played itself out. Now, having lost all of the loved ones in his life, Max truly felt alone. There were no more Coopers in Routt

County and the ranch was no longer referred to as the Cooper Ranch. All traces had been erased, and now everyone could go on with their lives and live as though the Coopers never existed.

PART THREE:

THE ORDEAL IS OVER

CHAPTER 29
THE END OF AN ERA

When the plane touched down at Yampa Valley Regional Airport shortly after 10:00 p.m., Max had regained his composure. With the coffee intake, the adrenalin pumping and an air of confidence, he was preparing for whatever awaited him. Mr. Whittaker or Uncle Larry, as Max fondly referred to him, met him at the airport. When Max deplaned and entered the terminal, he noticed the changes that had taken place over the years. Nothing felt familiar and the Steamboat area no longer felt like home. Max and Uncle Larry hadn't seen each other in years and Max wasn't sure they would recognize each other. Time and space, as it turned out, hadn't been an impediment. They gravitated towards each other as if drawn by a magnet. "Uncle Larry!" Max shouted.

"Max" Larry echoed back. They shook hands, embraced, cried, laughed and patted each other on the back all at the same time. While they embraced, Larry whispered in Max's ear "Max, the ordeal is over!"

Taking Uncle Larry aside, Max said, "The suspense has been killing me ever since you called.

What happened that caused you to summon me and what do you mean when you say the ordeal is over?" Larry stood there beaming, apparently trying to find the right words to respond. Max babbled on, "I couldn't tell if it was good news or bad news when you told me to drop everything and get here ASAP."

After stumbling around, apparently still searching for just the right words, Larry finally said, "Max, it's about time you just called me Larry. You've earned that with your law degree and all that we've been through together."

"Okay…but you could have told me that on the phone," Max teased.

"Very funny! To cut to the chase, Alden Stillwell died a few days ago." When Max started to reply, Larry held up a restraining hand. "But I'm told that before he died, he made a death bed confession admitting he was the one who embezzled the bank's funds your father was convicted of stealing and that your father was innocent. He admitted to framing your father and said he had lived with his sin far too long and wanted to make peace with those he wronged—especially his Maker."

Max stood speechless and in shock. *Dad died in prison and many lives were ruined as a result of Alden's greed and jealousy. he thought. Now he wants to make peace with those he wronged and his Maker? Too little, too late, at least as far as the Coopers are concerned!*

Larry continued, "Alden was able to describe where the money had been stashed, that the bank remodel had prevented its retrieval and that he was afraid of getting caught if he ever attempted to remove it."

Max, controlling his anger the best he could, said, "I assume they recovered the money?"

"No, not yet. The recovery process is being executed as we speak."

Max asked Larry if he had any idea what Alden had done with the money. Larry told him that Alden's wife, Debbie, and one of their daughters contacted him with the news the previous Saturday. Alden had told them that back in 1972 there was a trap door in his office covered by a throw rug, with a large oak roll top desk that had been atop the throw rug for years.

The trap door, which was undetectable, led to a cellar where some old metal file cabinets containing early bank records were stored. His grandfather, the late Wellington D. Stillwell, had conscripted Alden for help in moving the roll top desk to gain access to these records. Alden was only twelve or thirteen years old at the time and the grandfather and grandson were the only ones at the bank. The grandfather made Alden promise he would never divulge the existence or location of what he called their secret hideaway.

The trap door and oak desk were located in a storeroom accessible only by what later would become Alden's office. In 1972, Alden, who was then thirty-four years of age and an employee of the bank, had somehow obtained an override combination to the vault, whereby he could access the vault while the timer was running. He was the only one who had the override combination which ordinarily the manufacturer solely possessed.

Alden then requisitioned without authority, $30,000 in various strapped bills each containing $1,000, bearing the stamp of the Federal Reserve Bank of Denver. He then claimed he found the $1,000 in the bottom drawer of Max's father's desk. The remaining $29,000 was put in the drawers of one of the file cabinets stored in the secret hideaway until it could later be retrieved.

When Alden went to a banking conference in Salt Lake City, Utah, in early 1973, his father, Brandon Stillwell, still president of Steamboat Bank & Trust Co., surprised his son upon the latter's return with a newly remodeled office. The remodel included new flooring. Since no one made mention of the trap door and it couldn't easily be seen, it was covered over. Alden never gained access and was never able to retrieve the $29,000.00.

"The look of shock on Alden's face when he returned to find the secret hideaway sealed was no doubt construed as an expression of surprise and joy," said Larry with a chuckle.

"No doubt," Max muttered.

"Alden's widow and daughter recorded the death bed confession and have allowed me to duplicate it. Would you like to listen to it?"

"I don't think so, at least not right now. What happens next?"

"The Steamboat PD has the tape as well as a written statement from the widow and daughter. They also gave written permission to have the carpet removed to expose the trap door."

"Can we be there to witness the recovery?"

"They've included me in the recovery process, and I assume they'll have no objection to you accompanying me."

"Did Alden say anything about the slip of paper with the override combination written on it?"

"He apparently told his wife and daughter that while his father was at a conference in Salt Lake City and while looking in his father's desk, accidently stumbled upon the strange combination.

Suspecting it might be an override combo, he tried it while the bank vault timer was on and it worked. He said that's how he accessed the cash when no one was around."

"How did the combination end up in my father's belongings?"

"Alden confessed he planted it there. He, of course, thought that would probably be the nail in the coffin that would cement your father's conviction."

"So Alden falsely claimed the thousand dollars that he took from the vault was in Dad's desk drawer and that the vault's time lock override combo was in Dad's belongings to make it appear as though Dad snuck in after hours, accessed the vault, and stole the money?"

"Exactly!"

"If everything pans out as expected, what do you think our chances are of having my father's conviction vacated and his record expunged?"

"With the cooperation of everyone, including the district attorney's office, the police department and SB&T Co., it's a slam dunk!"

"I hope you're right. Only then will justice truly be served."

CHAPTER 30
THE LAST GOODBYES

When Larry and Max arrived at the Steamboat Bank & Trust Co. that snowy February day, the carpet layer was busy peeling the carpet away from the east wall of the annex to Alden's old office. The large oak roll top desk originally belonging to Alden's grandfather had been moved to the opposite wall. It was not long before the hidden trap door was exposed and opened. A Steamboat police detective and the investigator from the district attorney's office descended into the darkness below with flashlights, returning with a musty money bag bearing SB&T Co. on the outside. Inside was the $29,000 Max's father had been accused of taking.

"All roads did lead to Alden after all," Larry said, barely audible.

"What did you say?" Max asked.

"Twenty-seven years ago, almost to the day, Gordie and I argued to the jury in your father's case that the road of guilt led to Alden Stillwell, not to your father."

"I wonder what the jury would say today if they were here to witness this recovery," Max said.

"They would find your father not guilty and

join us in having your father's conviction vacated posthumously and beg for forgiveness for having bet on the wrong horse."

"I hope the police department and DA's office will issue a joint press release, and I hope the headlines reach from end to end on the front page of all the newspapers in the valley proclaiming 'Cooper Vindicated in Death,'" Max said with tears running down his cheeks.

• • •

Larry met with the new district attorney and together they drafted a motion in arrest of judgment/motion to vacate judgment of conviction/motion to dismiss with prejudice/motion to expunge records. It was immediately presented to Judge Tibbits' successor the Honorable Horace T. L. Vickers. Judge Vickers knew about the famous case of *People v. Cooper*. He had even read the file and a copy of the court transcript. He readily signed every place his signature was required.

"The court will make sure that everything is erased, even his incarceration in the Colorado State Penitentiary."

"Thank you, Judge," Max said.

"Mr. Whittaker, would you like my clerk to issue a press release on the ruling?"

"Yes, thank you, Judge."

• • •

"Larry?" Max asked.

"Yes," Larry replied.

"Would you drive me to the Hayden Memorial Cemetery so I can visit my parents' graves, maybe for the last time?"

"Absolutely."

It had been a number of years since Max had been there. He was surprised when he saw that two evergreens had been planted on each side of the headstone. "You and Bonnie?" Max asked.

"Yes."

Max and Larry brushed the snow off the large granite headstone that was shaped like the Roman arch that had spanned the two windows of Max's father's office at the bank. Along the curve was chiseled *Inseparable in Life—Inseparable in Death*. Near the peak of the semicircle in the middle were two angels holding hands.

On the left side of the gravestone was inscribed:

James Curtis Cooper
"Jamie"
Born July 15, 1938 — Died July 4, 1976

On the right side was inscribed:

Jennie Mae Cooper

Born September 15, 1938 — Died September 16, 1985

Max and Larry also visited the graves of Max's grandparents and great- grandparents.

On the way back to Steamboat Springs, Larry said he had a confession to make. Slowly and haltingly, Larry revealed that Collette hadn't run off. She had been institutionalized. She was in a private sanitarium near Steamboat. Larry, Bonnie, his mother and grandparents hadn't told Max for fear that he, too, with all that he had been through, would go off the deep end. They wanted to spare him the anguish.

Larry asked Max if he wanted to see her and give her the wonderful news.

Hesitating for an instant, Max asked in a subdued tone, "Will…will she recognize me?"

"I don't know. She recognizes Bonnie and me."

With tears in his eyes, Max asked, "Will she understand what I'm telling her?"

"Hard to say. Sometimes she appears to understand; other times not."

No longer hesitant, Max blurted, "I would like to see her!"

•••

At Strawberry Park Enrichment Center one of the attendants led Larry and Max into a wing that reminded Max of a college dormitory. The room had a door with wire-inlaid glass. Through the window Max could see a surprisingly attractive slim woman in a white flower-patterned gown. She had medium-length auburn hair and was wearing white stockings. No jewelry and no make-up. She appeared to be reading a book but there was no book.

"She's been like that ever since she was admitted," Larry said, and Max detected sadness in Larry's voice.

Before they arrived, Larry told Max that Collette had not uttered a word since she was institutionalized. "Outwardly she manifests no emotional reaction and has no facial expression. Be prepared."

The attendant opened the unlocked door for the two men then departed. Collette did not look up when Larry and Max entered. They positioned themselves in front of the motionless figure sitting on the rocker. When Larry asked how she was doing, she looked up. A faint glint appeared in her eyes. He took her hand and said, "I have a surprise for you. I brought someone you haven't seen in a long time."

When Larry said, "This is your brother," she looked with expressionless eyes at Max and several tears appeared on her cheeks. She appeared to smile as she stared at Max and him at her. Max, eyes watering, couldn't utter a word.

It seemed like forever, but Max finally regained his composure somewhat. Taking Collette's hand in his, and in a shaky voice, managed to say, "Our father has been completely vindicated of the bank theft charge for which he had been wrongfully accused and convicted of those many years ago. Alden Stillwell confessed to the theft and to setting Dad up. You can now rest in the peace knowing Dad was innocent. We can all rest in peace."

Collette just stared and said nothing. Larry and Max talked softly together. Max recounted some of the memorable times he and Collette had as children when they were with their parents and grandparents. Max then spoke to Collette about his wife and children and what he did for a living. He thought he detected some recognition and some reaction, but he couldn't be sure. As they were leaving and closing the door, Max turned back, and hesitating for a moment, stared in amazement as a faint smile appeared upon Collette's face as she looked heavenward and clasped her hands as if in prayer.

• • •

After her brother's visit, Collette's psychotherapist determined that her cognition was returning and within six-weeks she was starting to utter words and then whole sentences. Within fifteen-weeks, Collette was diagnosed as having overcome her psychotic disorder. Her mental competence having been restored; she was soon released.

Collette moved to Chicago to live with Max and his wife. And after receiving her share of the proceeds from her grandparents' estate which amounted to $1.4 million with accumulated interest, she purchased a home next to Max and Pam. She enrolled in college and graduated with honors with a degree in psychology. Collette would go on to write an inspirational book in her field entitled, *Shedding the Old to Make Room for the New*.

The period from her father's arrest until Max's visit spanned some thirty-six years and had been completely erased from her mind. Collette's psychotherapist described this as selective psychogenic amnesia, which he indicated occurred in a dissociative state. Max never spoke of the ordeal with Collette again. If he had, she would have had no idea what he was talking about.

With the ordeal behind him and all that he had recently experienced, he would be the type of father to his children, grandfather to his grandchildren and if God willing, great-grandfather to his great-grandchildren that they all deserved.

Whether visitor or prisoner, everyone entering the Jamie Cooper Memorial Chapel at the Colorado State Penitentiary in Canon City, Colorado, passes a large brass plaque with the engraved inscription:

> *Welcome to the Jamie Cooper Memorial Chapel dedicated to the man who was unable to cheat destiny but was cheated by destiny instead. Not vindicated in life, he was vindicated in death. His legacy lives on for laying down his life for a fellow prisoner— judging neither the prisoner's innocence nor guilt. No greater love no man hath than he lay down his life for his fellow man.*

Max and Collette would not have been aware of the plaque had they not been invited to partake in the dedication of the extensive remodel of the chapel and library complex, made possible thanks to the generous contribution of a benefactor known only by the initials L.W.